P...
Stea...

D0427853

"*Stealing Home* is pure poetry wrapped in wisdom. Allison Pittman gifts us with characters deep and true, dialogue that's real, and a plot that moves us to laughter and to tears while keeping us turning pages. I want to go to Picksville and watch the next baseball game. I want to meet Duke and Ned and Ellie Jane and Morris especially and all the other people whom Pitman brought into my heart. When I grow up, I want to write like Allison Pittman."

—JANE KIRKPATRICK, award-winning author of *A Mending at the Edge* and *A Flickering Light*

"*Stealing Home* took me by surprise with gripping characters who dare to defy traditions of race, relationships, and what it means to be a woman, a man, a friend. With baseball in the 1900s as a metaphor, *Stealing Home* is a skillfully woven story about believing in the game of life, love, and ultimately in the victory of change."

—TINA ANN FORKNER, author of *Ruby Among Us* and *Rose House*

"There is no doubt about it. *Stealing Home* has earned a place on my keeper shelf. Allison Pittman's wonderfully drawn characters captured my heart and never let go. I hurt with them, laughed with them, loved with them, and cried with them, and I will surely never forget them. Don't miss this book!"

—ROBIN LEE HATCHER, best-selling author of *Wagered Heart* and *A Vote of Confidence*

"The fabulous ensemble cast of *Stealing Home* broadens the scope of Allison Pittman's well-crafted novel, setting it apart from typical period romances and grounding the story with historical relevance. Yes, readers will want Ellie Jane to find love, but they'll want much more than that, too—justice for Morris; hope for Ned; peace and victory for Duke. And they won't be disappointed. *Stealing Home* drew me in from the first pitch and held me until the final strikeout."

—CHRISTA PARRISH, author of *Home Another Way*

"Allison Pittman hit one out of the park with *Stealing Home*. The superb cast of characters in this tender story of hope, love, and healing settled in my soul and made me long to stroll down to the town square and linger a while. An unexpected delight in this lovely tale was the narration by Morris, an innocent yet perceptive young man who knows the citizens of Picksville better than they know themselves. More than the story of a few characters, *Stealing Home* is a study of small-town life at its very worst and its shining best."

—MEGAN DiMARIA, author of *Out of Her Hands* and *Searching for Spice*

"Allison Pittman is a master at creating a fictional world so real you'll never want to leave it. She balances light humor with insights into romance that make you reexamine your own heart and soul. She keeps you guessing all the way to the grand slam of an ending. And when she writes about baseball, you feel as if the bat's in your own hand, swinging at the fastest ball you ever saw. *Stealing Home* covers all the bases—a home run of a novel."

—CAROLINE COLEMAN O'NEILL, author of *Loving Soren*

"Written with an elegant flair, *Stealing Home* is a tremendous story of love, patience, and hope against hope."

—ALICE J. WISLER, author of *Rain Song* and *How Sweet It Is*

ALLISON PITTMAN

A NOVEL

STEALING
HOME

MULTNOMAH
BOOKS

STEALING HOME
PUBLISHED BY MULTNOMAH BOOKS
12265 Oracle Boulevard, Suite 200
Colorado Springs, Colorado 80921

All Scripture quotations, unless otherwise indicated, are taken from the King James Version. Scripture quotations marked (NIV) are taken from the Holy Bible, New International Version®. NIV®. Copyright © 1973, 1978, 1984 by International Bible Society. Used by permission of Zondervan Publishing House. All rights reserved.

The characters and events in this book are fictional, and any resemblance to actual persons or events is coincidental.

ISBN: 978-1-60142-136-4

ISBN: 978-1-60142-237-8 (electronic)

Published in association with the William K. Jensen Literary Agency, 119 Bampton Court, Eugene, OR 97404, bill@wkjagency.com.

Published in the United States by WaterBrook Multnomah,
an imprint of the Crown Publishing Group,
a division of Random House Inc., New York.

Library of Congress Cataloging-in-Publication Data
Pittman, Allison.
    Stealing home : a novel / Allison Pittman. — 1st ed.
      p. cm.
    ISBN 978-1-60142-136-4 — ISBN 978-1-60142-237-8 (electronic)
  1. Baseball stories. I. Title.
    PS3616.I885S74 2009
    813'.6—dc22

                                    2008052741

Printed in the United States of America
2009

10 9 8 7 6 5 4 3 2

For Mikey

PART 1

ON DECK

Cubs swing into Spring minus the Duke

by Davo Voyant

(March 5, 1905)—It seems the Chicago Cubs will start their '05 season without the talented stick of Donald "Duke" Dennison, whose name has been pulled from the roster.

Despite signing a lucrative contract, the Duke has been conspicuously absent for much of the team's training exercises. When asked about the high-priced no-show, manager Frank Chance seemed unconcerned, saying only that he expected to see the Duke back in the lineup in June. This doesn't answer many questions for the fans who want to see their favorite royal knock a few out of the park.

Other players seem to be as much in the dark as anybody regarding Duke's whereabouts. When asked, first baseman Ken "Long Legs" Berg said, "As for me, I wouldn't care if Duke Dennison took a long walk off a short pier."

Dwight Institute for the Treatment
of Alcoholics and Inebriants

Patient Name: Donald Dennison (Male)

Date of Birth: August 15, 1877

Admitted: February 6, 1905

Discharged: May 1, 1905

Diagnosis: Acute alcoholism

Physician Summative Comments: Patient has responded well to isolation treatment. Night terrors have discontinued. Hand/bodily tremors have greatly reduced. Violent tendencies subdued.

Recommendations upon release: Because patient reports continued occasional cravings, it is suggested that he is released to a transitional environment where access to alcohol is limited for no fewer than twenty days. Recommended: the close supervision of a family member.

Physician assessment of patient's continued success: Guardedly optimistic

Person(s) responsible for patient release: Frank Chance, Dave Voyant

ELLIE JANE

S he took the job at the railroad ticket office quite by accident when her father, Sheriff Floyd Voyant, was summoned to the station to arrest the ticket agent who had shown up drunk to work.

It was early June, just after graduation, and Ellie Jane—needing to stop by the post office anyway—had accompanied her father. At the insistence of Mr. Coleman, the station manager, she settled behind the desk to fill in for the afternoon.

She had been seventeen years old. She never left.

Some people, she supposed, might find it monotonous to sit in a little glass booth, day after day, but not Ellie Jane. These were her finest hours, chatting with her fellow townspeople. She might ask, "Oh, do you have family in Tennessee?" or "Didn't you just travel to Boston last month?" And the person would be forced to reply, even if grudgingly so, with averted eyes and terse comments.

If she were to run into any of these same people in the town square, while running errands in the Picksville shops, they might walk right past her or make a quick detour into the butcher's shop. But here, if they wanted her to slide that ticket through the little archway cut into the glass, they'd have to engage in a bit of conversation.

This afternoon, the first Tuesday in May, Ellie Jane was finishing her modest lunch of an apple, cinnamon butter bread, and tea, when a tentative knock at the glass window got her attention. It was Morris Bennett, a little early to take advantage of passengers needing help with their bags.

"Miss Ellie Jane?" His voice was soft and muffled. "I gots a tele-graph message for you." He slid a slip of paper through the arched opening at the bottom of the glass.

"Why thank you, Morris." Ellie Jane sent him a smile few peo-ple outside of her family had ever seen. It was carefully controlled—an attempt to hide the excitement of such an occasion.

Other people might receive telegrams every day from friends and family who lived in places they took the train to visit. But Ellie Jane's whole life was here—equally divided between her little glass booth and the home she shared with her father. There was, of course, her brother, Dave, in Chicago, but his was a busy, exciting life that left little time for frivolous messages home.

She fished around in her handbag to slip the boy a dime, which he took with a toothy grin and dropped immediately into his pocket.

"Anything else today, m'am?"

Ellie Jane checked the watch pinned to her blouse.

"The two-o'clock will be here soon, Morris. Perhaps you'd like to stay and see if any passengers need help with their bags?"

"Yes, m'am." He touched the rim of his cap and sauntered toward the platform, hands in his pockets and whistling.

Despite her curiosity, before opening the telegram, Ellie Jane carefully put away the remains of her lunch in her bucket, wiped the corners of her mouth with a pretty floral napkin, and removed the square sign saying the window was closed for lunchtime.

Then, with nervous fingers, she opened the envelope and saw that the message was indeed from her brother. Her reaction differed each time she read the short note: first a giggle, then confusion, then a rather cold fear.

Dave was sending her a man. And he was coming on the two-o'clock train.

N ed Clovis had just drawn a straight black line under which he wrote a precise black total. He smiled at the number. Spring was a busy time for the feed store—new life all over the neighboring farms. So busy, in fact, that he thought maybe he should stay open all afternoon. But then he felt the vibration of the office clock chiming the hour. Two o'clock.

After blowing the ink dry on the page, he closed the ledger, stacked it neatly against the others, and took his well-worn newsboy cap from its hook beside the door. It was his store, after all. He was the reigning Clovis of Clovis Feeds. Had been since his father died. He could leave any time he wanted. And he always wanted to leave at two o'clock.

Six days a week for the past five years, Ned's path to the two-o'clock train's baggage car led him straight past the little ticket booth where Ellie Jane Voyant sat behind the glass.

Six days a week for the past five years, the window standing between him and Ellie Jane gave Ned the courage to offer her a wave, or a smile or, on days when he was feeling especially brave, a tip of his hat.

Six days a week for the past five years, two o'clock was his favorite hour, bested only by the time spent in church on Sundays where she sat two pews ahead of him, slightly to the left.

Although she often returned his greetings in kind—a wave for a wave, a nod for a nod—in five years, Ellie Jane never left the confines of her little ticket office. As Ned slicked back his curly dark hair in preparation for his daily greeting, he had no reason to suspect that this day would be any different. Perfecting an air of nonchalance, he measured his pace so he would turn and smile just as he passed the center of the window. Today, however, something was wrong.

Ellie Jane wasn't there.

Not wanting to appear affected, lest *she* be watching *him,* he cast a careful glance up and down the platform that rumbled with the approach of the train. Seeing it in the distance, he abandoned his search for Ellie Jane for just a moment as he closed his eyes and imagined the sound of its whistle—the only noise capable of penetrating the thick packing of silence he'd lived with since he was twelve years old. As long as he kept his eyes closed, he could listen to the train and feel whole.

When the whistle stopped, he opened his eyes and saw Ellie Jane halfway down the platform. Her crisp white blouse billowed about her, standing out in clean contrast to those who wore their coats to combat a surprisingly chilly spring afternoon. Her hair reminded him of hazelnuts, both in its color and its undisciplined pile on top of her head. She seemed to be battling the breeze to keep all the strands tucked away.

This was his chance. He could make his way through the crowd, sidle up to her, tap her elbow, tip his hat. Maybe some miracle would give him the voice of a man rather than a goose when he asked, "Who are you meeting today?" Or maybe he could just gesture toward the train and assume an inquisitive expression on his face, which she would immediately understand.

He imagined her turning and giving him a response in a voice so loud it would capture the attention of the other people waiting on the platform. He wouldn't take his eyes off her lips, watching them for clues, knowing that she'd replied, "My brother, Dave," or

"Miss Higgins's aunt." No matter, he would nod in understanding, and they could stand there together, side by side, waiting for the train.

But he didn't make his way through the crowd—if such a small gathering could be called a crowd. He was about to take a step, really, when Ellie Jane motioned for Morris, ever ready to lend an open hand, to come to her. She bent to talk to him, her dainty hand resting on the boy's shoulder. When she was finished, the shock and smile on Morris's face made Ned wonder if she hadn't told him that he would be carrying trunks full of pretty girls and candy, a percentage of each he could keep as a tip.

Whatever the prize, Morris stuck close to Ellie Jane's side. When the train finally came to a halt, a blur of movement materialized behind the windows of the passenger cars. Ned imagined people gathering their belongings—umbrellas, books, children—and making their way to the front.

Meanwhile, the porter set out the tiny flight of stairs to carry the passengers safely from the car to the platform. One by one, disheveled women and men descended and made their way to waiting loved ones. Ellie Jane and Morris stood, expectant with each new arrival, then shrugged to each other as the former travelers filed right past them.

Finally, when the hands planted on her hips gave Ellie Jane a posture of resignation, one more passenger stood at the top of the steps. He was miraculously unrumpled in a pressed brown wool suit and a bowler hat sitting at a perfected angle over his left eye. His thin brown moustache was trimmed to symmetrical proportion, and the rest of his face seemed so cleanly shaven as to rival the smoothness of his patent leather shoes.

Morris's face fell into slack-jawed rapture, and after Ellie Jane reminded him to hold out his hand for a handshake, he seemed entranced by whatever the man had pressed into his palm. So much so, in fact, that he had to be nudged in the direction of the baggage car.

Having dispatched the boy, Ellie Jane held out her own hand. The man took it, bent low, and gave it a kiss. Ned cringed at Ellie Jane's girlish reaction, bringing her other hand up to capture what must be a lovely giggle while allowing herself to languish in this forward embrace.

Worried about her honor, Ned strode across the platform toward the couple, ready to wedge himself between them, but just as he got close, the stranger stood to his full height, giving a clear view of his face.

Shocked, Ned stopped midstride and turned on his heel, but not before tipping his hat to what must be the luckiest woman in Picksville, Missouri.

MORRIS

Tuesday, May 2

*Mama says spending time with white folks will warp my soul.
Well today those white folks sent me home with nearly seven dollars. I could spend a year toting for folks on Lincoln Street and
never make half that. Course I only showed Mama the nickels
and dimes—shakin them in my hand like it was the biggest
treasure ever. If she seen deep in my pocket she'd snatch it all and
give it over to that fool Darnell who's always sniffin around here
just in case Mama gets lonely for a man.*

*Now if my daddy was around I'd let him take it down to
Bozie's, roll some bones, and come back with it doubled. But
I guess he's back to Georgia for good this time—where he says
blacks is blacks and whites is whites and the two walk a wide
enough circle around each other that a colored man with good
timing can live a life without any trouble.*

*But I like it here in Picksville. Not on my side of the tracks—
where every day seems to be the same kind of nothin over and over.
But in town bein around all them white people. Learnin what
they know, hearin how they speak, seein how they live. I figure it's
trainin me up for when I get out of here. When I head out west to
California or some other part of the country where everybody's new
and a boy can make his own life.*

*Darnell slaps the back of my head and says, Boy don't you
have any pride at all? You know you ain't nothin but a grinnin
fool to them, scrapin around for pennies.*

*Maybe so. But I get more than pennies when Mayor Birdiff
sends me with a package to one of them pretty ladies on Sharon
Street (boy wouldn't Mama rip into me if she knew I went
there!) and I don't scrape for nothin. They like it when you look
them straight in the eye, hand at your side—not holdin out but
not in your pocket—and say somethin like, There you are sir.
Anything else?*

And there's always somethin else.

*So today I'm outside the post office and Mr. Steve calls out,
Can you run a telegram over to Miss Voyant at the train station?
I just run right over and say, Yessir. Anything else? I don't hold
my hand out for nothin even though I know in some towns there's
people who have it a job to take telegrams. But Mr. Steve hands
over the quarter anyway—like he always does—and motions for
me to come a little closer.*

*Yeah, he says, There's another two bits in it for you if you
come back and tell me who gets off the two o'clock train.*

*I almost don't knock on the ticket window—Miss Ellie Jane
had the sign turned to Closed. But if word ever got back that I
held on to a telegram too long that would be the end of the
quarters from Mr. Steve. So I knock real gentle and slide the
paper under the glass.*

*For just a minute I pretend I'm me a few years from now
buyin my ticket to California and gettin away from here and
Mama and Darnell and the ghost of my daddy. But then Miss
Ellie Jane tips me a dime for handin over the telegram and I say,
Thank you m'am. Anything else?*

And she says, Yes Morris. I believe I'll need you to help with a passenger's bags. That brings me right back to my senses.

I ain't never seen Miss Ellie Jane so worked up over anything before. She even leaves the ticket booth window when that train pulls up—didn't close it up or nothin, just walked off and left it empty. Then on the platform she's just a bundle of fuss asking me, Do you think that's him?

I say over and over, Do I think that's who?

And she says, Why Mr. Dennison of course.

And I say, How should I know who Mr. Dennison is?

Then she fidgets a little more with her hair and asks, Do you think that's him?

And it starts all over again.

When he finally does come off the train it makes me wonder just how we could have thought he was anybody else. Now I know a rich white man when I see one. But this guy—he is almost pretty. He's wearin this suit the color of molasses cake and one of those dandy hats and more jewels than I've ever seen any man wear—diamond rings on each hand, gold watch, pearl tie clip and cuff-buttons.

Miss Ellie Jane is saying introductions, herself and me the boy to fetch his bags. She gives me a little nudge wantin me to hold out my hand to shake his but I guess she don't know that rich white men don't shake the hands of Negro boys. She keeps nudgin and nudgin until finally I hold out my hand and what do you know? He shakes it. Shakes my hand right there on the train platform in front of everybody.

I'm expectin a strong grip but his fingers never really wrap around mine. When he lets go I realize he wasn't shakin my hand at all. He was slippin me some money. He tells me he has two

bags in the baggage car and a hired cab—Mr. Coleman's own
automobile—waitin just outside the station and if I get a single
scratch on the leather he will take it out of my own skin.

I want to tell him that I'd like to see him try but then I look
and see what he gave me.

Five dollars. Five whole dollars in one bill. I never even seen
one of them before, let alone held one in my hand, let alone
know it was mine just for pickin up two leather bags and walkin
them twenty feet from one railroad car to a hired cab. When I see
that bill, all the hatefulness leaves me and all I can say is, Yessir.
Anything else?

And he says, Not now but stick close and I'll let you know.

I don't know when I ever carried anything as heavy as them
bags. When I'm done, I see Mr. Ned picking up a delivery and he
motions me over to talk to him. I like talkin to Mr. Ned because
it's not really like talkin at all—it's kind of a game where you
have to read his face and his hands and the little sounds he
makes and sort of put it all together. He taught me the whole
alphabet and some other signs too.

So he points over to the man on the platform with Miss Ellie
Jane and asks me if I know who he is. I spell out d-e-n-n-i-s-o-n
from Chicago and he asks me again do I know who he is and I
say yes and start spellin again and he sort of grabs me by my
shoulders and shakes me a little. If he could speak he'd be yellin
DO YOU KNOW WHO HE IS and I got no choice but to
shake my head no.

Then Mr. Ned grins like he had the winnin bid to share a
basket lunch with Miss Ellie Jane at the Sunday school picnic.
He points to the boxes waitin to be loaded onto his wagon and
asks if I can help.

Now I have five dollars in my pocket and I'm not about to let that rich man down. But then Mr. Ned just points to his wagon and then off in the direction of town, wantin me to help unload at the feed store. He rubs his fingers together to let me know there's a little money in it for me—and somethin more that I can't figure until I get there.

—

I been up to Mr. Ned's office once or twice before. He's the one got me writin my money in this ledger book so I wouldn't have to hand count it whenever I wanted to know what I have. Seem every time a person lets cash run through his fingers it's a temptation to hold out a few cents for ice cream or smokes and that's the type of thing that can keep a fellow from ever gettin to California. Got nearly thirty dollars already. Don't know when it's gonna be enough but I figure one of these days the Good Lord will let me know it's time to go.

Anyway I guess I knew he has that wall covered with newspaper clippings but I never paid them much attention. Today though he stands and runs his fingers over them until he finds what he wants. Then he pulls one of the tacks out real careful and hands me the paper.

Dennison Signs Record-Breaking Deal with Chicago Cubs

I read it and look at Mr. Ned and ask, This the same guy?

But he isn't payin no attention to me. He's diggin through a cigar box and hands me a card, one of those that comes in with

*Old Judge cigarettes. I never paid much mind to them but he had
a whole box full. The one he shows me has a picture of that man
from the train, only instead of the fancy suit he's wearing a baseball uniform, holding a bat like he's about to smack a ball right
out of the card and into your face and on the back there's a bunch
of nonsense. Mr. Ned let me keep it (he had about a dozen and he
don't even smoke), and someday I'm going to ask him what all
these letters and numbers mean.*

Donald "Duke" Dennison

\# 27 C

DOB 08-15-77

H 5-09

W 170

Hits-L

Throws-R

G 118

BA 388

I look up at Mr. Ned askin, What's he doing here?

*He shakes his head and shrugs and grins like someone just
handed him a million dollars. Then he gets real serious, looks at
me and says, Morris you need to go over to Ellie Jane's house and
find out.*

*(He has special hand signs for our names. Mine's the letter
M kind of dragged across his face. Miss Ellie Jane's an E that he
squiggles like a long lock of curly hair.)*

I point back at him. Why don't you go?

*He sort of laughs and walks to the other side of the room. He
puts a hand to his ear and makes like he's listenin through the
wall, then turns to me again and shrugs.*

Nothin, he says, and he says it right out loud in that funny voice he has and I have to laugh. He has a good point. There's not much I don't know about nearly everyone in this town. If Duke Dennison is here with a secret I don't figure it will take much to find out just what it is.

So I smile and shake Mr. Ned's hand and just as I'm turnin to leave he calls me back. He fishes in his pocket and I almost wave it off, feelin like we was more like friends and that I shouldn't take no money from him. Then I see he has a silver dollar and you just don't turn down that kind of cash.

I take it and say, Thank you Mr. Ned. Anything else?

He leans down real close and touches one of those long fingers to my chest then back to his then back to mine then back to his.

Keep this between us.

I'm just down the steps of the feed store when I remember that Mr. Steve has two bits waiting for me if I tell him who was comin to meet Miss Ellie Jane. I figure a friend is a friend and a secret is a secret but a quarter is a quarter too. That two bits will be dropped down in my jar long before Mr. Steve realizes I'm just some ignorant Negro boy who isn't so good at rememberin names.

DUKE

The hired cab drove Duke Dennison and Miss Ellie Jane Voyant through town, down a street called Green Avenue, lined with impressive brick buildings and cobblestone walkways. People on the street turned and stared, like they'd never seen an automobile before.

The woman wouldn't stop talking. She pointed out the post office, the general store, the barbershop, the ladies' clothier, the tailor, the church, and the other churches.

No saloon. Just like Voyant told the doctor. Some kind of small town ordinance.

Welcome to Picksville. Doctor's orders. For at least thirty days.

She was straining to be heard above the engine's sound. Her hands were constant motion, flopping around like two freckled fish. The combination of that voice and those hands connected like the crack of a bat just behind Duke's left temple. When the cab turned a corner into a fashionable neighborhood and Miss Voyant made it clear she intended to identify the occupants of each house, he reached out and caught one little hand in mid-gesture and brought it to his lips.

"Mr. Dennison," Miss Voyant gasped, "please!"

"I could say the same to you." Duke ran her cleanly clipped fingernails across his moustache. He arched one eyebrow, gracing her with the look more than one woman had called a devil's snare. He puckered his lips and said, "Please."

Miss Voyant wrenched her hand away and tapped the cab driver on the shoulder. "Just three more houses down. On the left.

Number seventy-two." Then she folded her arms across her chest and sat up high in stony silence.

Duke felt better already.

∽

The house wasn't terrible. It wasn't the Stratford, but Duke had slept in worse. For most of his life, if the truth were known.

"You can see clear to the corner from the front porch," Miss Voyant was saying, even as Duke paid the cab fare and tipped the driver. "We often spend summer evenings out here watching the children play."

"You have children?"

This brought a snort of laughter from the cabbie, although he quickly stifled it at Miss Voyant's disapproving glance.

"Don't be ridiculous. I was referring to the children of the neighborhood. There's a dozen of them."

Duke's head began to throb again.

The interior of the house left little doubt that it was inhabited by a widower and his spinster daughter. The furniture was high quality and well worn. Shelves lined the walls, each full of leather-bound books and fussy trinkets. Heavy drapes blocked out the afternoon sun. And the rug was patterned with roses and vines.

Duke had spent many evenings in such homes, where the nubile woman from the pub transformed herself into a desperate bride-in-waiting. He rarely saw the same parlor twice.

"The kitchen's right through there." She indicated to the right. "I'm afraid we don't do much cooking. It's just my father and I here now. We serve breakfast promptly at seven and supper at six. For lunch, I'm afraid you're on your own."

"I thought so."

"Excuse me?"

"Nothing."

She gave him a look that oozed both distrust and dislike, and he wondered why he ever took that vow never to hate a woman.

"Your room is upstairs." She turned her back fully to him and ascended the steps.

Duke picked up his bag and lingered at the foot of the stairs for a while, watching her. She climbed with firm purpose. He'd never seen a woman walk with less sway. He shook his head and climbed after her.

The stairs opened to a generous landing overlooking the entry hall with a comfortable-looking chair and yet another set of book-filled shelves and a telephone. Just off to the left he noticed the porcelain sink and tiled floor of a bathroom. He smiled slyly to himself and silently dared Miss Voyant to point him to the toilet, which, of course, she didn't.

"You're just around that corner." She stepped back to let him move ahead of her. "It was my brother's room. I'm sure you'll find it quite roomy."

"Roomy enough for two is fine with me." Duke brushed past her as he maneuvered around the corner.

He didn't have to turn around to know she was giving him that look again. Her angry little footsteps told him enough.

"Mr. Dennison," she said, stopping short of following him into the room. "I know a little about your business here. That you're to rest and recover from a bout of nerves."

"That's all Voyant said?"

"No. He said I'm to be patient with you and show you all the warm kindness that I would my own brother."

"A brother."

"Yes. So I would ask that you refrain from such inappropriate innuendo."

Duke winked. "I'll do my best."

He set his suitcase down and took in his surroundings. The room was large, big enough for a full bed, a chest of drawers, and a cedar armoire in one corner. He went over to the chest of drawers and emptied the contents of his pockets—a handful of coins, his money clip, his watch. Amused at her discomfort with such an intimate moment, he shot her his most engaging smile as he shrugged off his jacket, laid it across the foot of the bed, and reached for a cigar from his breast pocket.

"We do not smoke in this house, Mr. Dennison." Miss Voyant immediately became a bossy big sister.

Duke had to laugh at her prissy authority. "I would hope not, Miss Voyant. Smoking is highly unattractive in a woman."

"And it is equally distasteful in a man. Your room has a balcony." She gestured toward the French door next to the armoire. "You may step out there to smoke, or you may smoke on the front porch downstairs, but I will not have you smoke in my house."

"Is that how you treat a guest?"

"You are not a guest, Mr. Dennison. I did not invite you here, and since we left the train station, your behavior has been nothing but brutish. You are here at the request of my brother, and be assured that I am going to write to him immediately to inform him of your shortcomings as a gentleman."

Duke repocketed his cigar and walked over to where she stood, her toe tapping furiously on the other side of the threshold.

"Trust me, Miss Voyant," he braced himself against the doorjamb, "your brother is quite aware of every one of my shortcomings."

With that, he shut the door right in her little freckled face.

Miss Elijah Jane Voyant
72 Parkway Lane
Picksville, Missouri

May 2

My Dearest David,

I must let you know, dear brother, that I have serious misgivings about our newly acquired houseguest. Mr. Dennison was highly improper in both conversation and gesture no less than eight times in just the few moments it took to transport him from the train station. I had intended to spend the afternoon getting acquainted with him, leaving the ticket window with notice that any emergency transactions could be settled at my home, but I felt that my very virtue was in grave danger were we to be alone in the house together for any length of time. In fact, my only measure of comfort regarding Mr. Dennison's presence is knowing that our dear father will be just down the hall with his gun.

If you feel this man is truly in need of lodging, I will not question your judgment. I will comply with all the graciousness expected of a good Christian. However, by the vast amounts of money he so lavishly extended to both young Morris and our cabbie, I hardly think the man is in need of charity.

Please put the troubled soul of your sister at ease and respond to this letter as quickly as possible.

Your loving sister,

Ellie Jane

PART 2

OPENING DAY

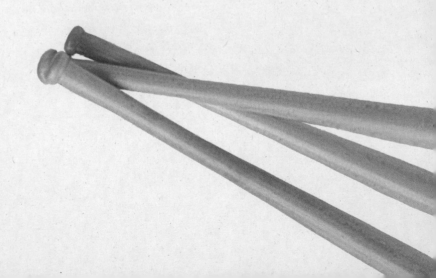

DUKE

For the third time that morning, Duke heard the series of three sharp raps on his door and Miss Voyant's equally sharp voice on the other side.

"Breakfast is at seven, Mr. Dennison. We'll not hold the meal for sluggish lagabeds. Keep an eye on the clock!"

Seconds later he heard an exasperated sigh, followed by the distinct sound of her quick little steps disappearing down the hall, then down the stairs.

The clock she referred to was a small, round ticking thing that had once sat on his bedside table. Now it was in the yard beneath his balcony.

It had been a bad night.

Not as bad as those first nights at the institute. Nothing like those endless hours of darkness, pacing the length of that small white room, his hands shaking so much he couldn't tie the drawstring of his pajama pants. He hadn't spent last night on his knees, vomiting into the chamber pot. Or curled in a quivering mass on the floor. He didn't wake anybody with his screaming at hundreds of crawling creatures only he could see.

No, it had been a quiet night, but a long one—starting well before the sun even went down—as he lay silent in this new bed, listening to the precise little footsteps of Miss Ellie Jane Voyant going about her household duties. Then, later, the addition of heavier footsteps when her father the sheriff came home. He heard their conversation as it seeped through the walls, and he ignored the knocks and requests that he come downstairs for supper.

But he couldn't ignore them forever.

Duke crawled out from under the bedsheet and walked to the open window. The morning breeze blew against yesterday's sweat-soaked shirt, and he shivered. He pulled the shirt away from his body, then reached for the top button. The tremors were back—not strong, but back. So he yanked the thing over his head and tossed it in the wicker hamper in the corner. His pants followed, then his drawers.

After wrapping himself in a heavy silk brocade robe, he grabbed a pair of silk pajamas and his shaving kit and stepped into his brown woolen slippers. One peek through the open door assured him that the hallway was clear, and he moved quickly to the bathroom across the hall.

No time for a full bath, so he filled the sink basin with warm water and splashed his face. He drew his hands away to stare at his reflection. He hadn't spent much time outside these past three months. Made his face a pale canvas for the stiff dark bristles of his morning beard. The stubble grated against his fingers, but he didn't trust himself with a razor. He'd have to find a barber in town. Still, he tapped a few drops of sweet-smelling lotion into his palm, rubbed his hands together, and brought them to his face and down his neck before indulging himself in one deep, satisfying whiff.

The robe hung on the hook behind the door. He worked the bar of soap into a lather and scrubbed his chest, shoulders, and under his arms. Duke dried himself with a thick white towel and wrapped it around his waist. A few steps back allowed him to see his torso in the mirror, and he took a deep breath, expanding his chest. Skin still taut, muscles defined. He lifted his arms, curled his biceps, and smiled at the thought of the power they held.

Or used to.

Now each bore the small, red, crescent-shaped mark. Not quite a scar, but well on its way. The reminder of weeks' worth of injections. Every day—molten gold and other secret elements. Taken without question or struggle or subterfuge. All part of the Keeley Cure.

He took off the towel, folded it carefully, and draped it over the bar before stepping into clean red silk pajama pants. His hands were still too shaky to make buttoning the matching shirt an easy task, so he simply fastened the top two and allowed the rest of the shirt to remain open underneath the silk robe that he knotted tightly at the waist.

He dipped his toothbrush into a jar of dentifrice cream and ran it through his mouth, grinning broadly into the mirror. His teeth were large and strong, perfectly straight. Last year a line drive caught him in the face and he'd feared his front teeth were knocked loose. He kept his mouth shut for two solid weeks—eating nothing that wasn't liquid or mashed—until they were firmly lodged in place again. Now he rinsed his mouth and engaged in a series of wide-mouth chomps, examining them from all angles. Then, one big flashing grin.

His hair tonic smelled of licorice and vanilla as he massaged a generous amount on his scalp, working from his temples, to his hairline, to the crown. Across the top and to the nape of his neck, working his way back to his temples. Once, twice, three times. Wider and deeper with each pass, just as the label recommended, before using a comb to make a part straight down the middle and urging two faint wings on either side. He took a small mirror from his shaving kit and closely examined the top of his head for any signs of recession.

Satisfied, he dropped his mirror, comb, dentifrice, and shaving lotion back into the kit. But not the hair tonic. Duke touched the tip of it to his nose and inhaled. Sweet…pungent. He met more than one fellow at the hospital who would drink this down when it got too bad.

He lowered the bottle and opened his other hand wide. Studied the palm still glistening with oil. He brought his hand closer and closer, until his fingers doubled and blurred before his eyes. Soon his own skin was warm against his lips, and he snaked his tongue between his teeth. Just a taste.

Once again three sharp raps sounded on the door, and his hand shook violently as he attempted to replace the cap.

"Mr. Dennison? Are you ready to come down? I am about to put breakfast on—"

Duke took one more glance in the mirror before grabbing the porcelain knob and pulling the door open.

"Good morning, Miss Voyant." He flashed a broad grin and ran his tongue across his teeth. "Didn't want you to see me before I was ready to face the day."

"And you consider yourself ready now? We are not accustomed to taking breakfast in a state of undress."

"And I do not get dressed until after breakfast."

"Then it seems we find ourselves at an impasse."

He waited for her to fidget, to blush at the sight of him, or titter behind her hand. Instead, she looked straight into his eyes, her head cocked to one side.

"As we were each unaware of the other's proclivities, today you may come down in your robe."

Duke braced one arm against the doorframe and leaned into the hall. "And tomorrow you may serve me in my room."

Miss Voyant merely cocked one eyebrow and turned on her heel. Duke smiled with every following step.

〜

The big man at the kitchen table must be the father. He looked up from his newspaper as Duke walked in, and in one motion folded the paper, stood, and extended a hand.

"Mr. Dennison?"

Duke stared at the man's hand. It was as wide as a catcher's mitt, and probably as tough. He willed his own to equal its steadiness as he reached out. "Call me Duke. And you're the sheriff?"

"Call me Floyd."

The two men took measure of each other, and Duke knew he came up short. A good four inches. And weak, based on the crumpling sensation in his hand. Floyd Voyant obviously didn't know what that hand was worth.

Duke's gaze traveled up the older man's strong arm, the broad shoulder, and finally met a pair of pale blue eyes sunk into a ruddy face. So this is where Miss Ellie Jane got her freckles—her father's bald pate, surrounded by a fringe of pale, rust-colored hair, was covered with them.

"Sorry I didn't get a chance to meet you last night." Floyd seemed to assess Duke's character with his grip.

"Yes, well," Duke said, unwilling to be the first to release, "you would think I'd be accustomed to travel, but I guess the trip down wore me out."

"Guess so."

Duke held himself steady under Floyd's scrutiny and counted it as triumph when the older man released his grip, sat down, and resumed his reading.

Meanwhile, Miss Ellie Jane rattled around the kitchen, then set a cup of steaming hot coffee on the table in front of her father. At least he thought it was coffee. Duke sat down to his own cup. With new steadiness, he brought the cup to his lips. The drink was thick, sweet, and faintly malty. If it came in a bottle, he might have kept it down. But this just wouldn't go.

"No offense, Miss Voyant, but that has to be the worst coffee I've ever tasted."

"None taken." Ellie Jane didn't turn around from the large pot on the stove. "And it isn't coffee. It's Postum."

"I can think of something else to call it."

Floyd chuckled behind his paper and looked up long enough to give Duke a commiserating glance.

"Do you have any idea of the dangers that lurk in a single cup of coffee?"

"Enlighten me," Duke said.

Floyd brought the newspaper closer to his face as his daughter walked over to the table, gesturing broadly with her long wooden spoon.

"It destroys your stomach, agitates your nerves, and—something *you* should be particularly interested in—hampers one's physical prowess."

Had the woman's father not been sitting at the table, Duke would have told her that his physical prowess was quite healthy, indeed. Instead, he curled his lip in a suggestive leer and pushed the cup away from him.

"I'll pick up some coffee at Jonas's this afternoon," Floyd said from behind his paper. "We'll have it for you tomorrow morning."

"Pop!" Ellie Jane used her spoon to force her father's arm to lower the paper. "We'll do no such thing."

"He's a guest in our home, Elijah Jane—"

"*Elijah* Jane?" Duke made no attempt to hide his amusement.

"I was named after my mother's favorite prophet."

"How unusual."

"I suppose you have a more noble origin for *Duke*?"

"Nope." He stroked the corner of his moustache. "I just made it up myself."

"*How unusual.*" She turned her back on the men, muttering and banging the contents of the pot into three white crockery bowls.

"Don't be so rude, sweetie. Remember he's a —"

"Please, Pop, not another word about Mr. Dennison being a *guest.*" She slammed a bowl of steaming, brownish stuff in front of both of them.

"She's right." Duke ignored the food in front of him. "The thing is, I'm a drunk."

Floyd set down the newspaper and picked up his spoon. "Now Dennison, there's no need —"

"There might be a more polite term for more polite society, but it boils down to the same thing. I'm a drunk, and the men who own me don't like that. They worry that I'll drink too much and lose a game. They don't trust a drunkard to get a hit. If my judgment's off by *this* much," Duke held up his hand and closed one eye, pinching Miss Elijah Jane Voyant's head between his thumb and forefinger, "I won't be able to pull a double play."

He picked up his own spoon and set it on top of the lump of food in front of him. It didn't sink in. "See, if we lose a game, they lose money, and they paid too high a price for me to take that kind of chance."

Now this was a quiet room. Ellie Jane stood, frozen to the floor. Her thumb hooked over the edge of a bowl. Like she was deciding whether to sit down and eat, or throw it to the floor.

She sat. Her little hands rested on the table. Then she reached one out. Not to the point of touching him. But just a little. Toward him.

"I am so sorry," she said, patting her fingertips on the table. "I had no idea."

"I spent the last three months in a Chicago hospital getting sober." Duke looked from Ellie Jane to her father. "I guess I'm here to be sure the cure sticks."

"Where you are most welcome," Floyd said.

For a few minutes, the only sound was the clicking of spoons against bowls. Ellie Jane taking dainty bites. Floyd digging up heaping mouthfuls. Duke trying to figure out exactly what had been served out of that pot. He looked up and saw the yellow box on the counter. Grape-Nuts. He took a bite and managed a polite smile as he worked his mouth around the warm, nutty, sticky mass. Nothing to wash it down with except the cooling cup of Postum.

"Why here?" Ellie Jane held her spoon aloft, looking at her father. When Floyd Voyant didn't respond, she turned her attention to Duke, who swallowed the lump of cereal before responding.

"Well, that's a good question, Miss Voyant. As far as I can tell, the only people who know I'm here are the team owners and that hack brother of yours."

Her eyes narrowed. "David is a fine, trusted journalist."

"Who sold me out. Week after week, writing about how Dennison's losing his edge. Headlines like: 'Duke Dennison: Dumb Decision.' My game wasn't slipping, but he just wouldn't leave it alone. Got the whole town talking about Duke's *problem.*"

"I'm sure he just wanted what was best for you."

"And I'm sure he wanted to sell newspapers."

"That still doesn't explain why he suggested you come here."

"That's easy," Floyd said, chewing thoughtfully. "Town's dry. Not a drop of liquor for sale within the city limits. Not legal, anyway. And I think folks'll worry about selling to the man taking board with the sheriff."

"You've got a smart boy there, Mr. Voyant."

"My brother's a very kind man, Mr. Dennison." Ellie Jane stood and took her father's empty bowl to the sink. "He must think very highly of you."

"He must indeed." Duke made one more attempt to penetrate the lump in his bowl.

"Forget about that." Floyd scooted his chair away from the table and swatted Duke on the shoulder with his newspaper. "You go upstairs and get some clothes on. I'll take you to Marlene's Diner for a real breakfast."

Duke looked at Ellie Jane.

"Oh, go on." She snatched his bowl away.

Duke went up to his room and examined the white suit he'd hung on the back of the closet door the night before. Not too wrinkled. Still, when he slipped his arms into the jacket, it hung on him much the same way. And it didn't seem as if Miss Voyant's cooking would beef him up anytime soon.

He grabbed his straw boater from its perch on the bedpost, put it on his head, and took one last look in the mirror. Finally, seeing himself with clear eyes, he tried to see what everybody else did. Fine clothes. Flashy jewelry. Every inch of him from his hair to his shoes a studied replica of high society.

But none of that fooled Duke. He was still Donny Dennison, stray son of a stinking drunk from a Wyoming sheep ranch. He was still just running away from home.

Floyd was talking on the telephone when Duke walked out of his room. Frantic, squawking noises spilled through the earpiece, and every now and then Floyd interrupted them to say something soothing. He motioned for Duke to wait downstairs.

With the parlor full of morning light, he saw the details of the room more clearly. In particular he was drawn to an ornate silver frame on the mantelpiece, and the picture within it. A woman. A beautiful one, with a shining mass of jet-black hair pinned up in some complicated style. Her face was turned away, showing a delicate jaw as she looked down at delicate hands resting on an open book.

Farther on was a picture of this same woman, holding a chubby, solemn child on her lap. Still another of her standing next to a much younger—but just as bald—Floyd Voyant. She had both hands lightly gripping the top of his head, and her face opened up in a knowing smile.

"That's my mother." Ellie Jane's voice surprised him.

"And is that you?" He pointed to the scowling baby.

"No." She reached out and ran a finger gently across the glass. "That's Dave. Mother died shortly after I was born."

"She was beautiful."

Duke had met Dave Voyant on three occasions. Once for an interview after Duke broke a league record in stealing bases. Once at a birthday party for the team's owner. And once at the asylum where

he showed up to offer Duke a place to stay for a few weeks before he
went back to the game. Dave looked like his mother. Slim and dark
and elegant.

Ellie Jane studied the picture of her mother. He knew they were
thinking the same thing, but Ellie Jane just nodded. "She was, wasn't
she?"

"What was her name?"

"Claire."

"Now *this* is an interesting picture." He pointed to the one of
Claire and Floyd.

"Oh, that's just a little joke. Mother used to go around with a
traveling phrenologist."

Every now and then a word came along to remind him that he
never stepped a single foot inside a school. Usually he'd just smile.
Gloss it over. Change the subject to one of his three favorite topics:
baseball, booze, and women. But not this time. He could tell by the
way Ellie Jane touched the photograph that she wanted to tell him.
So he asked.

"Some people say it's a true science." She put the picture back
on the mantle shelf. "And maybe it is for some. But for Mother, it
was a pure sideshow."

"But what exactly is phorn—"

"*Phrenology*? It's a way of deciphering somebody's health and
well-being by reading the bumps on their head."

Duke couldn't help it. He laughed.

"I know it seems silly, but remember. This was long before some
of the scientific advances we enjoy today."

"Ah yes. Medicine. Pure gold." He didn't mention the literal
gold—the painful daily injections that trademarked the Keeley Cure
for inebriants.

"Well, Mother traveled around with an uncle of hers, somebody just a generation away from being a gypsy. He was more of a mentalist, really, but he swore he could tell a person's future health by feeling his or her scalp. He brought Mother along because he soon learned that he'd get a lot more men to pay for a session if they could put their heads in the hands of a beautiful woman."

Duke looked at the photograph again. Claire Voyant's broad smile; Floyd Voyant's humorous, skeptical sneer.

"And your father was one of those willing customers?"

Ellie Jane laughed. "Hardly. He was the sheriff charged with running them out of town."

"She didn't run far."

"No. See, when my father put them in jail, Mother's uncle paid his own bail, then skipped town. At first Pop felt sorry for her, and then, eventually, he fell in love with her."

"So he bailed her out?"

"Mmm-hmm." She wrinkled her nose when she smiled. "And realized he was in love with her. They got married just a few days later, in the same courthouse."

"Very romantic." He just might use this story again someday.

"Yes, well, the town didn't exactly think so. There was always a kind of cloud over our family because of that. Picksville has a rather long, unforgiving memory."

"But she did give up her bump-reading ways?"

"Completely. She became a devout Christian woman. Pop says sometimes she'd stay up all night reading her Bible." Ellie Jane moved on and ran her fingers down the spine of a large black book. *The Holy Bible.* "She was reading about the prophet Elijah the night she gave birth to me and made Pop promise to give me his name."

"You ever wish she was reading about someone else? Like…" He tried to think of an example.

"Mary? Ruth? Esther? Good heavens, no. The world has enough of those, I should think."

True. He could think of several and could clearly remember at least three.

"But enough about me. What of your parents? Are they still living?"

Thankfully Floyd chose that moment to come down the stairs, hat in hand, ready to leave.

Duke didn't have the heart to tell her he didn't have a clue about his parents.

NED

Marlene's Diner was a long, narrow building on the corner of Spring Street and Green Avenue. During the afternoons and early evenings, she did a brisk business selling wax paper–wrapped sandwiches and bottled ginger ale to the passengers from the train. But in the mornings, Marlene was devoted to the locals who gathered daily for breakfast and gossip.

Ned always sat at the counter, right on the corner stool where he could have an uninterrupted view of the door. Marlene had a little silver bell hanging above it, and each time the door opened, every head in the place would turn to see who walked inside.

Before he moved to the corner seat, he'd been startled plenty of times with a hand slapped on his back, causing him to spew his coffee or drop the last corner of his toast into the remaining runny yolk on Marlene's robin's-egg blue plate. But now he could see who was coming into the diner before anybody else had a clue, thanks to the big glass window that looked out into the street.

Of course, other patrons could look through it too, but those who weren't bent over the morning edition of the daily paper were caught up in heated debates over the latest headline *in* the paper, and they would read or rant until the signal from Marlene's little silver bell interrupted their pursuits.

This morning Ned kept his eyes on the window and drummed his fingers on the countertop. He felt a touch on his hand and looked up to see Marlene's quizzical expression. She wore her thin blond hair in two braids wrapped around the top of her head and an apron that—no matter what time of day was meticulously starched and white.

Now she brought her hand up to hold an invisible cup. *Coffee?* Ned nodded.

She mimed cracking an egg into a skillet.

He nodded again and stirred his finger. *Scrambled.* He wasn't going to risk dribbling yolk on his shirt.

Ellie Jane never came in for breakfast, but she walked past the window every day at exactly a quarter 'til eight. Often, she was with her father who *would* stop in, after suffering what seemed a disapproving look from his daughter. So this morning when Ned saw Floyd's bald head skimming over the top of the enormous Marlene's Diner painted on the plate-glass window, he sat up a little straighter hoping, as he did every day, to catch Ellie Jane's eye. Today, however, she wasn't scowling at all. In fact, she walked arm and arm with Floyd, and even offered a kiss to his bent cheek before he walked inside.

The swinging of the door triggered the usual disruption of Marlene's clients, but instead of returning immediately to their plates of hotcakes and eggs, they remained a frozen image of twisted necks and suspended forks.

Floyd looked as intimidating as ever in his black leather vest and sheriff's star. When he lifted his hand in greeting to the patrons, they responded in one movement back to their meals.

But not Ned.

The steaming cup of coffee Marlene had set in front of him remained untouched, and though he felt the nudge of the plate as she placed it on the counter, he ignored it.

Duke Dennison, wearing a white suit and a straw boater, was in Marlene's Diner.

Floyd and Duke navigated through the narrow passages between tables to where two empty stools were on the end of the counter's long side, just around the corner from him. Ned kept his eyes locked on Floyd, willing him to take these two places, and minutes later, Ned was shaking his hero's hand.

His head filled with conversation. *I know who you are. I've seen you play twice—once in Chicago where you hit three doubles and chased down an overthrow to tag out the winning run at third. Once in St. Louis when someone threw a bottle of beer that missed your head by about an inch. You bat left, throw right, and—*

Ned recognized the name on Floyd Voyant's lips as the sheriff introduced the men to each other. Ned tried not to wince as Floyd pointed at his own ear, something people always seemed to do when introducing him. At this point Duke tightened his grip and mouthed *Nice to meet you!* exaggerating the words and contorting his face.

"It doesn't help if you yell," Ned said out loud.

Duke gave him a tight-lipped smile before sitting on the stool next to Ned. Floyd settled on the next one over.

For a while Ned's world was reduced to a pile of fluffy yellow eggs on a blue plate and pale gold toast. He watched his own hand move in and out of his line of vision, pleased with this new development in his otherwise ordinary life. With the slightest turn of his head, he saw Duke order hotcakes, sausage, and coffee, and he could see the flush on Marlene's face.

After that, though, he kept his eyes downcast, fascinated with Duke's hands. For a catcher, they were smaller than he would have thought, considering their uncanny ability to pluck a ball out of midair and shoot it to second. This soft, pale, quivering thing next to him seemed incapable of any such feat.

Ned looked at his own hands, one resting in an open, empty fist next to his plate; the other gripping a fork. His fingers were long and limber, having borne the responsibility of speech for so long. The tips were stained with ink; his left thumbnail permanently split from the time he'd been distracted and smashed it with a hammer. That was nearly a year ago. The memory of the pain had long since faded. In fact, it was the last time he remembered feeling much of anything.

Duke and Floyd were in deep conversation next to him, so Ned ventured a look around to see how his fellow townspeople were reacting to the arrival of such a celebrity in their little town.

At the table next to the door, Mayor Birdiff and his former campaign opponent (who was now his current advisor) sat nearly nose to nose with an impressive pile of paper strewn over the tabletop between them.

Two tables over, Steve, the postmaster, sat alone, sipping coffee while keeping his eyes glued to the clock on the back wall. He would sit there until five minutes 'til eight, when he would double-check the time against the watch in his pocket, stand, and walk the half block to the post office, where a line of people were already gathered and grumbling.

In the corner, Mr. Headley, the new teacher at the high school, ignored the half-eaten stack of hotcakes as he scribbled furiously in the leather-bound journal he carried everywhere.

No different from any other day. Maybe they were all choking down their excitement the way Ned was, but after a time he realized nobody was offering the least furtive glance. It was possible that they didn't know who Duke was. After all, these people had real lives and real relationships with wives and children and lovers and friends. He watched them all day, every day, their faces alive in conversation, hands flailing about in emphasis. He saw men cup their hands around their mouths to shout greetings to each other across the street; he witnessed young men leaning close to whisper in their best girl's ear. The people in Picksville were far too busy to pour over every word of the weekly sports page. They had more important things to do than to note scores and statistics in the back pages of a clerk's ledger book.

These people threw away the players' cards that came with their cigarettes—or gave them to Ned if he happened to be hanging around the drugstore. Of course, Ned would buy cigarettes too. He used to give them to his father, until his father died. Now he just kept them in a wooden box on the counter in the store—free to any patron—while he filed the cards neatly away in labeled cigar boxes.

He stretched up a bit to study Floyd, but Ned couldn't get a clear enough view to discern what he and Duke were talking about. The older man's face held the same steady, sober expression it always did. He could have been talking to anybody.

Ned was just finishing the last bit of egg and the last corner of toast when Marlene set two steaming plates of food in front of the two men next to him. His last swallow of coffee was almost cold, so he inched the cup across the counter, asking Marlene for a refill. She frowned a bit, because Ned simply wasn't a second-cup-of-coffee man. Any other morning, and he'd be reaching into his pocket for the two bits to slap down on the counter. But now he nudged his cup a little closer and raised his eyebrows.

Please?

She shook her head but obliged.

Meanwhile, behind him, the postmaster reached over Ned's shoulder to lay his money on the counter, as Mr. Headley tied the fraying ribbon around his leather journal. Mayor Birdiff and his advisor arranged their papers into neat piles and stuffed them into dark green folders. Within minutes the little restaurant was empty save for the three men at the counter, Marlene, and Gustav, her ruddy-faced husband who cooked the food and helped clear the dishes. Ned had never lingered this long, and he kept his elbows planted firmly on the countertop, his second cup of coffee cooling in front of him.

Back in the kitchen, Gustav was slicing loaf after loaf of bread for Marlene's lunchwagon sandwiches, and while they didn't speak to each other, they moved in companionable silence that seemed close to dancing.

At the counter, Floyd and Duke were tucking into their food, their forks and jaws moving in tandem. Occasionally one would speak to the other, keeping his eyes on the plate, the words lost in the motion of chewing and swallowing and sipping. Soon both plates were empty, and Floyd, despite Duke's protests, reached deep into his pocket to pay for their meals. Each man nodded to Ned, who nodded back, and gathered their hats from the rack by the door before shaking the bell in exit.

MORRIS

Wednesday, May 3

I stayed at school today clear up until morning recess then didn't see no point in goin back. Teacher was just up front readin from some book about a wild white boy and his adventures with a runaway slave. She says it's some great work of literature and how it tells about how terrible the slave days was but I can't see much point in spendin an afternoon listenin to Miss Teacher scrunchin up her face and puttin on a voice to talk like that slave Big Jim.

Besides, I never put no money in the jar by sittin in a desk.

So once we was set loose I walk across the tracks and come into town. There ain't a train due in until noon so I won't be carryin bags. But I figure I'll just hang around. There's always somethin needs done.

Next thing I know Miss Ellie Jane is tappin on the window of that little ticket booth and callin me over. She says, Good mornin Morris, and I say, Good mornin, back.

I know there's a lot of people in this town think she's kind of odd but she hasn't ever been anything but nice to me.

She's diggin around inside this little purse of hers and that gets my attention real quick. She hands me two quarters and tells me to go to the grocery store and get a pound of coffee.

Yes m'am, I say. Do you want me to bring it back to you here?

No Morris, she says. Take it back to the house. Mr. Dennison will be there to receive it.

I look down at that fifty cents in my hand and ask her if she wants me to give the change to Mr. Dennison. But she tells me I'm to keep it just like I knew she would.

Yes m'am, I say, and does she need anything else?

Not for her, she says, but I should ask Mr. Dennison if he'd like me to show him around the town a little.

The grocer gives me a look when I walk in. Not mean but questionin. He's not like most the people in this town who don't seem so bothered doin trade with a Negro. So I tell him I'm here on errand for Miss Ellie Jane Voyant.

He rolls his eyes and wipes his hands on his apron and asks, What'll it be?

I tell him a pound of coffee and while he scoops the beans on the scale I'm lookin at all the shelves behind him with every sort of box and bag and tin you can imagine. I wish Mama could shop here. Seems like there's a lot of food to be had that don't have meat. But Mama's work doin laundry for Dr. Ryan don't get her to the stores here much and we got our own shops to buy in. But I still wish she could walk in here just one time.

After the grocer cinches up the sack of coffee he tells me he'll put it on Miss Ellie Jane's account.

No sir, I say. She gave me money to pay for it.

He asks, How much money do you have?

And I ask, How much is the pound of coffee?

We just stare at each other for a minute and after a while he tells me thirty-five cents.

I hand over the two quarters and I can see he don't like the thought of givin me change so he holds on to it and asks, Do you want anything else?

I see a barrel of apples in the corner—two for a penny— and remember that I haven't eaten yet today so I ask for half-a- dozen and two peppermint sticks. He puts it all in a brown paper bag and hands me the dime but I don't put it in my pocket until I'm out the door.

I don't figure it's much of a hurry gettin the coffee to Miss Ellie Jane's house this late in the mornin, so after the grocer's I poke my head in at the post office to see if Mr. Steve has any telegrams to deliver. He don't. So I take my lunch over to the little park across the street from Mayor Birdiff's office. Sometimes he has little jobs for me to do and he'll glance out his window every now and again to see if I'm around. I keep thinkin that someday he'll make it a regular job and this tree could be like my own office, seein as I'm not supposed to sit on the bench right next to it.

I'm leanin up against it and finishin the first apple when Mayor Birdiff walks past his window. I make a sound—like a cough that don't quite leave my throat—and he sees me. I take off my hat to show him a little respect and he touches his nose. That means there's someone else in his office so he can't get away. I scratch my head asking if he'll need me later today and if I didn't know what I was lookin for I'd never known that he shook his head. No.

It's shapin up to be a one-dime day.

DUKE

His first priority was to find someplace to buy a decent cigar. If not, based on what he saw on the walk to and from the diner, he'd have to send a telegram to Carlos back home and tell him to ship a box down here to rube-town. Scratch that. The deal was for him to lay low. Four months sober and then back in June. Play a clean season, get a big check.

One more drink, and no team would touch him.

Lounging on the Voyant's front porch, Duke seemed to have everything the doctor ordered. A quiet, tree-lined lane, fresh air, stomach full of good food. A clear head. He closed his eyes and listened. Nothing but the irregular squeak of the chain as he left one foot on the white-washed floor and the other stretched out on the swinging bench.

He clamped the cigar in his mouth and savored the sweet taste of the tobacco on his tongue. His right arm hung limply off the side of the swing, hand curled as if holding a glass. It was noon— had to be near noon—and he had a whole long day stretched in front of him. Alone.

Miss Voyant had filled two milk cans with a cold lunch for her and the sheriff, telling Duke he would be left to his own devices for his noon meal and that he was welcome to whatever he found in the cupboards. He'd started looking the moment he got home from breakfast.

Cooking sherry? Wine? None. No apple brandy, sweet rum, or rosemary cordial. He checked the cabinets over the sink, under the sink, behind every box and jar and bottle in the pantry. Nothing in the pie safe. Nothing in the icebox. And, after thirty minutes by the light of a single lantern, nothing in the cellar.

Off in the distance, he heard a familiar grating sound. He opened one eye and craned his head to look down the street. There were at least a dozen kids coming home from school for lunch. Duke steeled himself and waited for the onslaught. The little boys would barrage him with questions about what it felt like to hit one out of the park. Or they'd beg him to put on a glove and go throw a few. Little girls were quieter but just as annoying, looking at him with great big eyes and giggling behind their hands.

Might as well get ready for it.

He set his burning cigar in the small glass dish on the porch railing and stood on the top step, one hand in his pocket, the other adjusting his hat brim. A few of the children broke off, going through their own gates and into their own houses up the street. Others made their way past the Voyant place. Several cast him curious glances but didn't slow their paces. Soon he was alone again. He picked up his cigar, clamped it back in his mouth, and sat back down on the swing.

"Stupid kids," he said to the empty street.

"Beg pardon, sir?"

It was that boy from yesterday. The one who carried his bags. He stood now on the other side of the gate at the end of the Voyant's walkway.

Duke leaned back, crossing one leg over the other. "What do you want?"

"Miss Ellie Jane asked me to deliver some coffee. You want I should take it inside? Or leave it here with you?"

Ah, she'd bought the coffee after all. He closed his eyes, smiled, and gestured toward the door. "Take it on in."

The iron gate scraped against the sidewalk. "Guess I'll just go 'round back."

"You know where the kitchen is?"

"I can find it."

He sensed the return of the boy minutes later. Probably standing there, waiting for a tip.

"You can go on home now, kid." Duke settled his hat a little lower on his face.

"Nothin' I can get done for you today, sir?"

Duke looked at him under the shadow of his boater. "Like what?"

"Miss Ellie Jane said I was to show you around the town if you like."

"I've seen the town."

"Yes, sir."

Just as the boy was turning to leave, Duke noticed the brown bag clutched in the boy's hand. "Hold on a minute." He sat up in the swing. "What do you have in there?"

"My lunch." The boy looked Duke straight in the eye.

"Did you take that from Miss Voyant's kitchen?"

"No, sir."

Duke was determined to make the boy squirm. "And just how do I know that?"

"They's apples."

"The apples could have come from Miss Voyant's kitchen."

The boy let the slightest smile tug at the corner of his mouth. "Looked to me like you went through that kitchen pretty good yourself. Seems you'd know whether or not apples was in there."

Duke allowed his own little smile. "Then you must have gone through the cupboards, didn't you, boy?"

"Just saw inside where the door was left open. If you gonna snoop around, you best learn to cover your tracks a little better."

"Perhaps that's simply the way Miss Voyant keeps her kitchen."

The boy shook his head. "I known Miss Ellie Jane all my life. Ain't no way she keeps nothin' that messy. You might want to straighten it up a bit before she get home."

"I don't suppose you'd care to come in and help me?"

The boy seemed to consider the possibility before replying. "No, thank you, sir. But I'll keep it under my hat that you wrecked it up so."

Duke actually chuckled. "Well, I can't ask for much more than that."

The boy touched his hat and turned to walk away again when Duke called out to him. "Hey, kid!"

"Yes, sir?"

"You know who I am?"

"Yes, sir. You that big baseball player here from Chicago. Mr. Ned showed me all about you."

"That's right."

"Sir? You know who I am?"

Duke Dennison was rarely at a loss for words, but this question took him by surprise. "No."

The boy grinned, a smile so warm and wide it took everything Duke had not to try to match it. "I'm Morris Bennett. You want an apple?"

Duke held up a hand. The boy, Morris, looked down inside the bag. "Red or gold?"

"Gold," Duke said. Dr. Keeley would be proud.

Morris produced a perfect gold apple from the sack and held it up. "You want me to throw it?"

"Yep."

"Might bruise."

"Not if you throw it right."

The kid tossed the apple gently—up and down in his hand—and smiled again. "What if I don't?"

"If you can't lob an apple twenty feet, then you're a sorry excuse for a boy."

Less than a second later, the apple was in Duke's hand. He hadn't seen the boy throw it, didn't see it flying toward him. There was just a golden zip out of the corner of his eye, and his fingers clutched instinctively once the skin of his palm touched the skin of the fruit.

"Nice. Can you catch it?"

Morris smiled. "Might bruise."

"Not if I throw it right." Duke curled his fingers around the apple, imagining a pattern of laces on its smooth skin. "Put your hand up. Get ready."

The boy tucked the brown paper sack under one arm and held the other out at his side.

Duke laughed. "You never caught a ball before?"

"'Course I have." Morris planted his feet a little more firmly.

"Put your hand in front of you." Duke demonstrated. "Like this."

"And have you hit me in my face? No, sir."

"That's the first lesson in fielding a ball. You and me, we have to find each other. Look each other straight in the eye. If you put your hand up—right in the center—it gives me a target."

"You can just consider this your target way out here." Morris reached his hand out a little farther and wiggled his fingers.

Duke picked the cigar up from its resting place on the porch railing and clamped it between his teeth. "Tell you what, kid. Catch it my way, and I'll give you a nickel."

The boy's face remained impassive. "How 'bout if I catch it my way and you pay me two?"

"I'm not aiming for that hand."

"I ain't askin' you to."

Duke tipped the rim of his hat and moved the cigar to the left side of his mouth. The porch was three feet off the ground; the boy was close enough for an easy toss. Ignoring Morris's outstretched hand, Duke trained his eye on a spot right at the base of the boy's throat. He wouldn't throw hard enough to hurt him, just hard enough to make his point.

And he let go.

With confidence equal to any player Duke had ever thrown a ball to, Morris tracked the missile, took half-a-step back, and brought his hand in front of him. There was a soft sound when the apple's golden skin connected with the boy's palm. A humble, perfect catch. Then, as if to end the game, Morris brought the apple to his mouth and took a large, gaping bite.

"Nice catch." Duke fished in his pocket for the two nickels as he made his way down the porch steps to meet the boy at the gate.

Morris dropped the apple—bite and all—into the bag and held out his hand. "Thank you, sir. Anything else?"

"Yeah." Duke took the cigar out of his mouth. "Come back tomorrow. And bring a glove."

"Ain't got a glove."

"Come back anyway. I'll let you use mine."

Enclosed please find $15.34 intended as payment for the following items. Please note I have included the price of shipment:

Item # 6R6886
Spalding league baseball   Qty: 2   ea = 1.15   2.30
   .35
   2.65

Item # 6R6888
Intercollegiate baseball   Qty: 10   ea = .75   7.50
   .70
   8.20

Item # 6R6934
Victor prof.
    baseman's glove   Qty: 1   ea = 1.95   1.95
   .12
   2.07

Item # 6R6964
Boys' fielder's glove   Qty: 1   ea = .35   .35
   .03
   .38

Item # 6R6975
Men's prof. league mask   Qty: 1   ea = 1.75   1.75
   .29
   2.04

Please ship items to
Donald Dennison
c/o Poplin General Store
Picksville, Missouri

Picksville Promenade Season Set to Begin

(May 13, 1905)—For those young people who plan to engage in our fine town's Promenade, several members of our community will be offering reception activities.

Mr. and Mrs. Gustav and Marlene Geist will host a pie and coffee reception in Marlene's Diner at the corner of Green Avenue and Spring Street. Cost is 15 cents for bachelors and 20 cents for couples.

The First Congregational Church of Picksville is offering free popcorn and lemonade in exchange for a donation to their African Missions fund.

Other businesses and would-be entrepreneurs will have several snack and beverage stands throughout our town's Center Park. Please bear in mind that permits are required, as per Mayor Birdiff. Anyone attempting to sell refreshments without having filed the proper paperwork will be subject to civil consequences.

ELLIE JANE

At precisely three o'clock on Saturday afternoon, Ellie Jane slid the Closed sign across the little arched opening of the ticket booth window. She arranged the schedule book, ledger, and tickets in a long metal box fitted with specialized compartments for each. The day's cash nestled in a flat leather pouch right atop the schedule book. She brought down the lid and locked it with a tiny key she wore on a ribbon around her neck.

Of course, nobody knew she kept the key there, as the ribbon was undetectable beneath the high collar of her shirtwaist, and she secretly relished the brief wanton moment when she unfastened the three pearlesque buttons at the back of her neck and ran her finger to the nape, capturing the ribbon and tugging it up over her head. Once the box was locked, Ellie Jane dropped the key into her little handbag and snapped it closed. It would stay there until she placed it back around her neck Monday morning.

Looping the handbag's thin strap over her wrist, she picked up the box and stepped out of the booth, closing the door behind her. She walked across the station platform and into the main office where Mr. Coleman sat behind his desk.

He was a tall man with thin, pale blond hair that seemed to float, strand by strand, above his head. His eyes drooped behind rimless spectacles, and his cheeks drooped beneath them. In fact, his entire body was nothing more than a series of droops lending him a prevailing air of melancholy even as he sat, awash in dusty sunlight, punching the keys of his adding machine.

"Mr. Coleman?" Ellie Jane knocked softly on the open door. "I have the day's receipts."

"Leave 'em right there." He tipped his head toward the least-cluttered spot on his desk.

Ellie Jane complied and was turning to leave when Mr. Coleman called her back.

"Yes, sir?"

He looked up from the machine, fingers poised over the keys. "Do I have any reason to be concerned about the—ah—situation at your house?"

"Situation, sir?"

"It's no secret that you've had a man staying there with you for well over a week."

"I've never intended it to be a secret," Ellie Jane said, but she felt the heat rising on her neck.

"You realize that you are a representative of the railroad, Miss Voyant, and the railroad does have a reputation to uphold."

"Mr. Coleman, I can assure you nothing untoward is—"

"Perhaps if I were to have the opportunity to meet the gentleman myself"—he leaned forward, resting his forearms on a loose pile of papers on his desk—"then I could ascertain his intentions and perhaps halt any—ah—undue gossip."

"With all due respect, Mr. Coleman, my father is present in the house, and I believe he is quite capable of ascertaining both Mr. Dennison's character and his intentions."

"Of course, of course." The pile of papers slipped beneath his weight, but he quickly righted himself. "I just thought that—ah—in the interest of the railroad, it might be best if I were to make his acquaintance."

"Perhaps," Ellie Jane said, softening, "I could arrange an introduction. I believe that should allay your fears."

"Well, I don't want to be a bother…"

"It's no bother, I assure you," Ellie Jane said, surprised once again at the level of mystique Mr. Dennison seemed to project.

From what she had seen of him, his only social outing was the daily breakfast at Marlene's and long conversations with her father. She came home to find Mr. Dennison sitting on the front porch, smoking his ever-present cigar, or on the sofa in the parlor snoozing quietly. What he did during the hours between breakfast and supper were a mystery, and he often refused the latter, saying his stomach was not quite up to Ellie Jane's sophisticated cuisine.

"That'll be fine, then." Mr. Coleman adjusted his glasses and turned back to his adding machine with new fervor.

"I'll see you Monday morning, Mr. Coleman." Ellie Jane moved one foot behind her, prepared to leave, but remained facing the desk lest Mr. Coleman have anything else to say. But the man simply continued punching his keys, and after a few quiet seconds, Ellie Jane turned and walked out of the office.

It was a perfect, cloudless spring day as Ellie Jane made her way from the railroad station, past the livery, and onto the sidewalk of Picksville's town square. She reached inside her little handbag and found her shopping list.

Tomorrow would be Mr. Dennison's second Sunday in town, and she hoped the idea of a special supper might entice him to accompany them to church. It would be nice to prepare something he wouldn't snap and sneer at. He might be an athlete, but he knew precious little about the deleterious effects of red meat and rich foods. If she had to endure one more of his complaints, she'd be sorely tempted to throw him out on his ear.

After all, her father had long ago accepted her dietary restrictions, and he was a man. In fact, he was twice the man as Mr. Dennison. Nevertheless, tomorrow's supper would be fried beefsteak and creamy potatoes, with a tinned-peach cobbler and heavy cream for dessert. And coffee—the *real* coffee she'd supplied without further comment or complaint. That should hold him for a few days.

Her first stop was the butcher's. The little bell above the door rang, calling Mr. Samms out of his back room. Ellie Jane tried not to shudder as he wiped his hands on his blood-stained apron.

"You're too late." He turned away from her almost as soon as he saw her. "Your pa's already come pick up your order."

"Did he?" Ellie Jane still stood in the doorway. "I'd wanted to be sure—"

"And the man himself was with him."

"The man?"

"The Duke!" Mr. Samms picked up a meat cleaver and cut into the roast sitting on the butcher's block. "Right here in my shop. So I told him, don't you worry about it, Duke. I cut the best steaks in town."

"You're the only butcher in town," Ellie Jane said, not trying to hide her disdain. Not only did she have an aversion to Mr. Samms's product, but to his business practices as well. It was a known fact in Picksville that the man was a cheat, and only the most naive townsperson would buy anything he didn't see cut and weighed before his very eyes.

Mr. Samms ignored her comment and continued. "So I says, 'Won't find a bit of fat on that one, Duke.' And he says, 'After many more days of Miss Voyant's cooking, you won't find much on me either.'"

Mr. Samms howled at the joke as if hearing it for the first time, and Ellie Jane turned on her heel and left, letting the door slam behind her. She would not stoop to defend herself to some blood-stained carcass peddler, no matter how rankling the laughter behind the closed door.

"Well, it's one item off my list, anyway," she muttered. "You would think that any man who could develop such a tolerance for the taste of whiskey could stomach just about anything. You'd think there was nothing more important in the world besides satisfying the physical appetite—"

"Are you quite all right, dear?"

Ellie Jane had been walking and talking aloud since leaving Samms's butcher shop three doors down and didn't stop until she felt a gentle pressure on her elbow and looked down into the sweet, concerned face of Mrs. Lewiston.

She'd been Ellie Jane's Sunday school teacher throughout her childhood, and she looked at Ellie Jane now with the same worried expression she always had whenever she caught the girl at the peak of peculiarity.

"I'm fine, Mrs. Lewiston," Ellie Jane said more harshly than she intended. The older woman's mass of gray curls fairly quivered beneath her neat straw bonnet. "I mean, thank you for your concern," she continued, softening her tone, "but I'm afraid you've caught me deep in thought."

"About tonight?" The startled look in Mrs. Lewiston's eyes turned into a twinkle.

Ellie Jane glanced up and down the street, wondering just what she'd been saying and how loud she'd been saying it. "Tonight?"

"Well, of course." The older lady patted Ellie Jane's arm. "Tonight's the first Spring Promenade."

"Oh, that." Ellie Jane took a step away from Mrs. Lewiston. "I hadn't given that much thought."

"No one to step out with?"

"Really, I must—"

"Such a shame, it is." The little woman's curls, bonnet ribbon, and jowls shook in unison. "A pretty young girl like you—"

"I haven't been a *young girl* for quite some time, Mrs. Lewiston. And I have far more pressing matters at hand than stepping on some silly walk—"

"It's not a *walk*, dear. It's a *promenade*. If you're lacking an escort—"

"Mrs. Lewiston, please—"

"—perhaps you could step out with that handsome young man. Mr. Dennison, isn't it?"

"Mrs. Lewiston." She dropped her voice to a whisper. "The man is a guest in our home, and I don't think it's proper to discuss him in such a manner."

"He may be a guest, my dear, but he's hardly a secret."

"So I'm learning," Ellie Jane said, not quite under her breath.

"And I can quite understand that some might think it unseemly if you were to step out with him tonight, seeing as he's"—Mrs. Lewiston leaned in closer and whispered—*"sleeping just down the hall."*

"I'm glad you understand." Ellie Jane took another step back and nodded to a pair of middle-aged women who flashed suspicious glares as they passed this sidewalk scene.

"You know my granddaughter, Charlotte, just turned nineteen." Mrs. Lewiston tapped one lace-gloved finger on her chin. "I wonder if your Mr. Dennison would like to step out with her this evening."

"He is hardly *my* Mr. Dennison." Ellie Jane formed her mouth into a wide smile and tried to speak without moving her lips. "And, no, I don't think he'd be interested at all. I'm sure Mr. Dennison's ideas of entertainment are far too cosmopolitan to include a small-town Spring Promenade."

"You're probably right, my dear."

To Ellie Jane's relief, Mrs. Lewiston offered a lacy wave and seemed to be on her way. Just as Ellie Jane was about to turn her back and continue her walk up the street, though, the older woman caught her attention one more time.

"All the same, though," she said, the twinkle back in her eye, "Charlotte will be walking with a few of her former schoolmates. I might just put it in her head to walk down your street."

Ellie Jane kept her frozen smile. "That would be lovely, Mrs. Lewiston. I'll be sure to look out for her."

She stared as the old woman made her doddering way down the street, wishing she had something to throw. Not that she *would,* of course. But it might have been nice to have the option. Instead, she squared her shoulders and continued on to her final errand.

Mr. Poplin's Dry Goods was known in town for stocking just about everything a person could need, and if he didn't stock it, well, come back in three days and check again. Mrs. Poplin considered herself somewhat of a mystic and spent hours pouring over catalogues at night, trying to pick up the unvoiced needs of her fellow townspeople to place her orders. Sometimes she claimed static electrical interference, and her timing might be off, but nobody's special order was ever a surprise.

Mr. Poplin, however, rarely ever left the store. He looked up from his task of sorting scented soaps into baskets to greet Ellie Jane as she walked through the door.

"Afternoon, Miss Ellie Jane. You want to try one of these new soaps? They're just in from Paris, France."

"No, thank you, Mr. Poplin." Ellie Jane never did like having to discuss such intimate decisions with Mr. Poplin, no matter how grandfatherly and harmless he seemed to be.

"You sure?" He held up a small, heart-shaped cake wrapped in pale green tissue. "Just seventy-nine cents to smell like a bouquet of fresh orchids."

"Or for half that," Ellie Jane clasped her little purse tighter, "I could have ten cakes of Snowberry."

"Ah, but the fellows, they don't stick around to smell Snowberry." Mr. Poplin shook a long, admonishing finger.

Ellie Jane, grateful to be the only customer in the store, felt instant heat rise to her cheeks. "*Mr. Poplin!* What would your wife say if she heard you speak to me this way?"

Just then the bell over the door rang, and a mother came in, dragging a less-than-cooperative child. Mr. Poplin curled his finger and used it to beckon Ellie Jane closer. She complied, and once she was close enough to smell the orchids in the green paper-wrapped soap, she leaned closer still until her ear was mere inches away from Mr. Poplin's thin lips.

"Who do you think she bought this for?"

"Maybe next time." Ellie Jane smiled warmly. "I've just come in to see if my catalogue order has arrived."

He looked up to the ceiling and ran his finger down an imaginary list, proclaiming "Bingo!" when he landed on her invisible name. "I'll just pop to the back and get it."

Following Mr. Poplin's retreat, Ellie Jane wandered through the store, inspecting the spools of lace and ribbons. Perhaps it was time to do something to spruce up her spring boater. She heard a little noise and looked down to see the child—a rather pretty little girl—eyeing her curiously.

"Aren't the ribbons pretty?" Ellie Jane lowered a spool of pink satin so the little girl could touch it.

"Come here, darling." The girl's mother grabbed the child by the shoulder and drew her protectively against her skirts, avoiding Ellie Jane's gaze.

"Good afternoon," Ellie Jane said through gritted teeth.

The woman gave a curt nod and backed toward the door.

"Oh, for Pete's sake, Miranda. We've known each other since we were children. There's really no call for—"

"We need to get home." The other woman continued her exit.

"But, Mama, what about my new stockings?" The child dug in her heels.

"I'm here to get new stockings too!" Ellie Jane spoke with affectionate enthusiasm, knowing it would irritate the little girl's mother.

"Another time, dear." This time Miranda was the one to grit her grin.

Ellie Jane lingered in the wake of her friend's exit. Well, not her friend, exactly. More like a former schoolmate. She thought about Charlotte, who would be strolling arm in arm with the same girls with whom she'd played jump rope and hopscotch and all those games little girls played together.

Ellie Jane stood alone in Mr. Poplin's store, haunted by the sounds of giggles and whispers behind her back. She remembered crying to her father who assured her they were all just silly girls, that they'd come around soon enough.

She carefully placed the spool of pink ribbon back on the shelf.

It's never going to change. All these years, and they hate me as much as they ever did.

Mr. Poplin came back into the room. "Did I hear the door?"

"That other woman left." As much as she tried to appear nonplussed, Mr. Poplin's face looked concerned. "I'm fine, really," Ellie Jane said, warning off his questions. Then she noticed the pile of packages in his arms and had a few questions of her own. "What is all that?"

"Why, your catalogue order." Mr. Poplin piled them on the counter.

"I ordered stockings. Five pair."

"That would be these." He held up a long, thin package.

"So what are these other things?"

"Let me see." He looked at a sheet of thin yellow paper. "Ah yes. Twelve baseballs, two gloves, and a catcher's mask."

"I didn't order these." Ellie Jane felt the tips of her ears burn. "I'm not paying for them."

"They're already paid for. By that fellow you've got staying at the house."

"Mr. Dennison?"

"That's the one." The old store owner's eyes took on a twinkle.

"And I suppose he just expects me to fetch them home," Ellie Jane said, intending the comment for herself.

"Doesn't matter one way or the other to me. I'd be happy to hold on to them here, and you can tell the Duke to come and get them for himself. Or, if you like, I can just drop them by your house sometime…"

"When did you incorporate a delivery service?" Ellie Jane leaned across the counter.

"Oh, it's never a problem to help out a loyal customer."

Ellie Jane *hmmphed* and gathered up the packages. "I'll remember that next time I order stockings."

DUKE

Duke himself manned the stove, his shirtsleeves rolled up past his elbows and one of Ellie Jane's aprons tied over his fine linen pants.

"Just about five minutes on each side," he said over the sound of the newly turned sizzling steak. "Keeps it a perfect warm pink right through the middle."

"Might want to cook Ellie Jane's a little longer." Floyd sat at the kitchen table, peeling a small pile of large potatoes. "Don't know that she's going to want—"

"Women don't know what they want." Duke turned another steak.

"You don't know my Ellie. She's a woman with some pretty strong opinions."

Duke chuckled. "Not the same thing. No offense to your lovely daughter, sir, but some of those strong opinions don't seem to come from her own mind." He reached for the peppermill and held it over the pan, turning the handle to grind a fine dusting of the black powder over each steak. "You think she comes up with these ideas herself? Let's see, what was that she fixed for supper last night?"

"Eggplant soufflé." Floyd grimaced, much as he had the previous night when Ellie Jane set the dish on the table.

"Exactly!" Duke turned his attention back to the steaks. "No woman in her right mind would ever think up something like that. No, my friend, that comes from all those books and magazines women are reading all the time. Telling them red meat's not healthy. Look at this—"

Duke stretched out and used the long fork to open one of the cabinets to the left of the stove. "All this stuff in little cans and boxes. When I was a kid, you wanted food, your pa went out and killed it. Now there's nothing but flakes and grains, coming from doctors who want to take away everything it means to be a man."

He found himself gripping the fork as tightly as he'd ever gripped any bat. Or any bottle. So slowly, relaxing his grip, he brought it down and jabbed at the meat in the pan, moving it around, and bringing forth fresh sizzles and pops.

"You know, son," Floyd's voice was quiet behind him, "sometimes those doctors are right."

"Sometimes." Duke didn't turn around. "But it does something to a man to tell him he can't even have a cold beer with a nice steak."

"Got nothing to do with being a man."

"So you say."

"It's like a disease with you, Dennison. No shame in that."

"Did I say I felt ashamed?" Duke faced the older man who, despite the fact that he was sitting behind a pile of potato peelings, created an imposing figure.

"I go every day of my life without taking a drink." Floyd used the tip of his knife to dig out an eye. "Think it makes me less of a man?"

"'Course not."

"There you go."

The room was silent. Just the sizzling of the meat in the pan and the intermittent sound of the slicing knife. Wearing a red quilted mitt to protect his hands, Duke opened the oven and took out the plate he'd placed in there. One by one he lifted the steaks out of the pan and set them on the plate, then put it back in the oven to keep the meat warm.

He brought the pan over to the table where Floyd had turned the potatoes into a pile of thin uniform sticks, which Duke scraped from the cutting board into the seasoned hot butter and grease. Back at the stove, he took a red-handled spatula from a crock and stirred the potatoes, spreading them evenly across the bottom of the pan.

For a few isolated moments, Duke felt perfect contentment. He still wanted a drink, but for the first time in a long time, he felt he might live through the night without it.

Then the storm hit.

During eleven days with the Voyants, Duke had noticed a certain placid tone that permeated everything these people did. Both father and daughter moved around each other in wide, silent circles, making polite conversation. Slipping in and out of the house. Appearing and disappearing from rooms. Like cats suddenly struck with human form.

But not today.

He heard the *whoosh* and *slam* of the front door clear over the sizzling of the potatoes. Then the series of quick, little footsteps bringing Ellie Jane storming into the kitchen. Her hair was a mess. Her face cardinal red. She clutched a disorganized pile of brown paper packages close to her with one hand. Her purse still dangled off the other.

"Exactly what is going on in here?"

She stomped her foot in never-before-seen irritation and threw—actually *threw*—her purse onto the kitchen table. Right into the potato peelings.

Duke had seen angry women before, and this one standing rigid in the kitchen doorway topped them all. He glanced over to Floyd, who seemed just as shocked as he was.

"I could smell this cooking halfway down the block!"

Duke puffed up his chest behind the floral apron and grinned. "Well, thank you, Miss Voyant. I picked up the technique from the head chef at the Chicago Tremont Hotel. Sometimes we'd go there after a game, and let me tell you, cutting into one of his steaks was like—"

"Oh, shut up!" Ellie Jane screamed, and to his own surprise, Duke did.

"Now, Elijah Jane, there's no call to be rude."

"Pop, how could you let this happen? Those steaks were for tomorrow. After *church*!" She practically spit the last word in Duke's direction.

"Well, sweetie, I don't see the harm—"

"Don't see the harm? Pop, you know what today is."

"Saturday."

"The *second* Saturday in May. You've lived in this town your whole life. How could you do this to me?"

A slow transformation came across Floyd's face. And then he knew. He rose from his chair and walked around the table. The very top of his daughter's head barely met his shoulder, and she looked like a very little girl as he folded her—brown paper packages and all—into his arms. For the first time since his arrival in this home, Duke felt like an intruder. No idea what they were talking about. No place in this tight little family.

He turned his attention to the potatoes browning nicely on the stove and would have been content to leave himself out of their befuddling conversation if it weren't for what Floyd said next.

"There, there, dear," he said, as if soothing a child, "we can put all this away in the icebox and warm it up tomorrow."

"The devil we will." Duke gave the spatula one last scrape across the pan before tossing it on the counter next to the stove. He turned around and fixed the pair of them with his most threatening glare, instantly wishing he wasn't wearing a knee-length floral apron.

"Watch your language, son." Floyd looked at him over the top of Ellie Jane's mound of frizzy hair.

"These steaks," Duke said, nearly salivating, "are cooked to perfection. This whole meal is—well, a *meal*. It's been nothing but canned food and vegetables since I got here, and I need food. I need meat. I paid for it. I cooked it. And I intend to eat it."

"Do as you please, Mr. Dennison." Ellie Jane backed out of her father's embrace and wiped her nose on her sleeve. "You've cooked it. The damage has been done." She strode toward the kitchen door, then stopped and turned. "By the way, I picked these up for you."

One by one she threw brown paper packages at Duke. Though her aim was true, he barely had time to register what she was doing, and he caught them clumsily, one after the other, clutching them tightly against the apron bib.

Then she left.

"What was all that?"

"Let's clean this up." The man seemed genuinely sad. "I'll tell you over supper."

"We're eating, then?"

"Yep. We're eating."

The two men worked together without conversation, but the companionable air was gone. While Floyd gathered the peelings to take outside to the compost heap, Duke dropped the packages on the table before removing the frilly apron and laying it on top of them.

"Want to tell me what's in there?" Floyd eyed the brown bundles with a hint of suspicion.

"Not right now." Duke wasn't ready to share the impact of that single, perfect catch the boy Morris made that first day. Or the bright spot in his day—and every day since—when the two got together to play a simple game of catch in the yard behind the Voyant's house. Right now he just wanted to know why this first attempt to repay their hospitality was met with such hysteria.

He picked up Ellie Jane's little purse and carried it out of the kitchen to deposit it in its rightful place in the entryway.

Given the huff she'd been in when she stormed out of the kitchen, Duke expected that Ellie Jane would have stomped herself clear up to her room, but there she was in the front parlor, standing in the narrow space between the back of the sofa and the front window. A thin, sheer curtain obscured the view outside, but she hadn't made any attempt to pull it aside. She seemed to be staring through it, her arms folded in front of her in grim determination.

Duke tried to incorporate his host family's gift for stealth and return the purse to the little table without calling any attention to himself, but his hands might as well have been catcher's mitts as he maneuvered around the intricate collection of figurines. He managed to catch a porcelain dancing girl before she crashed to the floor.

"Be careful with those. They aren't yours," she said without turning around.

"My apologies, Miss Voyant." He walked over to the window and looked out over her shoulder. "I'm sorry if I somehow offended you by cooking supper—"

"You didn't offend me, Mr. Dennison. It's much more complicated than that. And much more silly."

She put her hand to the sheer and pulled it aside—just an inch—and cocked her head to peer through the narrow opening. Duke followed suit, and for a brief moment the blurred vision on the other side became crystal clear. A man and a woman, arm in arm, strolled past the little iron gate at the entrance to the Voyant's front yard.

"Watch," Ellie Jane whispered, though there was no way the couple would be able to hear her voice. "You see them slowing down, almost stopping, and they're going to sniff the air."

They did. Right on cue.

"Who are they?" Duke was whispering now too.

"Emily Porthouse and Charles Gooding. I went to school with her older sister, and he's the new loan officer at the bank. And see? They know we're home. They know we're cooking a fine, hot supper in here. Ooh, I wish I could walk out there and slap the smirk off of Emily's face. But of course I wouldn't—oops!"

Just then young Emily cut her eyes straight to the window. Like she was listening to every word.

Ellie Jane not only dropped the curtain, but turned to step away from it, with no place to go but flat up against Duke. Acting on instinct, he put his hands on her waist to steady her, but it was more than instinct that kept them there. It had been a long time since he'd held a woman in his arms, and the last few were nothing more than blurry dark shadows.

Now this one. Forget about the steaks. All he could smell was the scent of her practical soap. As far as he could tell, she wasn't breathing. At all. He looked down, amused at the bird's nest atop her head, then tracked a loose copper-colored strand to where it landed at the base of her stiff, set jaw. She wore pretty earrings in her thin earlobes, and her neck was long and white, mere shades away from the high-collared blouse that—

"Miss Voyant?" Duke said, aiming his words at that delicate spot just below her ear.

"Yes, Mr. Dennison," she whispered.

"Are you aware that your blouse is unbuttoned?"

She was out of his arms that instant, hands at the back of her neck. Right now it looked like the color of a perfectly cooked steak.

"Can I help you with that?" Duke's fingers itched to touch those tiny, pearlescent buttons at the back of that perfect neck.

"Don't be ridiculous." Within seconds her small, deft hands had not only refastened her blouse, but also smoothed her skirt and trapped the loose strands of hair back behind her ears. "Now if you'll excuse me, I'm going upstairs to wash up."

"For supper?"

She sighed. "I might as well. The damage is done."

Duke worked his face into his best comic frown. "Keep talking like that and you're going to hurt my feelings." When she didn't laugh—or smile—he reached for her hand, holding it tighter as she tried to wrest it away. "Tell me, Miss Voyant. What's this all about?"

"I told you it's silly." Ellie Jane snuck a peek over her shoulder at the window. "It's something our little town does. We call it the Spring Promenade."

"Spring Promenade?"

"See? It sounds even sillier hearing somebody else say it." But there wasn't a hint of laughter in her eyes.

"Tell me." Duke brought her around to sit next to him on the sofa.

"I suppose it's a courtship ritual of sorts," Ellie Jane said, her newly freed hand gesturing wildly. "All through May and June, Saturday night is the night when couples, or at least young men and women who have a certain understanding, meet up with each other and…walk."

"Scandalous!" He looked out the window behind Ellie Jane and opened his eyes wide. "Especially so, given that there are two—wait, three—gentlemen *promenading* on your sidewalk as we speak."

"Oh, my goodness!" Ellie Jane hopped up from the sofa and moved out of the window's line of view. "Do you think they saw me?" She was whispering again.

"Do you want me to go outside and check?"

"Don't you dare." She moved back in front of him, as if to block him from doing so. "Those are young men who are currently… unattached, shall we say. Bachelors, if you will."

"Ah," Duke said as the picture became clearer. "And tell me, do the young women of your town also spend their Saturday evenings walking the streets?"

Ellie Jane pursed her lips. "I do not appreciate your crude implications. It is, in fact, completely different for women. We—well, they—meaning those women who are also unattached, might gather with other family or friends on their front porches."

"And when the eligible bachelor happens by this snare—or, porch, if you prefer."

She smiled. "They might stop and talk at the gate or, given there is adequate supervision or some other chaperone, they might be invited in for a light snack. Sandwiches, perhaps. Or a plate of three bean salad."

"So they meet pretty girls *and* get a free meal?"

"Something like that, yes."

"But not a juicy hunk of beefsteak and fried potatoes. I guess that's reserved for old married folks."

"No, Mr. Dennison. Even they like to sit out and watch the couples walk by, even invite them in sometimes. I'm afraid meals like the one you prepared tonight are reserved for those who no longer see courtship as an option or as entertainment."

She turned away from him then and was heading for the stairs. He cursed quietly when he nicked his leg on the coffee table before catching up with her, trapping her hand as she lay it on the banister.

"Please, Miss Voyant. There's no way I could have known."

She withdrew her hand and faced him. "Of course you couldn't. And I'm sorry to have subjected you to such histrionics."

"Perhaps we could sit outside after we eat?"

Ellie Jane threw her head back and let out a mirthless, bitter laugh. "My dear Mr. Dennison, it's been years since I've participated in such nonsense. I simply don't care to advertise my status to the street at large."

She then ascended the first, second, and third step before Duke called out for her to stop.

"If I could be so bold," he said once she'd turned around, "why?"

"Why, what, exactly?"

"Why hasn't some fellow come and swept you off your porch? You're young enough. I'd wager you're not yet thirty."

"I am twenty-five."

"See?" The edge in her voice made him choose his next words more carefully. "And you're not unattractive."

"Good heavens, Mr. Dennison." Ellie Jane brought a hand to her breast, as if to still a pounding heart. "I think it's a good thing you have your celebrity to save you from your dismal flattery."

Duke closed his eyes, wishing he had a drink. Good booze always seemed to smooth his tongue. "I mean, why are you alone? Certainly there have been—"

"Prospects?" She looked down at him from the fourth step, and he had never felt so small. "You'll do well to remember that you are a temporary guest in our home. My romantic past has absolutely no bearing on your stay. As I've said, we are a silly town, prone to silly things. I have weathered many a spring before you arrived, and I'll weather even more after you've left. Now I've grown tired of this conversation, and I wish to go upstairs and lie down. I don't think I could bear to stomach such a heavy meal. Good night, Mr. Dennison."

Duke watched her delicate step up the carpeted stairs, not knowing what he would say even if he could call her back. He turned around and saw Floyd standing in the middle of the parlor. Duke wasn't sure how much the older man heard, but he looked hurt. And embarrassed.

"Everything's set up in the kitchen, Duke. Whenever you're ready."

"I'm ready now." But his appetite had disappeared with Ellie Jane. He didn't want a steak, no matter how perfect. He just wanted a drink to wash it down.

"Now don't let her trouble you, son." Floyd clapped a hand on Duke's shoulder. "She gets that way sometimes."

"I'll try to remember that." Duke made his way to the kitchen. He was on the other side of the swinging door when he realized Floyd had not followed him. Duke poked his head back through the door just in time to see Ellie Jane's father close the heavy parlor drapes.

PART 3

THE GAMES BEGIN

GRACE METHODIST CHURCH

LADIES ACTIVITIES FOR THE WEEK OF MAY 15–19

Monday, 9 a.m. — Brunch

We welcome all women from Grace Methodist Church as well as members of Picksville's Ladies Auxiliary to come to this elegant event. We will serve an elegant buffet of many different pastries. Mrs. Herbert Lohman will also do us the honor of serving her award-winning creamed stuffed eggs.

After the meal, the First Lady of Picksville, Elizabeth Birdiff, will regale us with a brief glimpse into her life as the wife of a public servant.

The cost for this event is twenty-five cents. All proceeds will benefit the tireless work of our mayor and our church to give aid to our town's Tenth Street Mission.

Monday, May 15

I'm glad whatever I pray to God stays right between me and Him.

Saturday at church Bishop Tilley was up at the front, wailin and prayin sayin, Lord how we long for Your Promised Land. Jesus we toil here for a little while as we await our great and glorious eternity.

And everyone around is weepin and swayin. Yes Jesus. Thank You Lord. Cause they're thinkin about heaven and I guess that's fine. But there can't be any harm in wantin just a little bit of that right here in this lifetime.

Like that Mr. Duke has. I gone to see him every day since I met him and haven't ever seen him in the same shirt twice. Every one of them clean and starched and better than what the mayor wears in his own office. Me I don't have but three shirts to my name and when I tried to wear my good shirt over to play ball with Mr. Duke Mama had one of her fits—and she don't even know that's where I was headed.

That's what I was thinkin about in church. Not the Sweet By and By, not Blessed Be the Poor. I was thinkin what a shame it is to waste your only decent shirt sittin on this bench all Satur-

day afternoon. As much as I love Jesus I don't see the good of dressin up just for Him. Seems to me Jesus would love me in my rags so I can wear my good clothes for my work down here in the world.

And that's what I'm thinkin this mornin when I put on my good church shirt. And it ain't so good—just less stained and torn than my others. Figure if it's good enough for church it's good enough for school. After all it's the same building. But then I start thinkin that I don't have a head for school at all today. I mean with God all knowin He couldn't have intended this day as one for a boy to sit inside. So even though I can hear Teacher ringin the bell I head into town and walk right into Mr. Poplin's Dry Goods. I always like goin to his store because he doesn't get that nervous look like other white folks do whenever a Negro walks into the room. He smiles right at me like I'm a regular customer and asks me what he can do for me this fine morning.

I tell him I want to buy me a new shirt. Ready made with a finished hem. One with stripes like Mr. Duke wears only I don't say anything about Mr. Duke out loud cause I don't want to be gettin above myself.

Mr. Poplin starts hummin and lookin on some of the shelves behind the counter. Then he tells me to wait there while he checks somethin out in the back. Meantime I'm standin in the middle of this store all by myself, no white eyes to keep me honest. Those were the longest and proudest three minutes of my life yet.

When Mr. Poplin comes back he tells me he doesn't have anything that he thinks will fit me which is a lie because I seen some of the shirts he unfolded and held up.

I tell him, Thank you, and start to leave when he says, Wait a minute. Maybe we can try somethin else. Then he brings out a great big book, says it's a Sears catalogue, and we could get me a shirt from there.

I haven't ever had nothin from a catalogue before so I just wait while Mr. Poplin turns a bunch of pages and then calls me closer. Look here, he says, Maybe you see somethin on this page you like.

It's a whole page of pictures of white boys wearin striped shirts. They all look like miniature Mr. Dukes without the moustache, standin with their arms on their hips and their chests puffed out. Like they had some kind of power.

I look at that and figure that's why Mr. Duke is always tellin me to stand up straight like my mama hasn't ever told me to.

Mr. Poplin says all we have to do is get some measurements and then he takes this long tape from a drawer and comes over to my side of the counter. He measures my shoulders and my arms around my chest and my waist, tellin me to remember all the numbers so he can write them down. He gets to standin so close to me I was glad I just had my bath two nights ago cause I don't know that he'd order a brand new shirt for a smelly Negro boy. When we was done he takes out a little notebook and asks me to say all the numbers back to him which I do then he tells me to point out which shirt I want.

Now nobody has ever before asked me to choose anything I've ever owned. Every autumn a group of nice white people come to our church with boxes of clothes and shoes they spread out over all the benches. But that's not the same. Sometimes there's nothin there that fits me and I have to wait until spring when they come back again.

But this? There was five different shirts and I could have any one I wanted. And it would come special made for me, brand new with all its buttons attached. I have to choose so careful and I run my finger over all the pictures and all the words, tryin to put my face on one of those puffed-up bodies.

Then I see the price—one dollar—and I put my hand back in my pocket. I tell Mr. Poplin that I don't have more than fifty cents to spend on a shirt.

Fifty cents? he says. Well perhaps we'll have to strike up a business proposition.

I decide right then that I like Mr. Poplin even more because he doesn't talk to me any different than he does to anybody else. He says the shirt won't arrive for a few days yet and I can give him fifty cents now and the other fifty cents when it gets here. He says, Surely an enterprising young man like yourself can earn half-a-dollar?

And then I feel a little guilty because here he is trustin me and I have enough money sittin back at my house to buy myself a dozen of these shirts. But I just nod and tell him, Yessir.

Very good, he says, and starts fillin out a little paper after I show him which shirt I want. It's striped and has a pocket and pearl buttons. When he's finished fillin out the paper Mr. Poplin looks up at me and says, Will there be anything else?

I'm laughin inside because nobody's ever said that to me before and I tell him, Yes. Why don't you get me two of them?

When I leave Mr. Poplin's store it's still too early to meet up with Mr. Duke so I decide to start earnin some of the money I'll need for my new clothes. I walk through the little park in the center of town and stop at the bench just outside Mayor Birdiff's window. I was just about to think that it's too early even for the mayor to be at work when I see him walk past his window and I make my little sound—that cough that won't leave my throat.

I don't know how Mayor Birdiff can hear that sound from so far away but he always does—even if his window is closed like it is today. For all I know there's a bunch of real important men in that office with him but it wouldn't matter a bit because as soon as he hears me he comes to the window and looks straight down where I'm standin, hat in hand to show a little respect. He's movin his mouth talkin to whoever's in the office with him and gives me a signal—five fingers then two fingers with a swirlin motion. That means wait five minutes then meet him on the second floor landin of the back staircase.

The first time I ever walked in the back door of the city hall I was scared out of my head. But now nobody ever even gives me a look. At least not in a bad way. The back door leads right into the kitchen and if I'm lucky I'll be there right when Miss Cherine is settin up one of the mayor's snacks.

That happens today and I get a jam sandwich and a glass of cold milk before I even go upstairs and a shortbread cookie to eat while I'm waitin. I'm just finishin that up when the door opens and the mayor comes in, huffin a little bit even though he hasn't had to climb a single step. He has a little flat box wrapped with a red ribbon that he wants me to deliver to Miss LuAnn DeSalvo. And he hands me a nickel.

Do you know where she lives? he asks me and I say, Yes. Corner of Clinton and Tenth Street. But should I go back through the park? Or should I detour back and up Bellington Avenue?

He asks me, What's the difference?

I tell him that Mrs. Birdiff always has Monday brunch with the ladies of the Methodist church on Green Street so he gives me another dime and tells me to take the long way.

I don't even look up much when I'm walkin down Tenth Street, just watch my boots one step after another not too fast not too slow. I never had no dealings with any of the folks who live here but I know plenty of them that work here. And it's happened more than once that one of Mama's friends will holler at me through a side door and tell me I'm in for the whippin of my life when I get home. But nobody sees me today and as soon as I turn the corner of Clinton Avenue I feel more at home. It's not long until the houses start gettin smaller and then they start stackin up on top of each other. Miss LuAnn DeSalvo lives in one of those on the third floor up this little narrow iron staircase. I imagine it's quite a sight watchin that fat old man climb up here late at night.

When I get to Miss LuAnn's door I reach out and knock just three soft ones and step back away from the door. When she opens it I get hit with the smell of her perfume so strong it nearly knocks me off the stairs and I see her wrapped up in this pink feathery thing. Nothin like bein dressed even though it's nearly eleven o'clock in the morning. She's got long dark hair that's fallin all over and her face looks like somethin somebody painted then left out in the rain.

She says, Hello Morris baby, and grabs me.

Next thing I know I got a face full of soft feathers. I don't want to hurt her feelings so I don't push away even though I can't hardly breathe. And in just a minute she gives me one more little squeeze then lets me go and asks if I brought her a present.

Yes m'am, I say and hand her the little box. She hugs that box every bit as close as she did me then tells me to wait right here before she closes the door. I pull my hat down low over my eyes while I'm waitin just in case somebody were to walk by but nobody did. And after a few minutes Miss LuAnn is back with a little piece of paper. Now you take this right back to Mayor Birdiff, she says. And you tell him to give you a shiny new penny.

Yes m'am, I say again and I tip my hat a little. Anything else?

She hugs me real close again and makes me promise to come back and see her when I think I'm man enough. Well I don't know if I'll ever be man enough for Miss LuAnn DeSalvo but I promise anyway then walk real careful down the stairs.

I keep hold tight of the note until I'm halfway up Tenth Street when I think I'd better put it in my pocket just in case somebody stops me and wants to read it. But then I don't want it to wrinkle up so I just slip it up my sleeve. It's not sealed up or anything—probably because that lady don't think I can read—and I know I shouldn't look at it. But I figure it's my hide on the line if the wrong person reads it so I think I deserve to know what it says.

As soon as I get to the edge of the park I open it up. I don't read more than the first two lines before I learn two things. Miss LuAnn DeSalvo is not a nice lady and she spells worse than I do. I reach down into my pocket and find a little piece of string then I roll up the note real tight and tie the string around it.

When I get back to my bench outside Mayor Birdiff's window it's not long at all before he sees me and gives me the same *signal to meet him. By now everybody's workin on gettin lunch ready in the kitchen and Miss Cherine says I can have a chicken leg on the way out.*

Now that chicken smells good and I already done enough this mornin that my mama would say's gonna send me to hell but that chicken smells so good. Still a mama's a mama so I say, No thank you Miss Cherine.

Her eyes get real big and she takes a step back. She says, You sayin no to my chicken? Boy I know grown men to cry over this chicken.

I'm bout to cry myself but I just tell her that my mama says we ain't supposed to eat meat.

Then she scrunches up her lips and says, Hmm. You one of them Adventist people?

I say, Yes m'am.

Well, she says. You know it's Jesus who saved your soul?

And I say, Yes m'am.

Then she asks me if I got the Holy Spirit livin in me, and I say, Yes m'am. Cause I know that to be true. Then she bends real close and says, Boy don't you think the Holy Spirit of the livin God is stronger than one little old piece of chicken?

And it makes me think. I might of made a promise to Mama but I never made such a one to God so I say, Thank you m'am. I'd be glad to have it, and head upstairs where Mayor Birdiff's waitin.

Soon as I show up he asks, Do you have anything for me? He's rubbin his hands together like he's the one who's gonna get the chicken.

Yessir, I say and hand over the little note.

Then he asks me, Did she say anything? But I don't say
nothin about the shiny penny mostly because I don't work for
that kind of cheap. Instead I say that she says he should read this
as soon as possible but it turns out I didn't even have to tell that
lie because he's already tearing off the string.

Right there I pray to Jesus to forgive me for knowin exactly
what he's readin. The mayor's face turns bright red and he starts
to sweat a little before he rolls the note up tight and puts it in his
own pocket. When he brings his hand out again he has a whole
quarter in it that he holds out to me.

I slip it into my pocket quick before he realizes what he done
and say, Thank you sir. Will there be anything else? And he says,
Yes. Cherine's frying chicken for lunch. Make sure she gives you a
piece on your way out.

Not only does Miss Cherine give me a piece of chicken, she
gives me a whole sack lunch with chicken, cornbread, fried okra,
and a little peach tart. Now I know why Mayor Birdiff is as fat
as he is. And even though I'm hungry I decide to save it in case
this is one of those nights when Mama don't make it home for
supper.

I still have some time before I meet up with Mr. Duke so I
make my usual rounds seein if there's any telegrams or anything
else to deliver but it's a slow Monday morning and I'm out of
luck. So I head over early to the Voyant's house and stand at the
gate. It's not long before Mr. Duke himself is on the front porch.
He says, Ah young Morris. I have somethin for you.

Now so far this has turned out to be a million dollar day
and I can't even think of anything that would make it better.
Then Mr. Duke comes down off that front porch and he's smilin

bigger than a quarter moon. Come back here, he says, and I open the gate and follow him to the backyard. Then he says, Here you are, and hands me a brand new glove. I hold it up to my face and smell it deep. It's sweeter than Miss LuAnn DeSalvo's perfume and at that minute I want it more than Miss Cherine's fried chicken.

Now, Mr. Duke says, since I don't have to worry about breakin any fingers catchin what you throw, let's see just what you can really do.

NED

Ned brought the wagon to a stop at the storehouse entrance behind the store. Not much to unload today—a dozen sacks of chicken feed and half-a-dozen grain. If he tarried long enough, taking the sacks one by one, he could justify calling it a day. Not that he had anything much else to do. He'd finished updating the account books by noon and had read the morning newspaper while eating one of Marlene's wax paper–wrapped sandwiches at the train station.

He often did that on Mondays, hoping Ellie Jane would one day come out and join him. After all, they would have crossed each other's path at some point on the busy, errand-filled Saturday, and she'd sat just one aisle over and two pews up in church the day before. Maybe momentum would be on his side, and on a warm spring afternoon like this she would bring her little lunch bucket out of the booth and sit beside him on one of the benches on the platform.

Of course, he never invited her to join him, but he did sit in full view, slowly unwrapping his sandwich and opening a bottle of ginger ale. Then, when her eyes happened to catch his from the other side of the booth's glass window, he'd lift up his bottle (or sandwich, depending which was in his hand) in a friendly salute.

Care to join me?

She might return the salute with her own little cracker or piece of fruit, but without fail, every Monday—like this one—Ned was left alone on the bench. And there he would pray. *Lord, just let her look at me. Just once, let her see me, and I'll do the rest.*

Now he tasted Marlene's cheese-and-olive sandwich as he tugged open the wagon's tailgate and tossed the first sack of chicken feed over his shoulder. It took a moment for his eyes to adjust to the storeroom's darkness, so he stood perfectly still and waited for shelves and supplies to take solid form in the afternoon gray.

He dropped the sack at his feet and rearranged the shelves to make room for the new inventory, but when he bent to pick the sack up again, it was gone. Confused, he turned around to see young Morris, who held the sack out in two open arms.

There was, as always, that bit of shock at finding himself not alone. Just after his deafness set in, Ned started nearly every social encounter with a gasp and a jump, often scaring his visitor as much as he himself had been. Through the years he'd trained himself to stop that little jolt of surprise right at the tip of his throat, where it burned now like a funny little unspoken scream as he lifted a shaky hand in greeting.

Hey, Morris.

Morris nodded and handed up the feed sack.

Ned took it and shelved it before turning back to the boy. *What do you want?*

The boy said something, but his words were lost in the room's shadows. Ned leaned forward and Morris repeated his message, accompanied by an illustration of his two hands wrapped around an invisible stick, twisting his torso in a halfhearted swing.

I need a baseball bat.

Ned didn't answer right away. Instead, he headed back to the wagon, assuming that Morris followed, and when the two were back in the sunlight, he faced Morris head-on and asked, "Why do you need a bat?"

It's for Duke, Morris said, bringing his hand up to his lip to draw an invisible, perfectly groomed moustache.

Ned broke into a huge smile and let out a hoot. "Really?"

Morris nodded and crooked his finger. *C'mon, I'll take you.*

But there was work to do first. Ned piled sack after sack of chicken feed on Morris's outstretched arms, until the boy nearly staggered under the load, and pointed him toward the storeroom. Then he hauled two of the larger sacks of grain to the edge of the tailgate, squatted down, and positioned both on his shoulder. He stood, steadying himself under the weight, and strode inside, dumping them on the first available space.

Morris had somehow managed to unload his own, and it wasn't more than five minutes before the wagon was empty. Ten minutes later the horses were unhitched and settled in the stable, and Morris was following Ned up the back stairs to his room above the feed store.

Once there, he pointed to the overstuffed leather chair by the window, inviting Morris to sit down. There was a large steamer trunk in front of the chair—a place for Ned to prop his feet on when he sat reading his Bible every morning and *Spalding's Official Base Ball Guide* every long evening. That book topped the neat stack of other sporting magazines, and Ned carefully moved the collection to his desk before he knelt down and lifted the trunk's heavy lid. He looked up to see Morris's curious eyes peeping over the lid and invited the boy to sit next to him on the floor.

Across the top was a square of canvas that, if unfolded, would display in bright blue paint Connecticut Crickets—the name of a ragtag team Ned played with during his years attending the school for the deaf in Hartford. Underneath that, a neatly folded shirt with the same name stitched across the shoulders. It had been more than ten years since he'd worn this uniform, having packed it away the day his father declared that he'd paid enough for his education. If he wanted to waste time going to college, he could do so after he worked off the cost of high school.

Ned unfolded the shirt now and held it up between him and Morris. It was too big for the slender boy—not that Ned would ever consider giving it away—and, given the narrowness of the uniform's shoulders, too small for Ned. This was a young man's garment, tailored to a young man's form. He dropped it on the floor beside him and went back to the trunk's contents.

His hands pushed aside the rest of the uniform—hat and pants and socks. There was a long box full of photographs, but he wasn't going to go through those now. Too much to explain to the boy, all of the grand brick buildings and the slightly bewildered-looking young men posed in front of them. Then there were the silly ones— those same young men engaged in one sport after another, running races, and lifting papier-mâché barbells.

There were pictures of pretty girls in white dresses sitting on blankets with picnic baskets in the park, and small portraits of those same girls with sweet notes written on the back: *"For you, Silly-head Ned. Best wishes ever…"* and they were signed Sophie or Clara or Theresa, handed over to him with batting eyes and blushing cheeks.

And at the very bottom was a postcard with a picture of two little blue birds sitting on a blossoming tree branch. It was the first piece of mail he'd received when he went away to school. He turned it over, revealing the juvenile script on the back:

Dear Ned,

I am so sorry you had to go away to school.

I hope you learn all you need to know and that you get to come back to visit often.

Fondly,

Elijah Jane Voyant

Of course he hadn't been back to visit often. Train tickets were expensive, and jobs for young boys much more plentiful in the big city of Hartford. He was twelve when he left, eighteen when he returned for his mother's funeral. He wondered a million times what would have happened if he'd ever written back.

There were books he'd brought back from school—volumes of science and literature, all of which seemed frivolous now. But he closed his fingers around a thick green history tome, lifted it out, and presented it to Morris.

"Take that," Ned told him. He remembered most of the information in the pages, and what he couldn't remember, he didn't need to know.

The boy's eyes lit up when he saw it, and he took the book, holding it carefully as he ran his fingers over the gold engraved title. He flipped through the pages as Ned returned to the trunk. A few more textbooks, some writing tablets, one small notebook filled with the playing statistics of the Connecticut Crickets. This he handed over to Morris too, nudging the boy's arm to get his attention away from the history book.

Finally, clear at the bottom, there it was.

He was thirteen years old, out exploring a new city, when he found the split of ash in a heap of lumber outside a furniture shop.

He'd taken a silent walk through the shop until he found the wood-turner in the back.

It cost six months of pocket money and just as many Saturday afternoons sweeping up wood shavings, but by his second spring at school he had a beautiful bat—smooth and heavy with a perfect knot at the end of its handle. The shop owner had allowed him to use a small tool to burn his initials into the sweet spot. *N.C.* He could still remember the smell of the burning wood.

Ned lifted the bat out of the trunk and let the lid drop. He stood and tapped Morris on the shoulder. "Let's go."

They left by the back stairs. Once they were out of the alley and in the town square, Morris took the lead and it was Ned who followed, his bat resting on the tip of his shoulder. The boy walked much quicker than Ned was used to, and soon Morris was five paces ahead—such a distance that any of the townspeople they passed may not have even realized the two were on a mission together. That would explain why Morris was able to weave in and out of the crowd, never so much as brushing a sleeve, while Ned slowed intermittently to return a greeting, tipping his hat in response to the occasional touch of his sleeve. His anticipation grew as they kept walking through the park in the town square, and then they turned right on Parkway.

Then they were at the corner. Her corner. The corner where he'd stood last Saturday night—almost until dusk—wearing his second-best suit, wondering if Ellie Jane Voyant would come outside and sit on her porch.

If she had, he would have walked right up to the little iron gate in front, smiling until good manners forced her to invite him up for a glass of lemonade. After that he'd be ready, really ready this year, to ask her to walk with him.

If not this Saturday, the next.

But she hadn't come outside. An hour later, when he couldn't hear but could certainly suspect the pitying conversations of the happier couples and groups that passed him by, Ned went home.

Now here was Morris, opening that same gate as if he owned the place himself and glancing over his shoulder to urge Ned to follow. They walked around a little stone pathway to the back of the house where Morris stopped and looked up at a small second-floor balcony. Ned looked up too. The French-style door opened and Duke Dennison walked out and raised a hand in greeting, as if Ned and Morris had just arrived to save his life.

No steps led from the balcony to the backyard, so Duke ducked back inside and reappeared moments later and reached out for the bat. Ned handed it over carefully, holding on to it so tight that the other man had to give a little yank before it was fully in his hands. Duke turned it slowly, smiling when his eyes found the initials, then looked up at Ned.

You made this yourself?

"I had help."

Nice. Very nice.

The Duke took a few steps back and gripped the bat's handle. During his final years at school, Ned's hands had grown so much bigger he'd wrapped the handle in strips of leather to better accommodate his grip. He watched as Duke choked up, his diamond signet ring flashing in the afternoon sun. He was swinging it now— perfect stance, perfect cuts. He stopped after four and held the bat out again, admiringly. His lips pursed in a whistle before he looked at Ned again.

Can I use it?

Ned nodded.

Duke turned his head and said something to Morris, who trotted over to a canvas drawstring bag sitting up next to the house. He reached inside the bag, took out two gloves, and handed one to Ned.

Mr. Dennison says for you to catch me.

Ned took the mitt but remained rooted where he stood. This had to be a dream, standing in Ellie Jane Voyant's backyard, getting ready to pull batting practice with Morris the errand boy and Donald "The Duke" Dennison.

First of all, the yard wasn't nearly big enough, the width not more than twenty paces. And the length? Morris would have to stand in the middle of the vegetable garden to be far enough away from Duke to get any kind of decent pitch. Even then he'd have to throw it straight between the two oak trees in the middle of the yard, high enough to clear the ornate stone birdbath between the trees, low enough not to get it caught in the branches. Not to mention the problems when Duke got a hit—a line drive straight through the hedge into the next yard, or a high arc smack into Mrs. Finneworth's attic window. A foul tip up over the roof, onto the street, striking some innocent passerby in the head.

Meanwhile, Duke tugged on Ned's sleeve, leading him to a spot squarely in front of the back door, with the little three-step mud porch right at his ankles.

You know how to catch?

Ned nodded, muted by the ridiculousness of what was happening. He allowed the Duke to gently push on his shoulders until he was in a proper catcher's stance. He felt the faintest protest in his legs, so he bounced just a bit to work them in. He looked down the length of the yard, and there was Morris. He *was* standing in the middle of the vegetable garden, and that, along with the slight elevation of the yard, had him staring straight across—and down—at Ned. He felt a clap on his shoulder and glanced up to see Duke taking a few steps away before saying, *Let's warm up!*

Ready? Morris's posture asked from across the yard.

Ned nodded and moved the glove in front of him, staring at the boy beyond the stitches.

"Ready!"

At that, Morris brought the ball in the glove close to him and took on a pitcher's stance that rivaled any Ned had ever seen in any park. Morris lifted his foot, turned, and threw the ball—or at least Ned assumed he had, because there was a sudden stinging in his palm beneath the leather. He turned the glove to verify the ball was really there, before letting out a laugh. The Duke clapped him on the back again, and Ned saw the man grinning broadly, as if it were his own son who just threw a perfect pitch.

Ned took the ball out of the glove and held it for a minute. It had been years since he'd thrown a baseball—only once or twice since coming back home. Suddenly the Voyant's backyard seemed enormous. Morris might as well be on the mound at the Polo Grounds in New York. How would it look to send some sissy-lob splashing into the birdbath or a rainbow-arc into the tree? But he couldn't *not* throw, so he stood, drew back, and sent it out—rambling and unsteady—until it made its way into Morris's outstretched glove.

Feeling just slightly chagrined, Ned pounded his fist into the glove and squatted again, ready. This time he tracked the ball clear up to the moment it glanced off the tip of his glove, sending him scrambling on his knees to retrieve it. Then back to Morris. He lost count after a while as the two of them worked in a smooth, fluid rhythm, getting so caught up in the back-and-forth of it that he was actually startled when the Duke once again put his hand on Ned's shoulder.

The Duke was up to bat.

The imminence of this potential disaster brought Ned out of his reverie, and he stood to his full height, allowing just a flash of pleasure that he was a good three inches taller than the baseball hero. "Are you crazy?"

The Duke took one hand off the bat and held it up, placating. *Just wait.*

"You can't hit a ball right here."

Just hold off, and get back in your position.

Ned wasn't sure why he obeyed. Something in the Duke's eyes—a kind of impish desperation—made Ned believe, really *believe,* that wielding a baseball bat in the sheriff's backyard was the most natural thing in the world to do.

So down he went. He tried not to flinch as the Duke took a few swings, clearly outlining striking territory. Then he dug in his heels. Ned looked across the yard at Morris and, after saying a quick prayer for the neighborhood, nodded his readiness. Morris returned in kind and wound up.

The minute the ball left the boy's hand, Ned saw nothing but the gray leather orb barreling right down the line. As it came closer and closer, he tensed for impact. Out of the corner of his eye he saw the bat cut through the air, but just a breath too late because the ball was now cradled safely in his glove, and the bat dangled uselessly in Duke's hand.

Ned had never seen a man so proud to swing a strike.

ELLIE JANE

She often wondered why Mr. Coleman insisted the ticket booth remain open so late during the week. It was rare to have a train stop and go after three thirty, and certainly if there was an emergency, anybody in town could simply come to the Voyant house and bring Ellie Jane to the booth.

Still, Mr. Coleman seemed to think that staying open until five o'clock gave the station a cosmopolitan air, and if he was willing to pay her fifty cents an hour to sit in the booth and read her *Ladies Home Journal,* who was she to complain?

Ellie Jane flipped through the magazine now, whiling away the final hour. Her eyes skimmed over the articles—nothing caught her interest. Even the fashion illustrations seemed dull. Oh, she loved a new hat and a well-cut skirt as much as any woman, but who was here to appreciate how well her figure would fill that close-fitting striped suit? Not Mr. Dennison, surely. And not that it mattered if he would. She had enough problems with the people in this town without giving them the satisfaction of thinking her nothing more than some rogue's paramour.

She read the first and last paragraph of an article extolling the virtues of warm milk, thinking she was just as much an expert on the subject as the good lady doctor who wrote the thing. Then there were two pages of advertisements for tooth powder and cold cream, both of which featured pretty girls full of promise.

What caused her to stop, though, was the image on the facing page. It was a print of an artist's painting titled "The First Punishment." In it, a little girl with thick brown curls stood against a pretty pink-and-white striped wall. One could see that she should have had her little nose in the corner, but instead she was turning her head—just enough to show a single tear about to be wiped away by her soft, pudgy hand. On the floor next to her lay a broken doll, presumably the cause of such punishment. And though it was only a picture in a magazine, Ellie Jane's heart broke.

"Poor little one," she said, speaking right out loud to the girl. "Are you weeping for your dolly? Or because they've left you all alone?"

The last two pages of the magazine were devoted to the music for a popular song, and she hummed a few bars, finding the notes as well as her scant few years of piano lessons would allow. It was a silly song about lost lovers finding their way by the light of little glowing worms. Honestly, the thought of it. Still, she was humming when the little watch pinned to her blouse showed 4:45 and continued while she locked the cashbox and dropped the key in her purse. She kept the tune locked in her head while she delivered the box to Mr. Coleman, but the moment she walked out of his office, it came forth again, and she even allowed herself to sing a few lines just under her breath.

Shine, little glowworm, glimmer, glimmer,
Shine, little glowworm, glimmer, glimmer!
Lead us, lest too far we wander,
Love's sweet voice is calling yonder!

Only a blind woman would fail to notice the odd looks Ellie Jane received as she made her way past the shops along the town's main square and across the little corner of the park before reaching her street, and there was certainly nothing wrong with Ellie Jane's sight. In fact, she met the eyes of each and every neighbor and townsperson, as if daring them to join her in the chorus. Most merely gave her that same pitying look they always did before tipping their hats and moving on, but a few offered strange, weak smiles before sharply veering away to cross the street.

She herself had just about tired of the glimmering glowworm when she reached her front yard gate and would have stopped singing even if she hadn't been startled into silence by the sound coming from her backyard. Perhaps it wouldn't have been out of place for any other house on the block, but it was nothing that had ever greeted Ellie Jane upon her arrival home.

Laughter. Rich, hearty, rippling men's laughter.

Ellie Jane lifted the latch on the gate and squeezed through, catching her skirt on the iron bars. She winced at the tearing sound—this was her best spring gray—but couldn't be bothered to stop and assess the damage. Indeed, she didn't even take the time to go through the house and leave her purse on the entryway table. She walked on the narrow stone path straight around to the back and stopped cold at the corner.

There was Mr. Dennison stripped—not merely to his shirt-sleeves, but to his *undershirt,* bold as you please in her backyard. But he wasn't alone. There was her father, that boy Morris, and…Ned Clovis? They'd pulled the rattan furniture out from the shed, and the four of them sat, happy as you please, drinking bottles of Coca-Cola. Mr. Dennison held a cigar in one hand and a baseball bat in the other. Every now and then he swatted it lazily at something bundled in netting that hung suspended from her clothesline.

Young Morris was apparently the cause of the laughter she'd

heard, as he seemed to be in the midst of telling an amusing story. Unfortunately, Ellie Jane would never know the tale, because the minute his big, brown eyes saw her, he slammed his mouth shut and scrambled out of his chair.

"G-good afternoon, Miss Ellie Jane." He lifted the hand still holding the Coca-Cola bottle to tip his hat.

"Good evening, Morris." Amused at the boy's apparent terror, she softened her voice. "I'm sure it's past your dinnertime and your mother's quite worried about you."

"Yes, m'am." He put the bottle to his lips, drained the remaining drink in one gulp, and put it in the little wooden crate along with three others.

"Tomorrow afternoon, Morris?" Duke said. "Same time?"

Morris looked from Ellie Jane, to Duke, and back again before answering. "Yes, sir, Mr. Duke. Same time." He maintained some level of composure as he backed out of the yard, but there was no mistaking the scuttling sound of running footsteps once the little iron gate out front slammed shut.

Now Ellie Jane could turn her attention to the remaining three men.

"So, Pop," she planted her hands on her hips, "is this to be our new regime? Turning our home into some kind of gentlemen's club while I'm at work all day?"

"Maybe that's not such a bad idea," her father said, and for the first time Ellie Jane noticed that he too, was smoking one of Mr. Dennison's detestable cigars. "What do you say, Ned?"

Ned didn't say anything. He'd stood the moment Ellie Jane walked into the yard, but now he was staring at the ground between his feet. Her father reached his foot out to give him a nudge, and Ned looked up—straight up at Ellie Jane—and smiled.

She offered a short-lived, tight-lipped smile in return and twisted her head away to talk to Mr. Dennison. "I suppose this is all your doing."

"You know, Miss Voyant, that's pretty rude to turn your head like that. If he can't see your face, old Ned here doesn't know what you're saying."

"I know that." Ellie Jane repositioned herself. "I'm just surprised that Ned and my father were able to take time out of their busy schedules to accommodate your playtime." She spoke so loud the neighbors from two houses down might have heard her, and she stretched her lips and craned her neck, exaggerating each word for Ned's benefit.

"It's all right," Ned said in that odd, high-pitched nasal voice of his. "I should get home to supper."

"You're welcome to join us for supper here." Her father gestured meaningfully as he spoke.

She forced herself not to reach out and silence his hands. Wasn't there enough wagging gossip? Now, to force an evening with Ned Clovis of all people? But to rescind her father's offer would be insufferably rude, and she tried to force her face into one of pleasant anticipation, but it was too late.

Ned apparently noted her look of abject displeasure. His eyes met hers—and held them. Those few seconds marked the longest conversation she'd had with Ned since they were children, and his reassuring smile brought it to a close.

"No, thank you," he said, not breaking his gaze. "Some other time?"

Ellie Jane didn't respond right away. First, there was the issue of deciphering Ned's peculiar speech, and second, the shock at his bold self-invitation. Before she could answer—by nodding or shaking her head—her father clapped Ned on the shoulder, saying, "Any time, young man. Any time," as he walked with him out of the yard.

Once the two men got to the corner of the house, Ned turned around and looked at Ellie Jane one more time, smiled, and offered a little wave, just as he did every time he saw her at church, around town, or at the railroad station. And, just as she did on all those occasions, Ellie Jane waved back. But now her fingers lingered in the air a little longer, and she heard herself saying, "Bye, Ned," long after he had turned his head back around.

"So," Mr. Dennison's voice came from over her shoulder, "you two long-lost sweethearts?"

"Ned Clovis and I?" Ellie Jane said, buying time to settle her face before turning around. "Don't be ridiculous."

He hadn't bothered to stand when she walked into the yard, and here he still sat, his cigar clamped in his mouth, squinting up at her.

"Well, I think it's pretty obvious he's sweet on you. Seemed happy enough to be in your backyard."

"And you don't think the fact that he's playing catch with the famous Duke Dennison has anything to do with that? Given that opportunity I should think every man in town would soon find his way here."

Mr. Dennison laughed and leaned forward in his chair. "If that's what you want, Miss Voyant, I'm sure it could be arranged."

"No, it is not." Ellie Jane stood her ground, despite the flush growing on her face and the intense desire to run inside. "Having one is quite enough."

"One meaning Ned? Or me?"

Now this really was too much, as there was no mistaking the lascivious glint to his eye, so she spun on her heel to leave, only to realize her foot was caught in a tiny hole. Instead of the regal, intolerant exit she had planned, she found her body bent into a graceless corkscrew.

Worse than that, she felt Mr. Dennison's strong arms wrapped around her waist, holding her fast until she was on solid ground with both feet facing the same direction. Unfortunately, that direction brought her just inches away from his smirking face.

"And here we are again," he said. She could smell the cigar on his breath and found it wasn't as repulsive as she'd imagined.

"Yes." She dislodged herself from his grip. "Just imagine how freely I could move through life if you weren't lurking at my every turn."

She had little more than a breath's time to regret how inhospitable she must sound before the man's smirk turned into a smile, then a laugh, before the cigar was clamped between his perfect teeth. "Well, then, I guess that answers my question. Ned it is."

Her body turned to prickling fire. "You have no idea what you're talking about."

"Oh, I'm a pretty good judge of character. I think old Ned would love to have a chance to sweep you off your porch some Saturday night."

"You couldn't be more wrong."

"You've never noticed the way the man looks at you?"

"Of course he *looks* at me, Mr. Dennison. The entire town *looks* at me! Because of Ned Clovis, I can't walk down the street without people clearing their path."

Ellie Jane noticed a slight flare to Mr. Dennison's nose, a hard glint in his eye.

"What did he do to you?"

"Nothing." She wished she'd allowed their conversation to continue on a harmless, flirtatious path. Then again, maybe if Mr. Dennison knew the whole story, he'd refrain from involving her in this type of conversation again. So with a heavy heart, and a heavier sigh, she took a step back to gather her thoughts. "It's nothing he did to me. It's what I did to him."

Mr. Dennison took out his cigar and let loose a low whistle between his teeth. "Broke his heart, did you?"

"Something like that," she said, surprised at the chuckle behind the words. She'd never thought of any of this as funny before. "More like I broke his ears."

Now that wiped the smugness off the man's face. He took two steps backward and dropped into the chair; the rattan stems squeaked in protest against the sudden weight.

"Tell me." He gestured to the chair across from him, and without question she obeyed.

"We were children," Ellie Jane began, taking herself back to that awful day. "I was eleven years old; Ned was twelve. He wasn't always deaf, you know. He was a normal boy—a nice boy as I remember, although he teased me mercilessly."

"Because he was sweet on you?"

Ellie Jane picked at a reed that had escaped its weaving on the arm of the chair. "I don't think so. Children have always teased me, mostly because of my mother."

"The head-bump reader."

"Exactly. The town never really accepted her. And then I suppose I was a little shy, a little reclusive, and the other children saw that as suspicious too."

"So what does that have to do with Ned?"

Ellie Jane looked at the man across from her, speckled in the shade of the backyard's oak tree. The shock of seeing him in his undershirt had long worn away, and she quickly shifted her gaze to the rustling leaves above his head.

"We were in school. The teacher was guiding us through a read-ing of 'The Lady of Shalott'." She paused for a nod of recognition at the mention of the poem, and when there was none, she continued. "I thought the poem was beautiful, but most of the boys didn't. They were bored and silly. Ned sat behind me, and for some reason, he chose that day to put a caterpillar in my hair."

"Hoo boy!" Mr. Dennison slapped his thigh. "He must have been in young love."

"Nonsense." Ellie Jane smoothed her skirt. "He was just a typi-cal, teasing boy. I remember hearing him snickering behind me, but I thought he was just making fun of the way one of the other chil-dren was reading the poem. When it was my turn, I stood and was immediately lost in the verses. I can recite it to this day." She took a deep breath and prepared to launch into the words of Tennyson, but the disapproving shake of Mr. Dennison's head stopped her.

"Well, I'm sure you haven't noticed, but my hair is rather thick and curly—so much so that I couldn't feel the caterpillar crawling through it. But I noticed that more and more of the children were snickering while I was reading, despite our teacher's reprimands. Soon they were in an absolute uproar and then"—she shuddered at the thought of it—"the thing crawled onto my forehead. It scared me to death, and I slapped it. And—"

Mr. Dennison's face mirrored hers as she remembered the warm, sticky feel of the smashed creature.

"Well, then the children began to laugh harder. And I started to cry. The more I cried, the more they laughed, and I just wanted the floor to open up and swallow me."

"How did you know it was Ned?"

"Because he stood up, handed me a handkerchief, and helped me clean my face. And all the while, he was apologizing over and over." She could still hear his soft, earnest whisper rising above the cacophony of the classroom.

"Sounds like a good kid," Mr. Dennison said, his voice every bit as soft as Ned's had been back then.

"Yes, it does. Now. At the time, though, I was hurt and embarrassed."

"And so?"

"And so I hit him. I balled up my fist," she demonstrated, reliving the moment, "swung out my arm, and hit him on the side of his head. Right on his ear."

It was quiet in the backyard, save for the rustle of the leaves and the more distant sound of children being called home to supper. Ellie Jane studied Mr. Dennison's face, feeling just as embarrassed as she had that day she slugged Ned Clovis. The man's moustache was twitching, and he showed every sign of being on the verge of bursting into the same laughter that taunted her all those years ago. Somehow she sensed that one more word out of either of them would burst the dam of his resolve, so she sat quietly, studying the lace pattern on the cuff of her sleeve, waiting for the moment of mocking opportunity to pass.

"You know," he said at last, his voice full of restraint, "it's impossible for a little girl to hit a boy hard enough to strike him deaf."

"Yes, I know that." Ellie Jane felt like she'd just fallen into another little hole. "Everybody knows that. Our town is superstitious, not stupid."

"Then why—?"

"Because that was a Friday afternoon. And by Monday Ned was sick. He had a horrible rash and a fever. I prayed for him every night. The whole town prayed for him at church the next Sunday. His parents said he nearly died."

"But he didn't."

"No." She offered a wry smile. "He didn't. But by the time the fever was gone…"

"He was deaf."

Ellie Jane nodded.

"And you—and this whole town—"

"I know it seems odd. But what can I say? Old prejudices run deep."

"And this is why you're living here with your father. Watching happy couples parade by on a Saturday night. Because you slapped some kid twenty years ago?"

"Please, Mr. Dennison. It was fifteen years—" She felt herself growing smaller and smaller, facing a room full of ridicule in her own backyard.

"And you never talked to him about this?"

"I…I couldn't."

"Sure you can! I talked to the man all day. You just have to know—"

"I mean I *couldn't*. I wasn't allowed to. His parents wouldn't let me in their front door. Ned couldn't come to school. He went away shortly thereafter, to a special institute. I wrote him a letter once, but he never responded."

"Well, I guess I'll just have to look on the bright side of all this." Mr. Dennison settled back in his chair.

"Which is?"

"At least now I know who the one man is."

PART 4

TAKE THE FIELD

Tuesday "Tails"

Story Submitted by A. Nony Mouse
(the little reporter with BIG ears)

(May 16, 1905)—What are we squeaking about this week? Why, the long happy "tail" of the Spring Promenade, of course. What whiskery joy it is to see the lovely young people of Picksville arm-in-arm strolling through the town square. Lavender seems to be the color of choice for many a fine lady, as Miss Sophie Carson and Miss Emily Porthouse were both spotted in the pastel shade, which was perfectly set off by the greenery in the corsages presented to them by one of many dapper young men.

Speaking of the gents, there is no finer accessory than a well-groomed beau as our Mr. Pete Shiner was in a perfectly pressed linen suit.

One notable absence to the bevy of bachelors, however, was the rather anticipated introduction of Picksville's newest gentleman, the handsome heartthrob Donald "Duke" Dennison. It's not often the first night of the Spring Promenade finds homes with both drapes and doors sealed up tight, but this little mousy wonders if our own eccentric EJV finally found the right kind of cheese to trap herself.

DUKE

Routine kept him sane and sober in Picksville. Up and out of bed at the second round of raps on his door. Catching Miss Voyant with her little hand suspended mid-knock. Wash and shave, then downstairs for coffee and a bowl of medicinal gruel before heading to Marlene's with Floyd for a real breakfast.

But today at the diner everything seemed different. Rather than the usual genial chorus of "Morning" and "Coffee's hot," there was just the sound of one throat clearing after another. They barely looked at him.

He continued on to his usual place at the breakfast counter, Floyd Voyant on his left, Ned Clovis on the corner at his right. And a newspaper right in front of him.

Duke picked up the paper as he settled on the stool. "You didn't have this at the house this morning." He sent an accusing glance over to Floyd.

"Don't take the paper on Tuesdays," Floyd said, getting Marlene's attention for coffee. "Too upsetting for Ellie Jane."

The paper was open to the town Social Events page. At the top was a little section called "Picksville People." Duke skimmed the article. Spring Promenade. Women's fashion. Men's fashion. And…him. Rotten gossip and innuendo.

A burning sensation skimmed all along the top of his head, just under his scalp. This wasn't the first time he'd seen his name in print, not even the first time he'd been the object of an unflattering exposé. In the months before his hospitalization, the Chicago papers were full of stories of debauchery. Reckless behavior and exploits with women. Sportswriters loved to fill their columns with tales of his failure at the plate, jeering at every fall. At least once a week, in black and white, he'd been called a bum, a drunk, a lousy lush, and a surefire bet. Even from Dave Voyant, for a while. Before the guy decided that what Duke really needed was help.

But this was worse. Maybe because he was seeing it with a clear head; maybe because he was reading through Ellie Jane's eyes. He folded the paper up and slammed it down on the counter.

Ned clapped him on the shoulder. "Now you're famous," he said before turning his attention back to his hotcakes.

"This town is crazy." Duke looked over his shoulder at the restaurant at large.

"Now, son, you stop it right there," Floyd said. "We might be a bit smaller than what you're used to, but we have our ways."

"But how can you stand it? Having them write about your daughter that way?"

"They don't mean any harm. Ellie's managed to weather it well."

"You think so?" Duke thought back to the previous evening's conversation. The way Ellie Jane managed to look both defeated and defiant. "You think Ellie Jane likes to be the object of public humiliation?"

"I'm not saying she *likes* it." Floyd leaned in close, keeping his voice low. "I'm saying she can carry it. I love my girl, but she does have a strangeness to her. Like her mother did. Nobody takes it too serious."

Duke could have argued that point, given the way Marlene's customers were eyeing him this morning, but he chose instead to focus on the food in front of him. When he stabbed the fork into his perfectly cooked eggs, sunshine oozed across the plate. By the time he took his third bite, he'd decided if the town wanted to play a game of gossip, he just wouldn't step in. There were better games to play.

He tapped Ned's arm to bring him into the conversation but directed his question to Floyd. "So what do you think of the kid?"

"Morris? He's a good boy."

"I've never seen a kid who could throw like that."

Ned nodded and gestured that not many full-grown men could either.

Floyd's fork hovered over his breakfast. "That what you've been doing all these days while me and Ellie are out? Playing catch with Morris Bennett in our backyard?"

Duke sensed tension behind the older man's words, the same that had been present the previous afternoon when he first walked into the backyard. After being invited to play the fourth in a round of pepper-catch and take a few swings at the tethered ball, though, Floyd had relaxed, and Duke had chalked up his initial reaction to surprise.

"That a problem?" Duke asked. "I know I'm not allowed to step foot on a real field, but I didn't think I was banned from tossing a ball around a backyard."

"'Course not," Floyd said. "You just might want to be more careful."

Duke turned to Ned for confirmation but got only a shrug in response. His gaze shifted back to Floyd. "Just what do you mean?"

"You didn't notice I came home early yesterday?"

"Never been one to keep an eye on time."

"Wonder why?"

"I'm guessing there isn't much work being the law in Picksville."

Floyd glanced over his shoulder before leaning in close again. He dropped his voice to a whisper. "I got a telephone call at the office from Mrs. Finneworth. Do you know who she is?"

Duke shook his head.

"She's the old lady who lives in the house behind you." Ned's voice, uncontrolled in its volume, rang through the diner, much to the amusement of their fellow patrons.

Floyd rallied the men even closer. "She called me on the telephone to ask me if I knew that Negro boy was sniffing around my house."

"*Sniffing?*"

Floyd held up a placating hand. "Her word, not mine. But honestly, Duke, what were you thinking?"

"I was thinking there had to be something better to do all day than sit around smoking a cigar." He didn't add the fact that sitting around made him want a drink. Or that smoking cigars made him want a drink. Or that the only time he didn't want a drink was when he was on a field—any field—playing the game. "And I was thinking that this kid is the greatest natural talent I've ever seen."

Ned tapped him on the shoulder and pointed.

"Well, yes," Duke added, "since myself, that is."

Floyd didn't laugh. "Play all you want. Just not in the backyard. Neighbors are getting nervous."

Moments ago, Duke would have numbered this man as one of the kindest he'd ever met. The type of father he'd yearned for all his life. But the thread of intimidation in his voice bristled Duke's back.

He heard a sound over his shoulder and saw that Ned was back to his pancakes.

"Don't look at me like that," Floyd said. "He's a good kid. Whole town likes him. Have a hard time finding anybody who hasn't used him to run some errand or another."

"They trust him?"

"Yeah."

"Just not in their neighborhoods."

"And just what is it you plan to do? Are you going to take him back to Chicago with you? Get him on the team?"

"Of course not." Duke spoke in a low voice, hoping Floyd would follow. "He's just a kid."

"He's a Negro, Duke. He doesn't have any kind of future playing baseball."

"We're just playing a game, Floyd. Just passing the time."

"Passing *your* time. Feeding ideas into his head. Then a few more weeks, and you're gone. What's gonna happen to him then? You think he'll be happy going back to getting nickels and dimes all day?"

"That's more than I had when I was a kid." Duke kept shoveling his food, speaking around big, sloppy bites. "I never had nickels. Never had dimes. Never had baseball. Know what I had?" He swallowed. "Nothing. I got picked up off the streets and hauled out west so some drunk could beat me every day of my life until my ma kicked me out. That's what I had."

Floyd never took his eyes off Duke. "I'm so sorry, son."

"Don't be." Duke took a final swig of his coffee. "You're right. There's more to life than playing backyard catch."

He fished in his pocket for money to pay the bill and clapped his friend Ned on the shoulder saying, "See you later," and left, taking the rolled-up newspaper with him.

There was a cool breeze outside, promising a perfect day later on. Duke walked down to the post office, but it wouldn't be open for another thirty minutes. Good. He needed time to think, to compose exactly what he would say to his manager. *Come see this kid. He has a great arm.*

Maybe there weren't Negroes in the big leagues now, but that could change. So the kid couldn't walk onto West Side Park today. He was twelve years old. He couldn't walk on any field. And even if he never played for the Cubs, or any other major league teams, there were the Negro teams right there in Chicago. The Unions, the Giants, merging together to form one powerful team. They were fierce competitors. Fine athletes. Duke himself had gone to the games. Set himself up beyond the fence with a bottle of whiskey and watched the players just like any other fan. Those guys were fast and strong. Equal to any opponent Duke had ever faced from the plate.

He would bring Morris to them.

Just as the giant clock above the courthouse door showed nine o'clock, Postmaster Steve snapped up the window shade on the door and opened for business. Half-a-dozen people had gathered around Duke, waiting for just this moment, and he graciously stepped back and allowed them to enter the post office ahead of him. He still had to decide who to contact.

Nobody in the league would help. Plenty of them had been around for twenty years and talked with eerie amusement about those early days. Back when a few black men were allowed to play with the whites. Intentional injuries—hands ground under cleats, the foot-first slide designed to take down a colored man at his shins. Players who wouldn't be photographed alongside their black teammates.

But Duke didn't have an inroad with the Negro teams either. Why would they trust him? Or even listen? And his own people— the players, the fans—wouldn't like it. Sure they'd been willing to put up with the drinking, the women. Up to a point. But he'd been whisked away here to clean up his act. Come back a man ready to play the game. Their game. And there was no way an adolescent Negro, no matter how talented, fit into their game.

Assuming the boy even wanted to fit in.

Duke opened the post office door for an attractive middle-aged woman, who offered a sweet "Good morning" as he tipped his straw boater. Now there was quite a crowd gathered inside, so he walked across the street to sit on a bench in the grassy square. It was a bustling town at this hour. Shop doors ringing, neighbors offering friendly greetings to each other. Nothing like the gray, wind-torn Wyoming mountain town he'd grown up in, and nothing like the crowded, dirty streets of Chicago. Perfect, right here. Right at that moment, ten minutes after nine on a Tuesday morning in May, Duke could see himself staying. Forever. He could set up house with the Voyants. Never be tempted to have another drink. Never hear the cheer of another crowd…

At twelve minutes past nine he changed his mind.

Because this wasn't his town. Not his home. The only home he could ever claim was the three-room flat five blocks from West Side Park. But Morris? Floyd Voyant said the town liked him. To an extent. As long as he kept to his place. What could Duke offer that was any different? Bigger, maybe, but better?

Duke leaned back on the bench and twirled an imaginary cigar between his fingers, replaying the conversation he had with Floyd. He glanced over just in time to see the man walk out with Ned. The two shook hands before parting ways—Floyd headed to the sheriff's office on the next block and Ned to his store. Ned, in fact, glanced Duke's way and waved, pointing to the clock and holding up a single finger. *One o'clock?*

Duke waved back and nodded, but thought maybe he would go visit with Ned a little earlier. Talk to him about this whole mess before he sent any kind of wire to Chicago.

Then he heard a sound behind him and turned around to see a

streak of running boy—Morris himself tearing through the park like someone touched a match to his britches. As far as Duke knew, the kid had never been in town this early before. He took it as a sign.

"Morris!" Duke called, not bothering to stand.

But the boy blew right past him, like he was heading to first after putting one in the dirt.

"Hey, kid!" Now Duke was up and running, the smooth soles of his patent leather shoes slipping in the green grass as he tried to close the gap. "Kid!" His hat blew off his head, but he didn't consider slowing down. He took in great gulps of spring morning air and pumped his arms, propelling himself closer—close enough to reach out, grab a corner of the tattered shirt flapping behind his target, and pull it down.

By now they'd attracted the attention of every Picksville resident on the square, the majority of which paused briefly in their morning routine to point and laugh before going on with their daily affairs. Meanwhile, Duke worked to untangle himself, swatting in vain at the grass stains on his cream-colored slacks.

"Sorry 'bout that, Mr. Duke." Morris got to his feet and held out his hand.

"Didn't know you could run like that," Duke said, rising to his feet. "All that's left is to teach you how to hit."

"Yessir," Morris said, but Duke could tell the boy was distracted. "Anything else?"

"Yeah, come have a seat." Duke bent to pick up his hat on his way back to the bench.

"Sir?" Morris followed close behind. "Is it somethin' we can talk about later this afternoon?"

Duke turned around and saw the boy shifting from foot to foot, glancing over his shoulder at the city hall building.

"Let me ask you just one question, son. Do you like playing baseball?"

In an instant he was looking at a changed boy. Morris's face, the color of coffee and cream, lit up in a smile. He stood tall and straight, abandoning whatever else fought for his attention.

"Yes, sir, Mr. Duke. You don't even know."

Duke smiled. "Yes, I think I have some idea."

"So I see you this afternoon?"

"No," Duke said, then quickly corrected himself before the disappointment settled on Morris's face. "I mean, yes, but don't come out to the house. I need to find someplace bigger. There's no field in this town?"

Morris pursed his lips and thought. "No, sir. 'Cept that one by the white school. But I don't think that be a good idea to go there."

"You're probably right." This kid knew far more about life in this town than he did.

"I know." Morris snapped his fingers. "It's just a big open field at the railroad tracks. Got no trees, no buildings, nothin'."

"Sounds fine, Morris. I'll see you there later this afternoon?"

The worried look came across Morris's face again, and he glanced back at the city hall building. "I hope so, sir."

Duke had never seen Morris as anything other than cool and confident, and he worried now that Mrs. Finneworth had not stopped with her telephone call to the sheriff. He grabbed Morris by the shoulders. "Is everything all right?"

"Oh, yes, sir." Morris offered a weak smile. "Or it will be."

"Can I do anything for you?"

The big smile came back. "Maybe help me with my slider?"

Duke relaxed. "I'll do what I can."

He released Morris, who immediately turned and continued his run toward the red brick building at the top of the town square. Duke watched him, envious of the youth that would allow for such speed. The kid deserved a diamond under those feet. He was the only person who could make that happen.

And he couldn't do it alone.

With new resolve he planted his hat on top of his head and walked toward the post office. He opened the door for the same woman, wishing her "Good morning" again as she exited.

"Be with you in a minute," Steve said, lifting a large canvas bag down from a top shelf. He'd been in the diner earlier that morning but didn't seem to be affected by the story in this morning's paper. When Duke said he needed to send a telegram, Steve nodded toward a stack of small papers and a cup of pencils.

Duke took a slip of paper and set it on the smooth countertop. He touched the pencil to the tip of his tongue. Forget his manager. There was only one person who would understand this kind of problem.

Dave Voyant
Chicago Herald-Times
Chicago, Illinois

Dave.
You know a kid named Morris Bennett? Great
arm. See who you know with the Negro Baseball
League.
Duke.

P.S. This town has the worst cigars I ever seen.

MORRIS

Tuesday, May 16

I think I know why God wants to keep heaven such a secret. If we ever got even a glimpse of what was waitin on that side we'd never be able to stand another day livin here. I don't mean to blaspheme that Holy City, but I think I get a glimpse of it every time I'm at the Voyant house. I have to drag my shoes across the tracks every day when it's time to come home. Seems everythin there comes in pure colors. White house. Green grass. Blue sky. Course we got the same sky here on our side but it never stretches quite as clear. Spendin a day at Miss Ellie Jane's is like bein on the other side of the clouds and comin home just feels like fallin.

I fell hard yesterday.

I can still see that fool Darnell tryin to warn me, meetin me at the top of our row and sayin, Hoo son, your mama's gonna take the last two hours outta your hide.

Course he don't have no interest in savin my hide cause he follows me home and hollers, Here's your boy!

Mama's at the door reachin through it and grabbin my arm just in case I have a mind to make a run. The way she pulls me in makes me forget that sometime last winter I sprang up taller than her. Once I'm inside she says, We got a visitor here in the parlor.

I don't know what puzzles me most—the idea of a visitor or a parlor because our house ain't nothin but a front room where I sleep and a kitchen with one bedroom for Mama and sometimes Darnell. But sure enough I turn around and there's Miss Teacher sittin on the best chair in the room.

She's the first white person I ever remember seein in our house and there she is with that same half-smile she always has in class. The kind of smile that don't reach all the way to her eyes, like she's wearin half of her own face and half of someone else's. She's wearin her peppermint stripe dress today and her clothes are so clean. It's like there's some kind of a light shinin on them. When I look real close I see she's not sittin all the way on the chair. Mama had brought her out a cup coffee but from what I could tell she hadn't had even a sip of it.

Mama gives me a push and I sit on the other chair while she stands there in the middle. She folds up her arms and stares at me.

Go on now, she says. Why don't you explain to your teacher why you ain't been in school this past week.

I said that was a lie. I been to school every day.

Next thing I know Mama's hand is slappin my face—nearly hard enough to knock me off my chair.

She says, Don't you ever show that disrespect to Miss Teacher.

When I look over to apologize though it seems Miss Teacher's the one slapped. Her face is red and her mouth is hangin open like a fish off the line.

I make my voice softer and say, I'm sorry but I have been to school every day.

Miss Teacher gets herself together and says, Now Morris Bennett. You know you have not spent the entire day in school once this week.

I tell her I agree to that. But I was there every mornin for the Bible readin and the prayer and nothin else seemed important. I could read as good as her and write better than anybody I know. And I can cipher and speculate and pretty much think on my own about everythin that matters.

Miss Teacher says that was all fine and good but the state required that I be in school.

I say, I can't imagine the state gives a toss one way or another about what happened to some poor Negro boy. When I look over my shoulder I see Mama windin up her hand so I add that it's awful nice of the state to care just the same.

Then Miss Teacher looks up at Mama and says, Mrs. Bennett. What is it that Morris does all day when he's not in school?

That's when Mama looks at me like she'd like to chop me up and serve me on bread. She don't know but if it turned out I was rollin bones with that fool Darnell at the kooch house she would tie us together and throw us off the world.

The whole room's waitin for me to give an answer. I can hear Mama's bare foot tappin on the floor and Miss Teacher inches up a little off her chair.

I look from one woman to the other and say it might be better all around if they don't know. Miss Teacher starts in about the state again but I don't hear nothin she says because I'm lookin at my mama's face set in a mask that made every one of Miss Teacher's words bounce right off it. She's lookin at me like I'm some kind of hope and I don't want to let her down.

Now I haven't ever been one to tell a lie—not on purpose anyway—because I never had nothin to protect. I know if I said I spent all day playin baseball with some rich white man they

*would either lock me up for bein crazy or follow me over the
tracks and take it all away.*

So I take a deep breath and say, I am goin to school.

In town.

*Miss Teacher gets that just-slapped look again and Mama
makes a grab for me and says she'll twist the truth out of me if
she has to. But I swear up and down not meanin any offense to
Miss Teacher. Her lessons are fine for most of the Negro children
just not for me.*

*Then Miss Teacher laughs. She says there's laws and policies
about such things and I really shouldn't tell a lie so easily
uncovered.*

*I say I wasn't goin to the proper school. I was takin some
private lessons.*

*Mama asks, With who? And I answer straight up, With
the mayor. Then it's Mama's turn to laugh but Miss Teacher
just looks mad and says, Honestly Morris I've never heard such
a fib.*

*I say, I got my own books. Don't have to share them with
anybody. Then I get up out of my chair and go into my room and
pull the cardboard box from under my bed. I take out the green
history book Mr. Ned gave me—already read twenty pages of
it—and take it out to show Mama and Miss Teacher. I say when
we finished that I was gonna learn algebra and after that how to
speak French. I don't feel one bit of bad about a word I say until
Mama starts cryin and huggin me and sayin that she always
knew I was better than this place.*

*But Miss Teacher just makes a snortin sound and says she
still don't believe it.*

That makes me want to lie even more.

I tell her I can come first thing in the mornin with a letter from Mayor Birdiff hisself. She says if I don't she's goin to call the sheriff and then I'll be readin my fancy history book in jail.

All night long I'm tossin and turnin because I know God isn't about to honor a falsehood like the one I told my mama. I finally get out of my bed and down on my knees and pray, Lord I'm sorry I told such a fib. And if it's Your will that the truth be exposed so be it. I promise I'll keep goin to school for the Bible readin an the prayer because I know that's important, even if the lady leadin it isn't as much of a Christian as I am.

So this mornin I'm runnin through the town square like a thief on fire to get to the mayor's before Miss Teacher or the state or anybody has a chance to. All I can think of is what I'm goin to say and how I'm goin to say it so I don't even hear Mr. Duke callin my name—don't know he's even around until he grabs at me and we're both rollin on the grass. If it was anybody else I'd have been blazin mad because I got a new rip in my shirt. But I'm expectin two new ones any day now—already paid off what I owe—and it wasn't nothin compared to what Mr. Duke done to his own pants.

I admit I'm scared a little because I ain't never seen Mr. Duke's face lookin so serious as it did this mornin. Like he was about to tell me that Miss Teacher got to him and wrangled out the truth and our baseball days was over.

But he just asks me if I like playin baseball which seems a dumb question because here I am riskin the wrath of my mama just so I can keep on.

And when I say, Yessir, he looks downright sad when he tells me that we can't meet at Miss Ellie Jane's anymore.

He must of thought I was gonna take that hard—I guess he ain't as used to disappointment as I am. But I already figured that couldn't last much longer. White people are fine to let you work in their world but they sure don't want you to play there.

I tell him we can meet at the empty field by the tracks and he seems happy. I got to go take care of my business or else I'm not goin to be doin nothin but sit in Miss Teacher's room and feel myself get stupid. I can tell by the people on the street that this side of town is startin to jump and pretty soon I won't be able to get my face time with the mayor. So as soon as Mr. Duke gives me my leave I'm off like a shot again.

This is the first time I ever walked into the city hall kitchen without first bein called there so I don't know what they'll make of me. But Miss Cherine is the same woman in the mornin what she is in the afternoon. I had a good supper last night cause Mama was feelin proud and Darnell was off roamin but all I ate was long gone by now and the smell of bacon makes me feel like I been starvin for a week. Even if I ain't supposed to eat it.

Miss Cherine says I'm a welcome sight this mornin as she had fried up Mayor Birdiff's eggs too hard and didn't know what she was goin to do with them. She says I could eat them if I didn't mind that the yolks wasn't runny enough. Says she could slip them into a biscuit and I could eat it like a sandwich.

I told her, Thank you that sounds fine, and Is there any way I can get upstairs to the mayor's office before he starts his business for the day?

She asks, Can you carry a tray? And I say I can, so she shoos me into the washroom to fix my shirt and wash my hands, tellin me I can have my breakfast when I get back.

On the tray there's a plate covered with a silver dome, a little coffeepot, a folded-up newspaper, and a pretty blue napkin with a knife and fork sittin on it. I never took stairs so careful in my life, imaginin what it would sound like if I dropped this tray and myself with it all the way down. When I get to the second floor landin I lift one knee to balance the tray while I open the door to the stairwell. I'm hopin there won't be a lot of people on the other side because they'd all know I don't belong here. At least not deliverin breakfast.

When I'm outside the office door I knock four times just like Miss Cherine told me to before walkin straight in. To say Mayor Birdiff looks surprised is like sayin the world looks wide. His eyes bulge out a little bit and he jumps up from behind his desk to run behind me and close the door. The whole time he's askin does anybody know I'm here and has anybody seen me?

I tell him, Just Miss Cherine and the kitchen help but they probably don't care much.

He laughs a little and says, True—the woman can't remember how to cook eggs so she'd never remember who came upstairs.

I hate him just a little for sayin that but then I check it. The only thing that fool Darnell ever said that took in my head was that it was a dangerous thing for a Negro to hate a white man.

Pretty soon the mayor settles himself behind his desk and I set the tray down in front of him. He takes the silver dome off the plate and there's a mess of bacon, three eggs, biscuits, and a little bowl of gravy. Steam comes up from the food while he takes a big ol whiff of it before pokin the egg yolks with his fork and sayin,

Better when they run out yellow. He picks up his knife and makes a show of cuttin all the food together until you can't really tell what was what. Then he pours gravy over the bunch of it. Then he asks me what I'm doin here.

I tell him I need him to write me a letter sayin I have his permission not to go to school anymore. I tell him a little about Miss Teacher's visit and the state and my mama. (He smiles at that part.) I didn't tell him what I said about him bein my new teacher just that I didn't think I was learnin much and I'd rather spend my time workin here in town.

He's halfway through his plate of food by the time I finish talkin.

And just what do you want from me, he says, like he hasn't heard a word.

I tell him all I want is a letter signed by him that says I have the mayor of Picksville's permission to leave the Negro school every day in order to follow other pursuits of my better interest.

And just what pursuits might that be? he says.

Of course he knows that I'm always runnin somethin around for him but then I tell him that sometimes I like to just go off by myself and think or write. Or even play some baseball with Mr. Duke Dennison.

His eyes get round as corncakes when I mention that. He says, What does Mr. Dennison want with a boy like you? Though I like to think of myself as a modest sort I tell him that Mr. Duke says I can pitch a ball real good and he might even be teachin me to bat someday. But I need the letter to take to Miss Teacher so the state doesn't come and make me spend all day at the Negro school or in jail. Which of the two is worse I couldn't say.

Fascinatin, he says, and for half a tick I think he forgot I was in the room because he was shovelin food in his face and tellin his plate that he, the mayor himself, had sent Mr. Dennison a letter invitin him to luncheon in the office and hadn't heard a word. But this boy can straggle around the streets and become a bosom buddy?

Since I don't know if he's talkin to me or not I don't say anything until he puts his fork down and then I ask, So will you write the letter?

Darnell told me once if I ever wanted a white man to do me a favor I had to be sure not to look him in the eye. That I should keep my head down just enough to see his mouth. But if I looked him in the eye, well, they wasn't much better than dogs and would see it as a challenge and there wouldn't be any way to get nothin out of them. So I focus on Mayor Birdiff's little triangle of a moustache and beard and see that blue napkin come up to wipe away a few drops of eggs and gravy.

And I hear him say, No.

Then he shoves his tray across his desk and tells me I can have whatever mess is left on the plate.

I can't remember a time this man ever talked to me so harsh. His words hit me somewhere at the base of my throat because there is a swellin burn there makin it so I couldn't swallow none of those scraps even if I have a heart to. I figure I'd asked for somethin far and away from what I've earned so I just pick up the tray and say, Yessir. Will there be anything else? Because there's always somethin else.

Then like he hasn't just talked to me so mean he's back to what he always is and tells me that his wife was complainin of a headache last night and could I pick up some powders for her from the doctor.

I feel that burnin move from the bottom of my throat to all up and down my back, the whole time drawin my body up until I'm lookin straight into that man's eyes. I want to say I'd be careful if I was him, careful I don't take the wrong powders to the wrong woman. Be a shame if Miss LuAnn DeSalvo got his wife's headache powder by mistake. Even worse if Mrs. Birdiff ever got wind of some of those other brown paper packages that sometimes showed up in the mayor's mail.

But that seems cruel and I just got a glimpse of what this man could be if he takes it upon himself to get ugly. I'd be a fool to think that any power I have would come close to comparin to his so I just say, No.

He says, What did you say boy?

I tell him I can't run for him if I'm sittin in school all day and if I don't go back with a letter from him I'll be sittin in jail all day. So I best get back to that schoolhouse and settle in for my new routine. I give him a little smile and remind him that Tuesdays is the day Miss DeSalvo takes the newspaper because she likes that town gossip and he better find someone to take it out to her. Them women do love their gossip.

I'm standin there with the tray not makin a move to leave when Mayor Birdiff asks me do I know what position Duke Dennison plays for the Chicago Cubs?

I say, Catcher, and he makes this snortin sound. Says when he was a kid he played out in left field and he never did get a fair shot at playin infield even though he'd of been the best short-stop any team ever saw.

By the time he finishes talkin he's not lookin at me anymore and I'll bet my life I see a little quiver underneath that beard of his.

I tell him I don't know for sure what a shortstop is and if I didn't have to spend all day in school it might be nice if he would stop by some afternoon.

Even though it don't weigh nothin I hold that tray like a burden and pretty soon the man opens the top drawer of his desk and takes out a piece of paper.

Looks like I'm gonna be able to play some baseball after all.

NED

Once, when Ned was at the Hartford school, his teacher wrote a Bible verse on the blackboard: "Delight thyself also in the LORD: and he shall give thee the desires of thine heart" (Psalm 37:4). Each student was to write an essay explaining his or her heart's desire. Later, they were to present their essays in the language of signs.

The first student to present was a pretty girl, a year behind Ned in class, whose cheeks and throat were flushed before she even made it to the front of the room. Over the next few minutes, with trembling hands and a soft pink mouth rounding out the words, she told of her heart's desire to hear. To hear her mother's voice singing a favorite lullaby, to hear her father's laughter, and finally, with arms linked to form an imaginary cradle, to hear the sound of her own baby's sweet cry someday.

Despite being fifteen years old and nearly a man, Ned had felt himself dangerously close to tears, especially when he noticed those pooled in the younger girl's big blue eyes as she returned to her seat. He looked around, noticing that everybody in class seemed to be equally affected. But the mood quickly changed when the instructor, normally a gentle woman, strode to the front of the room.

That will never happen. Her signs were sharp, and her otherwise placid face was set to a firmness that spoke of her frustration. *There is more to the world than hearing. It is possible to live without noise.*

As the teacher continued her diatribe, Ned noticed a classwide shift in posture as students slumped in their seats and turned their papers over on their desks. When the teacher called for the second presentation, no one moved until Ned stood, walked to the front of the room, handed over the written essay, and turned to face the class.

"The desire of my heart," he said before bringing his fists together, as if gripping a bat, "is to play baseball. Every day."

Immediately the boys in class sat up a little straighter and, if he wasn't mistaken, the girls did too.

"I want to take the field with Cy Young and Cap Anson." He gave a little punch to each signed letter, his fingers moving deftly with each transition. "I want my face on a card in a package of Old Judge cigarettes." For added effect, he assumed the slouch he'd seen the older boys take on when they stood outside the dormitory and smoked under the gaslight. "And finally," he said, allowing a dramatic pause, "I want dozens of beautiful girls lined up to give me kisses after the game."

At that all the boys nearly burst out of their chairs and the girls simultaneously brought their hands to their mouths to stifle shocked giggles. The teacher herself seemed to be fighting back a smile. As Ned made his way back to his seat, he steeled himself for a reprimand, knowing that his heart's desire was just as unattainable as that of the girl before him, but when the teacher got up to face the class, she simply said, *I don't know if God would approve of kissing dozens of girls.*

From his desk Ned replied, "One would be fine."

Then the teacher *did* laugh.

The next three years at school were the fulfillment of that desire. He played first base for the school's team, even had a modest following of girls lined up at the fence to watch him play. More than one afternoon ended with a kiss after the match.

But that was years ago. What was meant to be a sojourn at home helping his father get the family store's accounts in order had turned into a life sentence when the old man died. Meanwhile, his heart's desire sat on the shelf along with the birdseed.

Then, that Tuesday morning, Duke Dennison came in to bust him out. He strode through the store's front door, bypassed old Mr. Shiner and the feed store regulars, and landed elbow-first at the counter where Ned stood, entering the last order in the ledger.

The look in Duke's eye took Ned back to the days when he was a boy—before the illness stole his hearing—when pals from school would show up to badger him to finish his chores so he could go out and play. Maybe it was the grass stain on the man's cream-colored suit or the straw boater that bore a distinct footprint, but the cigar-smoking athlete with the moustache was wearing the smile of a schoolboy when he leaned over the counter.

Let's go.

Ned shook his head, touched the top of his cheek just under his eye, and moved his hand in a sweeping motion encompassing the room.

Duke looked around and back at Ned.

What is there to watch?

"I have to stay here." At the sound of Ned's voice, the men gathered around the barrel of seed corn turned their grizzled faces toward him before resuming their own conversation.

Give me that. Duke snatched the ledger out from under Ned's hands and tore a blank page from the back. He picked up a pencil stub and, leaning over his work like the earnest schoolboy he'd become, made a series of broad, sweeping lines.

Intrigued, Ned leaned in for a closer look. A shape emerged on the columned paper. A diamond, precisely, with messy squares drawn for each base and a feathery arc marking the outfield boundary. A little oval mound rose up in its center, and numbers were written along the baselines in careful, cramped script.

When Duke paused to stand back and look at the finished product, Ned took the pencil and wrote *"Polo Grounds?"* at the top of the page.

Duke took the pencil back, drew an X through Ned's writing, and wrote *"RR"* beneath it.

Suddenly Ned could see it. Anyone who stood on the train station platform and looked to the west would see nothing but an expanse of open land flanking both sides of the railroad tracks. In fact, with the rest of the world shut away behind him, he'd watched many a train chug its way into oblivion and felt quite alone when the last puff of smoke disappeared on the horizon.

His attention returned to Duke when he felt the paper slide up against his fingers. He looked down and saw a list—*shovel, spade, rope, saks, mower*—all in painfully fashioned letters. Ned fought the urge to take the pencil and correct Duke's spelling.

"When?" Ned asked.

Duke pounded his finger on the counter. *Now.*

Ned eyed the men gathered in the corner. They would loiter there at least until lunchtime; any one of them could easily step behind the counter and stand for the rest of the day, ready to wait on the two or three other customers who might come in. Or Ned could do something he hadn't done since the day after his father's funeral.

He wrapped his knuckles on the counter and signaled to the little crowd to head out the door.

He was closing the store.

ELLIE JANE

She watched the plan unfold from behind the dome-shaped window of her platform ticket booth. At first just Ned Clovis and Duke Dennison were out there in the open field, mowing down the weeds. Then they were pacing back and forth, counting steps, driving stakes into the ground, and stringing rope between them.

It wasn't until young Morris Bennett showed up and broke the first ground that Ellie Jane thought this might be something Mr. Coleman might want to know about. She propped the little Will Return in 15 Minutes sign in her window and popped out of the booth. She faintly heard Mr. Dennison calling her name as she took the few short steps to the depot office.

Mr. Coleman was, as usual, sitting at his desk, with five open books laid out in front of him, each page displaying a complicated table of columns and numbers. But these were apparently not as important as whatever Mr. Coleman was reading in the day's newspaper. So absorbed was he that he didn't hear Ellie Jane's footsteps, didn't hear her soft knock on the open door.

Ellie Jane cleared her throat and said, "Mr. Coleman?" causing the man's surprised droopy face to jump out from behind the paper.

"Ah yes, Miss Voyant." He made a show of folding the paper into a sloppy triangle and slamming it inside one of the books. "It seems we have something of great importance to discuss."

"Yes, we do." She looked past his head and out the window behind him where Mr. Dennison and Ned seemed to be squabbling.

"I believe I voiced my concerns about your situation not three days ago."

"My situation?"

"And if you'll recall, my worry was not only for the reputation of the railroad—of which you are a representative—but your own reputation as a young lady in the town."

"Oh, that situation." Ellie Jane allowed her eyes to linger on the two men, now openly engaged in a silent argument. "I appreciate your concern, Mr. Coleman, but there's something else—"

"I assume you've read this morning's paper?"

"No, I haven't but—"

"I warned you of precisely this kind of thing, and now it seems to have come about. Miss Voyant if you are going to continue to associate yourself with this railroad, then I must insist that you curtail any opportunities for such scandalous reports."

As he spoke, Ellie Jane tore her eyes away from the scene outside and looked at the corner of newspaper sticking out from within the closed book. She instantly recognized the intricate drawing of a little mouse with an enormous feathered hat perched between two round ears. She could only imagine what it said. A stinging sensation tickled at the tip of her throat, and she swallowed hard, fighting to maintain her composure.

"I never read that rag," she said, her voice steady. "It's nothing but tittle-tattle penned by some cowardly scandalmonger with nothing better to do than wallow in meaningless rituals."

"But it does raise a concern. I think it would be best if I were to talk to Mr. Dennison myself."

The old man's eyes peered through rimless spectacles that seemed to be buoyed up by the soft folds beneath them. Ellie Jane realized he was not looking at her, rather up and beyond her as he tapped his fingers on the desk. Whatever tension she felt melted as she tried to ward off a smile.

"That's probably a good idea, Mr. Coleman. In fact, you might want to go speak with him now, as I believe he intends to build a baseball field just outside your office."

She pointed at the window behind him, causing Mr. Coleman to nearly fall out of his chair in his eagerness to turn around.

"What is this?" He stood, bracing his palms against the window.

Ellie Jane couldn't remember the last time she'd seen him standing. His body had a distinct beet shape—nearly pointed head, narrow shoulders, wide rump, and skinny legs. And if she'd rarely had the opportunity to see him stand, she'd never seen him move like he did at that moment, stumbling out from behind his desk, rushing past her without so much as an "Excuse me." Within a few seconds he was another silent animated figure in the scene beyond the window, walking straight up to Duke Dennison, hand extended in greeting.

Ellie Jane started to leave the office to return to her ticket booth, but the image of that awful column glared at her from the desk. She reached down to open the book and lifted the newspaper out of it. Taking a deep breath, she began to read. *Spring Promenade…fine ladies…corsages…* Everything she expected.

Then, *Duke Dennison…*and *our own eccentric EJV.*

Her cheeks burned, and she looked over her shoulder, although there was no one else who would possibly come upon her. Outside, Mr. Coleman, Duke, and Ned were all engaged in conversation, so she took a deep breath and continued reading. If the column were to be believed, she was keeping Mr. Dennison as a virtual prisoner, trapped by her sheer desperation to have a man. Any man. Not caring about his reputation and previous romantic conquests. She, EJV, had exhausted her chances of finding love in Picksville, but fortune had seen fit to drop a star on her doorstep.

Her throat closed up as she read. She clutched the paper tighter, wondering who could write such scurrilous things. Long ago she and her father entered an unspoken agreement not to take the Tuesday paper, as this was far from Ellie Jane's first appearance in the Tuesday "Tails" column. But surely he'd read it somewhere. These words guaranteed several weeks' worth of sidelong glances and whispered comments.

"Oh, Pop, I'm so sorry."

Mr. Coleman was on his way back inside, so she quickly folded the paper and stuffed it in the book. She was just turning around to greet him when he burst through the door. He had a lilt to his step and a smile that lifted his jowls to his ears.

"I take it everything is all right?" She stepped away from the desk.

"Ah yes." Mr. Coleman grabbed Ellie Jane by the shoulders, his long fingers crushing her carefully puffed sleeves, pulled her to him, and placed a wet, heavy kiss on each of her cheeks. "I'm going to play first base."

The next three days were full of just such odd occurrences. Oh, there had been a few raised eyebrows and snickers as she made her way through the Picksville shops on her daily errands, but no more than she was accustomed to. Added to her daily interactions was a distinct feeling of celebrity. More than one matron greeted her with an endearing, "Well, if it isn't our own darling eccentric Ellie Jane" and stopped to clasp her hands and inquire if all was well with her charming houseguest. And nearly every man—old and young— stopped to tip his hat and ask her to give their best to her father and the Duke.

The early mornings were just as they'd ever been, with a small healthy breakfast at home and the comfortable quiet of her booth on the platform. Then, just as the little watch pinned to her lapel was ticking toward noon, the townspeople came to work.

Ned Clovis was always first on the scene, driving his wagon of supplies to the place where an open field of weeds now served as a carefully crafted diamond. He would hop down from the wagon and survey their work before turning to give Ellie Jane a wave.

Soon after, Duke would arrive, followed shortly by young Morris, and the three of them would work—clearing the outfield weeds, mowing the infield grass, turning the dark soil to create baselines, and building up the pitcher's mound in the middle. They would work until the two-o'clock train, when Ned would reload their tools alongside whatever shipment came for the feed store and go home.

Then Duke and Morris would play catch.

The Picksville residents and visitors getting on and off the train were fascinated with the process. The normally terse transactions through the dome-shaped hole in her ticket booth window blossomed into questions about the field—when would it be completed? Who would play there? Was Mr. Dennison planning to bring the entire team to town? Had she ever in her life seen a boy who could throw like that?

If Ellie Jane had any answers to their questions, it was only because discussion about the field and the games that would be played upon it dominated the supper conversations at home. Duke, too distracted to complain about her eggplant soufflé, would sit at the table, his hands scrubbed raw and red, talking tirelessly about the next day's addition.

The high school teacher, Mr. Headley, didn't look like much, but he'd played on the first nine at his college, and was a sure thing at second. Ed Vick, who had a farm just east of town, was donating the chicken wire to build the backstop. Morris's fast ball was coming along nicely. Marlene was stocking up to sell sandwiches and ginger ale. The mayor himself promised a set of bleachers to be set up on the site.

And the first game would be Saturday night.

The three of them sat out on the Voyant porch the evening Duke made that announcement, and an astonished Ellie Jane planted her foot midswing, nearly jolting her father to the floor.

"What about the Promenade?" she asked.

"It's about time this town found something else to do," Pop said and started the swing in motion again.

The jangling ring of the telephone upstairs interrupted any further conversation, and Ellie Jane groaned a bit as she stood up from the swing. "Why can't we have a telephone downstairs in the kitchen like everyone else?"

"Now, Ellie," Pop said, making no attempt to stand, "if it were one of those sheriff emergency calls we get in the middle of the night, you'd be complainin' about fallin' down the stairs."

"Yes." She reached for the front screen door. "And then I might just have to teach you how to answer the phone."

The satisfying sound of masculine laughter faded behind her as she trotted up the stairs.

"Hello?" she spoke breathlessly into the mouthpiece before bringing the earpiece to ear.

"Hey, sis!" Her brother's deep, rolling voice stretched to tin.

"Dave!" His presence, even stretched through thin black wire, never failed to lift her spirits, and whatever had troubled her about the Saturday Promenade disappeared. "How lovely to hear from you!"

"Does that mean you've forgiven me?"

"Forgiven you?"

"After reading your letter, I was worried there were assassins lurking around every corner. I take it you and Duke have come to some kind of understanding?"

"I guess you could say that." She glanced over her shoulder, lest she'd been followed, and brought the mouthpiece closer. "He's turning the whole town on its ear, you know."

"He is?" The change in his tone was distinct, and after years of being a tag-along sister, Ellie Jane could picture his furrowed brow. "He was supposed to lay low and relax."

"Apparently nobody told him that."

"They said—the doctors at the clinic, I mean—that rest was very important to his recovery. He isn't…"

His words trailed off, probably so as not to offend her sensibilities. She smiled at his chivalry, checked over her shoulder again, and answered anyway. "No, Dave. He's not drinking. Not a drop."

"You're sure?" He spoke with guarded relief.

"I think I would know. I'm with him practically every minute of the day."

"Really?" And here was the brother she adored. Warm, teasing. If he were in front of her now, his eyebrows would be dancing above his glasses. "You sure Pop's being an adequate chaperone?"

"Oh, now stop." She clutched the phone closer to her and leaned against the wall, keeping her eye on the staircase. "Surely you know me better than that."

"Yes." The word unfurled into her ear. "But I've been following Duke around a good while, so I know him pretty well too. Now tell me," he offered a welcome change of subject, "what's the story with the Bennett kid?"

"With Morris? What do you know about that?"

"Apparently nothing. Look, why don't you put Duke on the line?"

"He's out on the porch with Pop. I'll go—"

But there he was on the bottom step, his calfskin shoe noiseless on the carpet, his hand clutching the polished banister as he gazed up inquisitively.

"It's Dave." She held the telephone's mouthpiece against her shoulder. "He wants to talk to you."

Now it was Mr. Dennison's turn to bound up the stairs, an excursion that seemed to have no ill effect on his vigor. He took the phone from her—commandeered it, actually—and offered her nary another glance before saying, "Hello, Voyant."

Ellie Jane retreated to her room, leaving the door open, hoping to catch bits of conversation. She sat at her dressing table, quietly fussing with the powder box. Though it was nearly dark, she opted not to light the lamp, thinking the low rumbled conversation in the hall might have more clarity in the shadows. She took off her earrings and set them gently in the little pewter dish that held her other favorite pairs. Her fingers toyed with the bristles of her hairbrush, even as her brother's words echoed in her ear. Well, not his words exactly, but his low, teasing chuckle. As if she would ever be interested in a man like Duke Dennison. Moreover, as if *he* would ever be interested in a woman like *her*.

She caught a glimpse of her reflection. Just enough light in the room to pick up the paleness of her skin. The mound of hair that, just this morning, had been a respectable coiffure and was now straining at its pins, ready to mutiny against any semblance of order. Her fingers gripped the handle of her hairbrush as she longed to take it all down and run the comforting bristles through its length. But it was early yet, and she still had business about the house. It wouldn't do for Mr. Dennison to see her roaming around like some unbound banshee. Instead, she let go of the brush and dove in, her deft fingers searching out the pins, shoring up the tendrils. The success of her efforts were lost in the shadows, and it occurred to her that no man had ever seen her in such light.

A soft knock at her door startled her so that she grazed her scalp with a hairpin.

"Miss Voyant?" At some point, Mr. Dennison had lit the lamp on the landing, and he stood now a silhouette in profile in her doorway.

"You're off the phone," she said, controlling her voice.

"Did you manage to hear all you wanted to?" Even in profile, it was clear he was smiling.

"Don't be ridiculous. I was just—"

"Sitting in the dark? So you don't know the good news?"

Ellie Jane leaped from her cushioned stool, knocking her elbow against the carefully arranged powder brushes. "What good news?"

"That brother of yours wants to check on me. He's coming for the game."

∽

With the news of Dave's impending visit, Ellie Jane found herself all the more invested in Mr. Dennison's plan. After all the years her brother had worried about her, bemoaning her lack of friends, wouldn't he be pleased to see how everybody treated her these days? Parents now encouraged their children to say "hello" when they met her on the street. Her fellow women had begun to greet her in the shops. In fact, the same women who always gazed upon her with disdain and pity now added envy to the mix.

Before he left home, Dave was always trying to convince one chum or another to take up her romantic cause. Wouldn't he just love to see the men lined up at the little ticket booth? Of course, they were there to get information about the game, to try to wheedle some preferential treatment, but still she offered each one—no matter his age, stature, or size—the same tight-lipped little smile and simply repeated what Mr. Dennison had instructed her to say.

"Show up Saturday at four. That's when the teams will be chosen."

Undaunted, though, they loitered around the field, nonchalantly tossing a ball between them, or loudly recounting their childhood days on the field. They were out there now, vying for the star's attention. Duke glided from one to another, shaking hands, bearing up under good-natured slaps on his back.

She wondered what those men would think if they ever had the chance to see the Duke that she knew. They might be taken aback by the desperate grip he kept on his morning coffee cup, warding off the occasional tremor that threatened to slosh the hot drink over the side. Even from here she could see the boyish glint in his eye, but more than once she'd come across him unexpectedly—in the kitchen or at the little writing desk on the landing—and had seen those same eyes, deep set above blue shadows.

Still, she wouldn't begrudge him his hero's status. After all, she need only to be within his reach to be vulnerable to his charm. But here, safe behind her ticket window, she leaned forward, resting her chin on her hands, and enjoyed a most welcome view. Not Mr. Dennison, of course, but a whole host of men. Why, she'd never seen so many gathered in one place, except at the occasional funeral.

She allowed her imagination to take over, wondering which she would choose if she could be on the arm of any of them for a Saturday Night Promenade. Surely, after this foolishness was over, the Promenades would resume, and now that she wasn't such a stranger, it stood to reason that someone would—

She caught her breath as one of them broke free from the pack and made his way toward her. He was tall and broad-shouldered, his shirt open at the collar to reveal a narrow triangle of sun-darkened skin. A wide-brimmed hat was pulled low over his eyes, and the afternoon sun behind him made it impossible to see his face. But soon his loping gate became familiar, and when he lifted his hat to run his fingers through the short, brown curly hair, she realized it was Ned Clovis.

The shock of recognition surprised her. She'd seen Ned every day of her life—every day that he was in Picksville, at least. But something was different. It wasn't the way he looked so much as the way he moved. Maybe she'd never noticed the way he moved before. He was always merely present, or not present. Visible, or not visible.

Today, however, she watched his every step, moving her eyes from his scuffed boots to the top of his suspenders. He must be over six feet tall. Not that it mattered; it was merely an observation. Just as it was an observation that when he stopped moving, he stood on the platform outside the ticket booth with his hat in his hand, looking every bit like a young man come courting. And the minute his eyes met hers, he raised his hand to beckon her out of her booth, and she immediately complied.

"We have a job for you." His hands were closed fists, which he crossed over each other and waved once before opening the upper hand to briefly point at her. In just that flash, Ellie Jane realized she understood his hands as well as his voice.

"What is it?" she asked, wondering if she should offer some gesture too.

As a reply, he beckoned again, stepped off the platform, and walked toward the place where, earlier that day, a work crew sent by the mayor had stopped by to set up the band bleachers, usually reserved for the Independence Day townwide picnic.

Ellie Jane hesitated. She'd never abandoned her booth in the middle of the workday. She stopped just before stepping off the platform and started to call out to Ned that she simply couldn't, but he was ten steps ahead of her, not looking back. She had no choice but to follow. She hopped down and quickened her step until she caught up with him. Then she tapped him on the arm, just to let him know she was there.

Ned stopped briefly at his wagon and reached up to the seat. "We need you to make the bags. For the bases."

He held up an empty burlap sack. A small one that wouldn't hold more than ten pounds of anything.

Not understanding exactly what he meant, Ellie Jane smiled broadly and nodded her head, shouting, "Yes, Ned. That *is* a bag! But I do not know how to make them!" She gestured wildly, pointing at the bag, then at herself, shaking her head so hard she feared her hairpins would fly out, and making manic slashing motions across the space between them.

With his free hand, Ned reached out and caught hers. His fingers were so long they reached well above her wrist. Just an observation.

He smiled. "You don't need to yell. I can understand you."

"We were wondering if you could stuff them and sew them up." Duke's voice came from behind Ned's shoulder, and Ellie Jane snatched her hand away. Ned turned around and took a step back. Soon the space between them was filled with Duke Dennison.

"We've got the grass clippings over there." Duke pointed vaguely away. "Think of it as making a tiny ticking."

"Oh, of course," Ellie Jane said, working to reinforce the hairpins she'd dislodged. "Because I've stuffed so many tickings in my life."

She felt nervous somehow, as if she'd been interrupted from something more meaningful than a conversation and was chagrined at the harshness of her retort. Duke, of course, was no stranger to occasional sharpness of her tongue, but she hoped—deep down— that Ned wouldn't know her voice was anything less than sweetness itself. Still, to be sure, she softened her tone. "Besides, I don't have a sewing kit here, and I wouldn't have a needle heavy enough if I did."

"Get some twine and tie off the end," Duke said.

"I assume you have twine? Of course you do, just look at this mess."

"Look." Duke held up his hands in resignation. "I thought you'd like to help." He tapped the top of Ned's arm with the back of his hand. "Let's go finish the backstop."

Duke headed off toward the small gathering of men who were setting posts at the top corner of the diamond. A roll of chicken wire sat on the ground nearby.

"You don't have to if you don't want to," Ned said as soon as Duke stepped away.

Once again the sun was behind him. Ellie Jane looked up into

his face, shadowed by his hat, and found herself smiling at his sheepish grin.

"I don't want to bring a bunch of weeds into my booth."

"Then stay out here." He opened his arms wide. "It's a beautiful
day."

Ellie Jane laughed and held out her hands for the sacks. After all,
she could see the booth from here, and it was lovely outside. "How
many?"

"You're kidding," Ned said before holding up three fingers.

"Very well." She walked over to sit beside the pile of cut grass.
No hat, no gloves, just the sun on her neck and the low sound of
men talking all around her.

Looking up, she saw her little ticket booth in the distance. A
waning sense of duty beckoned, but the breeze won out. This was a
day far too lovely to be hidden by a window.

PART 5

THE FIRST PITCH

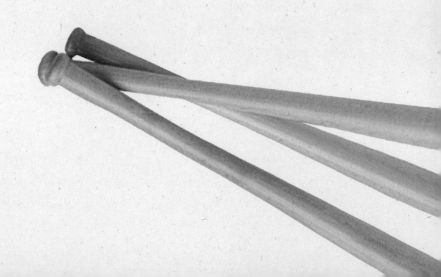

MORRIS

Saturday, May 20

It's one thing spendin days runnin for the people in town but
when Mr. Duke tells me to come in on a Saturday evenin well
that's somethin else. Still that's what he said. To be there Saturday at three o'clock and I'm throwin the first pitch at four.

He really don't know nothin about me.

He don't know what it is to be on the dark side of the tracks
on a Saturday afternoon. He doesn't have a mama who gets up
for her half-day's work and leaves a list of chores so long it'd be
hot afternoon before they're half done. Course she don't write the
list down. She can't write. So every Saturday mornin—the one
day a boy don't have to see the sunrise—she's standin at my head
barkin them all out.

Sweep up the house and borrow Hattie Mae's Bissell for the
carpets.

Put a pot of beans soakin.

Get our clothes pressed for church.

All the other boys'll be gatherin outside Bozie's playin like
they're as tough as the daddies and uncles drinkin hooch inside.
Mama's always tellin me I got to be the man of the family but it
seems more to me I got to be the girls.

As soon as Mama leaves for work I get up and put my blanket and pillow on Mama's bed. Seein it's payday she'll stop at the grocer's on her way home so I take it upon myself to clean up whatever we've got in the kitchen. It isn't much—some leftover cornbread and coffee—but enough to take off the hunger and more than Mama would've let me have. Before I leave for town I take a handful of coins that I got runnin yesterday and drop them in the blue speckled jar on the top shelf in the kitchen. She don't know I drop money in there. She just praises Jesus and brags to her friends that the Lord always sees we got enough.

I guess the Lord can use my money as good as anyone else's.

Mama's left a little bit of water in the wash basin so I splash my face and scrub my teeth with the new toothbrush Mr. Duke told me to buy at the drugstore. He said if I wanted to keep my chompers I'd better brush them every day and I can't think of nothin better to have than Mr. Duke's smile.

I'm ready to get started on my chores but it's too early to call on Miss Hattie Mae so I figure I'll go into town and see who needs what done this mornin. Sometimes just by walkin in the right neighborhood a boy can get himself a quarter by scrapin out a gutter or paintin a shutter. Most times it's just boys like me—cept white boys—who want to buy their way out of the chores their own mama gave them. But I don't care. Honest work is honest work and every dime I get takes me farther out of this town when I won't never work for nobody but me.

Anyway I think my first stop's gonna be the baseball field Mr. Duke's buildin at the railroad station. He's been payin me a dollar every day just to work it there for him and it turns out he's callin my name before I even get myself across the tracks.

I say, Good mornin, to Miss Ellie Jane in her ticket booth

before goin over to the field. Mr. Duke is there wavin and wavin his hand wantin me to run. But I ain't never been one to run at someone's command. Instead what do you think? That Mr. Duke comes runnin up to me and he's got such a smile on his face as I ain't never seen on a white man before.

He says, What do you think Morris?

And by this time I'm halfway out to the field and I just stop cold. I ain't never seen nothin like it before cept on the pictures of them cards I give over to Mr. Ned. There's a clear diamond of red dirt and a little mound right in the middle.

Mr. Duke says, That's where you stand when you pitch son.

We're standin side by side and he has his arm just sittin on my shoulder. And when he calls me son well I think both of us stopped breathin for just a bit. I ain't never considered myself to be any man's son since my daddy left, let alone a man as fine as he is. So I take a second to pretend it's true. That I'm the only son of a rich white man who spends every day of his life playin base-ball. Now I've been buildin dreams for myself for as long as I've been able to put thoughts together but I ain't never dreamed of anything so fine as that. And you just can't take a breath when a dream is bein true.

Let's see how you like it, he says. He reaches down into a can-vas bag sittin at his feet and hands me my glove and a ball and tells me to head out to the mound.

When I get there I stand up on it and look around at the whole field. It was like seein it all for the first time because I had it all to myself. I feel like I'm just a little taller than the rest of the world up here and I can feel my fingers curled around the ball, itchin to throw it. Mr. Duke is at home plate crouched down behind a square of white board partway buried in the ground.

Looks like he's a mile away.

Mr. Duke tells me to toss him one across the plate but I tell him there's no way I'd ever be able to get the ball all the way over there. He puts his glove up and tells me it's no different from playin catch and somethin in his voice brings him a little closer. So I wind myself up, fix my eyes on the mitt, and let the ball go. A second later I hear it hit the leather and Mr. Duke gives a kind of a hoot and tosses it back to me.

We throw it back and forth for a while and I can't miss. I'm gettin them in fast, droppin them down late, and workin a curveball so pretty Mr. Duke hoots again. After a while though he says we got to stop or I won't have nothin left in my arm for tonight.

We walk over to a bench set up behind the first base line where he opens up a paper bag and hands me a sweet roll. It's still warm and there's a thin white icing swirled on top of it, prettier than anything I've ever seen. I try not to eat too fast, wantin to take my time with the sweet and the butter.

After I swallow the first bite I ask him, What's tonight?

He says, Gonna get a game goin. Choose up teams. These guys won't know what they're up against.

He goes on and on namin half the town and who's gonna play what and I'm gettin excited too, because we've always talked about playin a real game. I've pitched against Mr. Ned and Mr. Duke and he pays me a nickel for every strike and a dime for every hit—if I'm out of the zone I got to pay it all back and start over. So I'm addin it all up in my head—what I'd get in a real game—then two thoughts turn that sweet roll dry as a biscuit.

First Mr. Duke hasn't said he's gonna pay me at all to pitch in a real game.

Second it wouldn't matter if he did. Saturday afternoon means one thing. Church. There's no way my mama's gonna let me skip out on it to play baseball. So I tell him the problem— nothin about the money just about church.

He looks real surprised and says, On a Saturday?

I say, Yeah. We're Adventists and that's when we go. Every Saturday, four o'clock.

He kind of rubs his chin and asks, When do you get out?

I tell him that's kind of tricky because it all depends on when the Holy Spirit's done with us. Sometimes in the summer when it's real hot in that little church the Holy Spirit's there just in time to let us out into the cool evenin. But in the wintertime when it's cold outside and we got the church stove burnin the church coal we might take until late in the night to feel the anointin. Spring evenin like this there's no knowin.

Mr. Duke laughs and says that's why he never went in for church—might interfere with his baseball.

I tell him there ain't any reason why a fellow couldn't have both but if he had to choose well baseball couldn't ever offer up the kind of promises the Lord can. What kind of hope can you have in a game?

He picks up the ball and tosses it from hand to hand a few times before he talks again. He says when he was just about my age he had nothin to give him any kind of hope.

I say, That's a shame because God and baseball was both around back then.

He says his old man never would've let him have either one.

Right then Mr. Duke and I are at a place where we're just the same. Hard to tell who's the boy and who's the man because all I want to do is try to take away the sadness that's come over his face. *I'm thinkin maybe I can help him know God the way he helped me know baseball and in my heart I know there's room enough for both. So even though I'm not real sure how I'm gonna make it happen I tell him that I'll be here this afternoon for the game.*

He says, What about your Holy Spirit?

I tell him it's not my Holy Spirit it's God's and it's with me all the time. The rest of the church is on their own.

Then just because it seems the thing to do I rip off half of the sweet roll and hand it over to him. He puts the whole hunk in his mouth so I put the rest in mine and we just sit there and chew and chew while the minutes of the mornin waste away.

⟿

I leave Mr. Duke and head into town to see if there's any telegrams need deliverin (there aren't) or if the mayor's in his office (he isn't). I figure I'm gonna need a few things to build myself up in Mama's eyes so I go into the green grocer and buy her a few treats. Some sweet red peppers and three lemons the size of my fist for the collard greens she'll fix for tomorrow's lunch. None of the markets on our side of the tracks have anything like this and if the grocer's a little nervous when I walk in he's comfortable enough with my money after I leave.

I decide it's just about time to head back home and finish the chores Mama has waitin for me there when Mr. Poplin pokes his head out the door and says, I have a package waitin inside.

My shirts.

I try to put on the face of a boy who gets brand-new shirts every day and kind of roll my steps into Mr. Poplin's store. The

place is full of women, all of them with these little baskets
hangin off their arms, and the minute I walk in it's like they all
had their breath hooked to a fishin line and cast away. All their
eyes stared at me from those pretty white faces. They didn't look
mean or scared just surprised—like I'm some kind of a goat in
bloomers.

Mr. Poplin goes behind his counter and sets a flat brown
package on top of it.

He says, Here you are young man. Two shirts courtesy of
Sears and Roebuck. Then he makes a show out of lookin at his
ledger book and announcin to everybody that they're paid in full.

Now I know they're paid for because I brought him the last
of what I owed on Thursday and I know he remembers too. But
there's somethin in me that wishes I still owed a little so I could
set the money down on the counter same as all these other women
will.

Then Mr. Poplin asks if I want to open the package and take
the shirts out just to see that they fit the order specifications but I
tell him no. Somehow the thought of all these women seein my
clothes without me in them seems akin to them seein me without
my clothes. So I tell Mr. Poplin if it's all the same to him I'll just
take my package on home.

As I'm walkin out the door Mr. Poplin says, Those'll sure be
nice for wearin to church.

And I can barely bring myself to turn around and tell him
that they sure will.

When I get back home it takes less than an hour to finish a
mornin's worth of work. I'm scrubbin like a whirlwind not carin
about what splashes back on this old shirt. We only have one little piece of tacked-down carpet in our front room and I run Miss

Hattie's Bissell up and down it a dozen times, hummin a tune that seems to go with the rhythm of the brushes. When I take the sweeper back to Miss Hattie I give her one of the lemons I bought at the grocer, hopin that'll help her forget just how late in the day it was. By the time Mama walked through the door at three o'clock the whole place is scrubbed down and fluffed up and I'm buttoned up to my chin in stiff clean cotton.

ELLIE JANE

Ellie Jane looked out the window of her ticket booth and saw another one. This time it was Mr. Headley, the new teacher at the high school, hands in his pockets, standing on home plate, craning his neck in all directions. They'd been coming in a steady stream all day—local farmers with their goods, shopkeepers, the older boys from the high school—all of them looking slightly dazed.

She set aside her magazine, after folding the corner of the page with the extremely helpful gardening tips, and leaned forward until her nose was pressed against the glass and her mouth just outside the little round window.

"Hey!" she hollered. "He isn't here!"

Mr. Headley turned around, saw her, and made his way to the platform, stopping an arm's length from the window.

"You are looking for Mr. Dennison, aren't you?" Ellie Jane said, having backed a respectable distance away from the glass.

Mr. Headley nodded. "Do you know anything about a game today?"

Did she know anything about a game? Had there been any other conversation at home all week other than the game?

"It's later this afternoon. Around four o'clock. Bring your own glove." Exactly what Mr. Dennison had instructed her to say.

"And will you be attending?"

He leaned closer to the glass and smiled, revealing large gums and tiny teeth. Ellie Jane took this feature into consideration, alongside his thinning hair, upturned nose, and thin, feminine hands.

"If I am not otherwise engaged." She offered a smile of her own. It wasn't often she had the opportunity to be coy, even if she held no interest in the flirtation.

He offered a limp little wave and backed away from the platform, not turning around until he was dangerously close to falling off entirely.

Ellie Jane checked the watch pinned to her blouse.

Two more hours. Still no sign of Dave, and there wouldn't be another train today. It wouldn't be the first time he'd canceled a visit home.

She sighed and opened the magazine, filling her head with ideas for window boxes for the front of the house, when she saw another man leaning up against the backstop. Once again she set the magazine aside, put her face up to the window, and prepared to yell for his attention before realizing the man was Ned Clovis. Unlike the other visitors throughout the day who came to gaze longingly at the field, Ned was turned squarely toward the booth. And, though he didn't beckon her in any way, she found herself standing straight, smoothing her hair and skirt, and walking out her little door.

"He isn't here!" she hollered, but soon realized she was still too far away for him to understand. So she continued to walk until his face was so clearly in view she could see the individual whiskers that made up the scruff of a beard on his chin.

"Are you looking for Mr. Dennison?"

"Duke," he clarified, making an imaginary curled moustache with his fingers.

"Yes, well, *Duke* isn't here," she said, replicating the gesture.

"That's all right. I didn't come here to see him."

Immediately her nerves began to churn. "Oh—"

"I have the scoreboard." When he turned and pointed behind him, she saw the large board, painted black, with careful lettering and boxes in white. He was smiling, almost as if he could sense the turmoil just beneath her skin.

"Good, well, I need to get back to my booth." Ellie Jane wanted to stand there and shake herself to try to restore some sort of order to her mind, but instead she prattled on about it being nearly closing time and needing to count the day's money and take the cash box in to Mr. Coleman and getting home before Mr. Dennison took it upon himself to cook Saturday supper again.

Somewhere in the midst of her litany she realized that Ned was laughing—a strange silent laugh that was little more than a broad smile and the rhythmic shaking of his shoulders. She stopped mid-word and gave him a tight-lipped smile.

"I never knew you talked so much." His fingers created an invisible torrent pouring out of his mouth.

"That's because you never *talked* to me." Once again she found her hands mirroring his, speaking under their own power, just as her voice surprised her with its light, lilting laughter.

"I've wanted to." He reached out to her, palms up, fingers curled, and gathered the air between them back to him. For a second it seemed her body would follow. "For years, ever since I came back from school."

Her eyes darted between his face and his hands, which were in continuous motion, punctuating each word, underscoring the weakness in his voice. She thought about those years since his return from school, always seeing him on the town's periphery, a constant reminder of just why she felt so alone. She stared at the ground between them and was surprised by a memory she had tucked away long ago.

"I wrote to you."

She felt the lightest touch—his finger just under her chin, tilting her head up to meet his gaze. Then he took his hand away.

"I wrote to you," she repeated.

He nodded.

"You never wrote back to me."

"I was twelve years old."

Ellie Jane suddenly felt childish, sounding like she'd been pining away for something she hadn't thought about in years. And she hated being out here, exposed in this open field. The sun warmed her face; the breeze ruffled the wide sleeves of her blouse and brought one dislodged curl over to tickle her nose. Her mind was tumbling with unspoken words, desperate phrases to let him know that she hadn't thought a thing about that letter in years, not since she sent the silly thing. But she remembered now. She remembered running home from school every day for weeks to see if the mail carrier had left a letter for her. She even went into the post office to see if one had been delivered there. As each day went by with nothing, she'd known that Ned hadn't forgiven her, so she'd never forgiven herself, and the taunts of the town took hold.

Still, they were children then, as Ned had reminded her, and what kind of woman would she be, here on a spring afternoon, blaming her fate on a few lines she scribbled fifteen years ago?

She summoned her most polite smile. "Yes. It was long ago, wasn't it?"

A response was forming in Ned's eyes, but before he could reel her in further, she felt the comfort of her booth calling to her and began to turn away.

"Wait." He reached out, but she stopped before he touched her. Instead, she was held by his grin, as mischievous as it had ever been when he was a boy. "I thought you could help me put up the scoreboard."

He reached into the bed of his wagon and pulled out a large piece of plywood with two posts attached at either side.

Not sure what her part was in this endeavor, Ellie Jane simply followed—a safe enough distance that if the board became too heavy for him to carry, at least it wouldn't fall on her head. In the meantime, she studied the breadth of his shoulders, the narrowness of his waist, and everything else that came with walking behind him, hoping he wouldn't turn around anytime soon.

When they got to the backstop, he leaned the board against it and went back to get the post-hole digger from the wagon. He moved as if she wasn't there, never looking to the left or to the right, almost as if she'd already become a fixture in his life, even as she warmed to the very idea of being so.

She tried to picture the boy he'd been back then. She remembered dark curly hair and thick black eyelashes—so dark that when their teacher showed them a picture of an Egyptian pharaoh, the kids teased him saying he looked like his eyes were lined with kohl. What she remembered most, though, is that he was always laughing. Forever telling jokes or chanting rhymes or calling to his chums from across the schoolyard. He'd tell wild stories about things that might happen, dreaming up heroic scenarios for himself, holding an audience while he spun his tales.

Now, everything he did was punctuated with deep, perpetual silence. Even as he dug the earth out of the ground, there was no grunting or huffing as she often heard when her father did similar work in their yard. Ned didn't whistle or hum or break into short, chatty conversation. The only sound came from the blade hitting the ground and the moist earth piling up next to the deepening hole.

The next thing she knew, that sound had stopped and Ned was standing upright, wiping the sweat from his brow. She didn't know how many times he said her name before she finally heard him.

"Ellie Jane?"

She jumped up to her feet, ready to do his bidding.

He brought the sign back to where he'd dug the holes and asked her to help him lower the posts down into them. She complied without complaint. He then asked her to go back to his wagon and bring a third post while he held the board steady. She complied again, wondering just what he might be thinking as she walked away.

Minutes later, with the scoreboard fully planted and braced, Ned stepped back to observe his handiwork. Ellie Jane stood beside him.

"There," he said, still looking at the board, "it's all ready for you."

Then they looked at each other.

"You want me to keep score?"

"Do you want to?"

"Oh, I don't know," she said, working a girlish lilt into her voice. "I wouldn't know what to do."

"I'll show you." He took a piece of chalk out of his pocket and turned to the board. With bold, sure strokes, he showed her how to indicate the innings, the pitch count, the outs, and the score. He disappeared in his lesson, losing his careful enunciation. The faster he spoke, the less she understood as some words seemed to be lost entirely, while others ran together to become little more than nasal noise. But the concept was clear enough, and rather than prolong the tortuous monologue, she reached out and touched his shoulder, stopping him in the middle of the proper way to record a strike.

"I understand all of this," she said, her hands making large, swooping circles toward the board. "It's the game—"

"Just watch me." He drew an invisible line between her eyes and his. "I'll tell you everything you need to know."

He opened his arms wide, palms up, inviting her to the inner circle of this event that seemed to have taken over the town, and she felt herself being drawn to him, to the game, to a Saturday night outside of her darkened parlor. She took the chalk from Ned's hand and attempted to record a third out. She'd need to bring a stepstool to use during the game, but for now she merely stretched, drawing in a deep breath as she arched her back just a little in an attempt to elongate her body. She could only imagine the appreciative look on Ned's face at the fine figure she was creating.

"Is that Dave?"

Ned's words were hardly the response she'd hoped to get. She spun around and saw the approach of an impressive, sleek black automobile and blushed thinking how full her head must have been not to have heard its guttural engine, not to mention the scene she was presenting to its driver—her big brother.

"Dave!" she called out as he brought the car to a smooth stop just outside the first base line. She slipped the piece of chalk into her skirt pocket as she ran toward him, making just enough effort to hold her arms at an attractive angle so she wouldn't seem, even from behind, like she was exerting any undue effort.

By the time she got to him, Dave had removed his lightweight camel-colored riding coat, draping it carefully across the car's open door, and was in the midst of taking off the protective goggles, revealing his familiar spectacles beneath.

Ellie Jane threw herself into his arms, burying her face in his shoulder and breathing in the satisfying scent of warmth. She felt the deep rumble of his greeting, then stepped back to snap his suspender in playful chiding.

"Since when do you drive? Why couldn't you come on the train like a normal person?"

"I didn't want you to worry." He bent to plant a dry kiss on her cheek. "I figure if I had to break away from my glamorous city life to cover some small-town story, I may as well take the new girl out for a ride."

Ellie Jane craned to look behind him. "What new girl?"

"This one." He closed the door with a grand gesture. "She's the only love of my life right now."

At that moment, Ned joined the little reunion, and the two men shook hands before stepping back, assuming identical postures as they gazed at the automobile.

"Mercedes?" Ned asked before looking to Dave for confirmation.

"American duplicate." His voice echoed pride. "Got her about a month ago."

Ellie Jane found herself growing more and more annoyed at the increasing insignificance of her presence.

"Honestly." She wedged herself within Ned's line of vision. "It's just a car."

Ned gave her an indulgent smile, then looked over her head at Dave and shrugged before moving around to examine the back.

"Well, then." Ellie Jane turned her attention to her brother. "Shall we push it to the nearest museum? Or do you think you can take me for a drive?"

Dave grasped her hand and walked her around to the passenger side with exaggerated grandness. "Mademoiselle?" He opened the door with a flourish. "Your chariot awaits."

Ellie Jane joined in the game, puffing herself up and holding her nose high. She settled in the seat and busied herself smoothing her skirt to hide the disappointment when Ned declined to join them. She sensed him moving to the front of the car, and then he was there, right in front of her, his elbows resting on top of the door.

"See you this afternoon?"

She swallowed, nodded, and held up four fingers. "Four o'clock."

Meanwhile, Dave brought the engine to a smooth rumble with a single crank and interrupted his fiddling with various levers to reach across Ellie Jane and shake Ned's hand again.

Then, after a benedictory slap on the rear fender courtesy of Ned, they were touring the streets of Picksville, turning every head they passed.

"It's surprisingly quiet," Ellie Jane said, hardly needing to raise her voice.

"Want to know what's under the hood?" Dave took his eyes off the road long enough to offer a boyish grin.

"Oh, not now. You'll want to save something to talk about at supper tomorrow."

They came to the town square where, ignoring the unwritten town ordinance, Dave took a left-hand turn and lifted his hand in response to the greetings and appreciative stares offered by the people on the Picksville sidewalks.

"I won't be here for Sunday dinner." He doffed his cap to Mrs. Lewiston. "I really do need to leave first thing in the morning."

"You're not even staying for church?"

He shouted a greeting to Mr. Poplin before taking the corner a little more sharply than she would have liked.

"Nope. Got to head out at first light."

Ellie Jane turned in her seat. "You drove all this way just to turn around and go back again? That doesn't make any sense. The train is much faster."

"Maybe so." He eased them through the final intersection before turning onto their home street. "But there's something alluring about the open road, and I thought I might try to convince our Mr. Dennison to come back with me a little early."

"A *little* early? He's supposed to stay for two more weeks."

Dave applied the brake and brought the automobile to a halt right in front of the Voyant home and waved to the neighbors whose heads popped out of their doors. Then, though nobody could possibly hear them over the rumbling engine, he leaned in close and said, "What's the matter? From the sound of your letter you couldn't get rid of him fast enough."

"I'm just concerned about his well-being is all," she said, stiffening. "He's still not, I think, quite ready."

"Wouldn't have any romantic interests there, now would you?" His brows were waggling again. "Because it looked to me like you and Ned Clovis were a pretty cozy pair."

"Certainly not," Ellie Jane said before returning a greeting to the elderly lady across the street. "On both counts."

Dave's countenance turned serious, and he reached out to take her hand. "I just want you to be happy, EJ. I know it hasn't always been easy—"

She gave him a reassuring pat. "I'm fine. And any man who refers to his automobile as the 'love of his life' has absolutely no business offering me romantic advice."

"True," he said, taking off his plaid driving cap and running his fingers through his hair. It was still the same jet-black color as their mother's, although thinner on top than she remembered. "But a big brother can still worry, can't he?"

"Better than anyone I know."

NED

There had been a few uneasy minutes when Ned worried that nobody would come. That all of the hard work and sacrifice was nothing but some overgrown child's folly. He'd encountered more than a few quizzical looks from customers who hunted him down at the railroad tracks only to be told to write down their order, leave it on the nail in the door, and come back to pick it up before ten o'clock the next morning. He'd gone home at night, sore from the day's labor, but exhilarated from the day's play, as he and Duke and Morris would stop everything for a quick round of pepper.

Sometimes, when Ned stood poised at home plate, ready to toss the ball into the air and hit it out to where Duke and Morris stood ready to field it, he'd close his eyes and imagine the roaring of a crowd. He'd never heard such a thing, but he'd been to a White Sox game in Chicago and even one excursion to the Polo Grounds in New York where he'd certainly *seen* the crowd—a blurred mass of movement, everybody's mouths open in one collective cheer, a sea of fists pummeling the air, an ocean of hat-tossing, back-slapping, beer-sloshing joy.

When he tried to pull a memory to match the vision, the closest he could come was a storm. So to make the experience complete, he'd stand on home plate, close his eyes, and summon not only the roar of the wind, but the pelting power of rain. He imagined tossing the ball up into thick, dark clouds, and when it came down and connected with the bat, he was sure Duke and Morris could hear the thunder.

But this Saturday afternoon was nowhere near a storm, although much to his satisfaction there seemed to be a slow, steady drizzle. This must be how Noah felt, standing on the deck of the ark watching God's promises arrive in pairs. That's how the first of the crowd arrived—courting couples. Men dressed in their Saturday Promenade suits, minus the traditional boater hats; women in frothy layers of lace and bonnets, gloves and lace. The men seemed just as happy to be here as the women seemed surprised, then annoyed. More than one surveyed the ball field, pursed her lips, crossed her arms, and engaged in a foot-stomping argument that could only be summed up in one sentence.

Take me home.

The men, however, didn't take them home, and Ned didn't blame them. These fellows had little opportunity to show off for their women. Being tethered at the elbow for long strolls around the town square gave no chance to be cock of the yard, strutting to get the females' attention. Tonight, the diamond was the yard, the bats and balls their feathers. They would puff up, hit, and strut as fast as they could around the bases, hoping to later reap the benefits of their best girl's ardent arousal.

Oh, and what Ned wouldn't give to be one of them. To be part of the game, running the bases, looking out the corner of his eye to see the scramble of the opponents trying to make the play. But yesterday, as Ned was raking the baseline, Duke had approached him and made it clear that he wanted Ned to officiate.

You're the only one I trust.

So he would stand beside the plate, taking careful inventory of the whole game, and then turn to relay the information to the scorekeeper. That's when he decided to ask Ellie Jane. She'd never be able to take her eyes off him.

The modest gathering of young men wasn't surprising, but then there were the others. Mr. Coleman and his pear-shaped body wrapped in stained trousers shook hands with Mayor Birdiff, who wore a college sweater stretched to its threads across his bulging stomach. The mayor's equally round wife was there too, but Ned noticed a decidedly less savory woman perched on the end of one of the bleachers, offering the occasional surreptitious waves to Picksville's civic leader. There was Mr. Samms, the butcher, and even Mr. Poplin, so thin it seemed the weight of the bat would knock him over.

And then, like the wayward prince coming to claim his kingdom, Duke Dennison arrived on the scene. Not strolling up on a sunny afternoon like the others. No, he sat tall in the backseat of Dave's automobile, behind Floyd Voyant, with Ellie Jane by his side.

Ned swallowed hard and wrapped his hope around the conversation he shared with her earlier. The warmth in her eyes, the genuine affection he sensed. He'd spent the balance of the afternoon wondering if it was wishful thinking on his part or an answer to prayer; he decided to thank God for those few moments and pray for a torrent of more to come.

Dave parked the car close to the station, and the four piled out. Ned held up his hand, beckoning Ellie Jane over. She and Duke—both dressed in clean, white linen—broke away from the others, walking together in matching strides. Easy to do, given the shortness of Dennison's legs.

Duke was the first to offer his hand in greeting; Ellie Jane echoed, *Hello.* For just a moment Ned worried about their seamless interaction, but he reminded himself that, despite her friendliness over the past few days, he had no right to be jealous. And, most likely, no reason. By the end of the night, Duke would have a dozen of Picksville's prettiest girls competing for his affection. He wouldn't even notice Ned walking Ellie Jane home.

They were shortly joined by Floyd and Dave, who was toting a large leather case.

Mind if I take a few pictures?

Something flitted across Duke's face, the briefest ripple beneath the mask, before his cajoling smile was back.

There's no story yet, Voyant. Wait until the kid gets here.

Dave brought his free hand up to tap his breast pocket, where he'd carried a small notebook long before leaving Picksville for the world of big city journalism.

I'm the writer, Duke. I'll decide what the story is. He looped his arm through Ellie Jane's. *Come on, sis. Introduce me around.*

But before Ellie Jane could lead him away, Duke grabbed Dave's sleeve, his face that of a desperate man.

Leave me out of it, Dave. Out of the pictures and out of the story.

It was a moment, Ned was sure, that was meant to be held between the two men. Ellie Jane and Floyd both looked away, embarrassed, but Ned stood transfixed by the transformation of his hero. The great Duke Dennison seemed hollow, and the rumors and suspicions about what he'd been filling himself up with before his disappearance from the world of baseball were suddenly indisputable. The man was scared, and everybody in this little circle knew it. Perhaps Dave, most of all, because he offered a quick, reassuring nod before setting off with Ellie Jane to find more interesting subjects among the gathered townspeople. They weren't more than three steps away before Duke had composed himself again, and the three men put their heads together to plan the course of the afternoon's game.

Duke would head up one team, Floyd Voyant the other—each

of them choosing one player at a time from the assembled crowd until they each had nine. Duke would choose first, and he would choose Morris.

He looked around the assembled crowd. *Where is he?*

Ned shrugged. He'd seen the boy briefly earlier in the day, but that was well before noon. The big, white clock face on the front of Ellie Jane's ticket booth read five minutes to four, the agreed-upon start time. Any longer and the assembled crowd would become restless, maybe take the privilege of being captain away from the very man who organized the game.

Duke rubbed his hands together. *Let's get started!* He strode over to where the men stood and gathered them around. Ned couldn't see anything he said, but when he watched Duke Dennison from the back, he looked like an orchestra conductor, his arms wide and animated.

Every now and then the men reared back in unison laughter, and Ned tried to imagine the joke. When Duke pointed left, their heads swung in one accord. When he brought Floyd to stand next to him, they offered a giant, respectful acknowledgment. Then, at the backhanded beckoning of the Duke, they shuffled toward the bleachers to sit with the women and wait to see just who would be worthy to be chosen.

The man was good.

Ned felt the smallest touch on his shoulder and turned to Ellie Jane.

Sure you don't want to be on a team?

He smiled. "Positive."

Back at the bleachers, Duke and Floyd shook hands and adopted identical hands-on-hips stances on the third base line. After one long, craning look, Duke pointed to his first player.

Mr. Coleman.

The old station master got up from the bleachers and waddled himself to the field. Ned might never have noticed how disproportionately small the old man's hands were, except that Mr. Coleman held one fist high in triumph long after taking his place behind Duke.

Floyd chose Gustav Geist, fresh from mopping up Marlene's Diner, who covered the distance from the bleachers to the baseline in two enormous strides.

Next, Duke chose Mayor Birdiff in his ridiculous overstretched sweater. He might be the only player wearing actual baseball clothes, but he also seemed the one least likely to be able to play the game.

Again, the gentle touch on his shoulder. *What is he doing?*

"Gratitude." Ned pointed and twirled his fingers in big, encompassing circles. *For all this. The field, the bleachers, the town…* And a certain strategy too. They'd talked about it during those long hours working side by side, cutting grass, hauling weeds. He didn't catch every word, of course, but the gist was clear. Duke wanted to win the game with one star, one boy, and a host of old men.

Floyd's next two picks were Ed and Tommy Vick, a pair of brothers from a nearby farm, each of them with arms the size of oak branches. They rolled the sleeves of their starched striped shirts past the elbows and flexed their biceps, much to the clapping delight of two fresh-faced girls in the bleachers.

Meanwhile, Dave scribbled furiously in his little notebook, shaking his head after each of Duke's unlikely choices.

For Duke, those next few choices were Mr. Poplin, whose arms looked like kindling, and Mr. Samms, the butcher whose shirt still bore the bloody smear of his trade.

Floyd chose the young man responsible for keeping the grounds for Picksville High School; Duke called up Mr. Headley who was so intent on cleaning his glasses he stood with the wrong team and had to be directed—none too gently—by Gustav Geist. Floyd summoned the carpenter who oversaw the construction of the new Catholic church; Duke, the middle-aged priest who'd shown up in his religious garb.

The pickings were getting slimmer and slimmer, and by now Ned kept his eyes focused on the dirt road that led up to the station from the south side of Picksville. Floyd was shaking the hand of Pete Shiner—a man who left town for a while to work a cattle ranch in Texas—while Duke took on the elder Mr. Shiner, who had always been faithful in sharing his son's exploits with the crowd gathered at the feed store.

There was only one spot left on each team, and despite his earlier thoughts, when the last plausible player had been chosen, Ned held a faint flutter of hope that Duke might just decide to round out his nine with the town deaf man, when he caught sight of Morris— running like the devil was chasing him. He pointed the boy out to Ellie Jane, who hollered for Duke's attention. She and Ned pointed together, and when Duke saw Morris, he had the look of a man who'd just been acquitted.

Morris slowed his pace as he got closer and was down to a trot by the time he came alongside Ned. *I'm not too late?*

Ned drew an invisible line across the top of his nose. *Just made it.*

If the others on the field had any objection to Duke's final choice, they didn't show it. Floyd rounded out his team with a red-headed high school senior. When a coin flip gave Duke's team first at bat, their opponents huddled to decide who would play what position.

Morris headed over to join his team, turning for just a moment to tip his cap to Ellie Jane, and Ned was struck by how different the boy looked this afternoon. It was more than the clean shirt, although that was the most obvious change in Morris's appearance. For the first time, Ned noticed the kid had a thin, fuzzy layer sprouted across his upper lip, and he wore his hair with a definite part combed in one side. Mostly, though, he noticed how tall the young man stood, having left his subservient slouch on the other side of the tracks. Duke had buried Morris sixth in the lineup—probably so he could get to the second inning as quickly as possible—and Morris claimed his place in line with the rest of Picksville's elite.

Dave had settled himself in the front bleacher seat, and even from this distance, it was obvious he'd opened up his little notebook to a brand-new page.

Ned looked over to Ellie Jane. "Ready?"

She held up her chalk. *Just tell me what to do.*

He made his promises, then moved into position. Batting first for Duke's team, Mayor Birdiff walked to the plate and took a few feeble practice swings that brought the bat up short at the widest part of his girth.

Gustav Geist took the mound, and Pete Shiner settled down at home to catch.

Ned stood to the right of the batter. Once he'd found the perfect haunch to gauge the throw, he stood straight, held up his hand and, in what he hoped was a bold, clear voice, yelled, "Play ball!"

It didn't matter that none of Gustav's throws were anywhere near the strike zone; the mayor swung hard at all of them and was summarily sent back to his team.

Ned signaled to Ellie Jane to put a single checkmark in the box labeled Out before turning back to the second batter, Mr. Coleman, who summarily offered a repeat performance. Third up was Mr. Samms who fared no better, though he did have the sense to let two bad pitches go by without swinging.

As the teams prepared to switch sides, Ned stepped over to the scoreboard and instructed Ellie Jane to draw a large "0" under Duke's name.

She frowned. *That seems sad.*

"Don't worry. This is baseball. There's always a second chance."

Duke and Morris were conferring on the mound when Ned called time and Duke came to take his place behind home plate. The expression on Duke's face was every bit that of a proud father.

This is it.

First up for Floyd's team was the smug-faced high school kid, sauntering up to the plate, practically twirling the bat.

Ned steeled himself to remain neutral as Morris wound up for his first pitch. Minutes later, after three blinding fastballs, the smug expression was one of shock. Poor kid never even moved the bat. Next, Gustav swung madly at pitches long after they were snug in Duke's glove. Then the first of the Vick boys managed to hit a couple of foul tips straight up, the second of which dropped nicely into Duke's lofty glove, and it was time for another "0" on the scoreboard.

Dave Voyant's pencil stub hovered, frozen, above his little pad.

Ellie Jane planted her hands on her hips. *Not a very exciting match.*

Ned took the chalk from her and reached to the top of the scoreboard to write the change in inning. Instead of handing it back directly, he held on to it while she tugged on the chalk playfully.

"Just wait," he said before relinquishing his grip. "It'll get better."

She was missing out on the beauty of the game. Sometimes all it took was one spark of life to turn everything around, and that spark was on deck.

Ned imagined Duke probably looked just like this every time he took the plate—confident stride, bat resting on his shoulder. For now, that flash of weakness moments ago was forgotten. All those newspaper articles, baseball cards, nothing compared to this moment, seeing his hero—no more than three feet away—taking his stance, readying himself to do what made him famous. What made him the highest-paid player in the league.

Then Gustav released the ball, and Duke swung. Late.

Before he knew what he was saying, Ned was standing straight up, sending the signal with his right hand. "Strike one!"

So, Duke Dennison was just a man after all.

The pro had the good grace to send Ned a self-conscious smile before choking up and readying himself for the second pitch.

High and outside. Duke didn't budge.

"Ball."

For the first time, Gustav looked unhappy with the call, but Ned simply bent again, leveling his eyes with the strike zone and prepared for the third pitch.

There were a few sounds Ned carried in his memory, and the sound of a bat hitting a ball was one he felt as a tingle in the palms of his hands. This one he could feel all the way up to his elbows. It was a hard line drive, cutting straight through two startled brothers who scrambled to find it, then proceeded to fight over it while Duke flew by, touching first base, then second, and finally shoring up at third.

The faces on the players and the crowd all registered the same. They were awake. Ned turned to Ellie Jane who was jumping in place and clapping her hands. But she wasn't looking at Duke; she was looking at Ned, and he fought with everything he had not to run back to her, swoop her up, and say, *See? I told you things could change.*

Mr. Headley was up next with a pop fly straight back to Gustav.

Ned turned back to Ellie Jane to tell her to mark the out but, much to his pride and pleasure, she already had.

Then Morris took the plate, stood stock-still, and took his base after watching four bad pitches roll by.

Now Dave was writing, flipping through his pages like a man possessed, interrupted only by the occasions when he shouldered the camera and took to the edge of the field, poised to snap a photo of the next great play.

Mr. Poplin managed a weak hit good enough to confuse Floyd's team and allow himself to take first while Morris advanced to second. Again, Ned found himself fighting his instincts, as he would have loved to see Duke run home. He'd get his chance soon enough when Mr. Samms, after two strikes, swung and missed a third. He shouldn't have swung; it was a bad pitch that went wild, sending Pete Shiner into a spinning dervish looking for it in the dirt while Duke seized the opportunity and flew across the plate.

Leave it to Duke to steal home.

Ned left Duke's team to their celebration and walked back to the scoreboard where Ellie Jane was using the square of blue felt to erase the "0" and write "1" in its place.

Surged with the adrenaline of the play, Ned leaned over Ellie Jane's shoulder and spoke directly into her ear.

"See? One hit, and it's a whole new game."

When she turned around she was so close, and he was fighting a whole new instinct. But something in her eyes told him she was fighting too, and for the first time in six years, Ned thought he might have a chance.

Bottom of the second. Morris still pitched like fire, but there was an occasional hit, and even a couple of walks. The old men on Duke's team seemed to step out of their graying skin and recapture some of the vigor they must have had when they were the life force of the town—before desks and shops and farms took their hearts. And Floyd Voyant's assembly of strength took on a grudging respect of both young and old as each took his turn at bat. Often, facing Morris, they muttered something that was lost on Ned but served to harden the glint in the boy's eye.

And Ellie Jane. They worked together, sending each other signals and messages, communicating and verifying. She motioned him to her side and he trotted over, eager to answer whatever question she'd fabricated. When he recorded the change of each inning, she beckoned him to lean close while she repeated to him the latest muttering insult of a disgruntled player. How odd to see such sweet lips, the color of a summer peach, mouthing some of that spite-filled speech. But some of what she conveyed—especially that of the hot-tempered Catholic priest—was genuinely funny, and he loved sharing a secret laugh with her while keeping the others at bay.

So it went on through the late afternoon and into the early evening when the sun descended behind the scoreboard. More than once, when Ned looked over to catch Ellie Jane's eye, she'd stepped away, and the sunset kissed the copper tendrils of her hair, and she was wholly outlined in fiery light. Once, after a close play at first base, he completely forgot how he had called it, remembering only when Ellie Jane moved to the board to mark the out. At that moment he gave himself a stern reminder to keep his mind on the game and sent up a hopeful prayer that there would be other sunsets.

It was the sixth inning, with Duke's team clinging to a 5-4 lead, when Ned noticed a rare break in Morris's concentration. Nothing had been able to shake him—not the taunts from the other team, not the idea of an enormous farm boy poised to steal a base behind him. All of a sudden, though, Morris dropped his head and his glove, looking like a wounded animal on the mound.

Duke was standing now, and he touched Ned's shoulder directing his attention to the new arrival making his way onto the field across second base.

He was a small man, black as night. His clothing hung loosely on his thin frame; his shirt lay open, exposing a gaunt, dark chest. Misshapen hair topped a slack face, and he came onto the field by way of a staggering, unsteady gait—some steps taken sideways. He was yelling something, but the unnatural twist to his lips made it impossible for Ned to understand. He turned to Duke for confirmation, but he'd already taken off for the mound where he put a protective arm around Morris, putting himself between the boy and this angry apparition.

So, as he'd already grown accustomed to doing, he went to Ellie Jane whose eyes were open pools of shock. He leaned close. "What is he saying?"

She shook her head. *Such awful things. I can't repeat. Such horrible, horrible names. Who is he?*

Darnell. The boy had talked about him often enough—nothing good.

Now the man grabbed Morris, attempting to pull him off the mound, but soon gave up the quest as everybody—young and old men alike—rallied around the pitcher, becoming one huge defensive mass pushing Darnell off the hill.

He stumbled back a few steps, hollered something else, and made a new attempt to push through the dome of fat and tall and muscled men. But when he bounced off without making a dent, he found his fall broken by Sheriff Floyd Voyant, who twisted the man's arm behind him marching the two of them past third and to the bleachers where Dave was pocketing his little notebook and closing the snaps on the camera's leather case. After a brief conversation that seemed to involve much convincing on Dave's part, the three of them—Dave, Floyd, and the inebriated Darnell—headed off the field toward the station house, where an American duplicate of a fine Mercedes would take them into town.

Apparently Picksville's single cell would be occupied tonight.

A new stillness came over the still interlocked players. Morris emerged from the middle of his human armor, handed his glove over to Mr. Poplin and, without so much as glancing back, walked off the field.

Nobody moved until the boy was well out of range, close to disappearing at the top of the dirt road that connected the darker side of Picksville with the rest of the town. There was a shifting restlessness, and every eye turned to Ned.

He held up his hands. "That's the ball game!"

After one last, long look, he wished Ellie Jane a good night, and headed home. Alone.

DUKE

It felt good. All of it. The way it felt the first time he ever stepped up to the plate, the first big hit. Never mind that there weren't any cheering crowds or a fat check hiding behind every play.

Never mind that it wasn't perfect.

This was love.

Maybe tomorrow he'd mix it up a bit. Give himself a chance to hit against the boy.

That is, if the boy came back.

Duke clamped his cigar between his teeth and relived every pitch. The kid was better than he'd thought. Sure he was throwing to a bunch of farmers, but they were young and strong and hadn't been able to get more than a couple lucky rolling grounders late in the game. Just enough to keep it interesting. Enough to cut the lead to one run—5 to 4 in his team's favor.

Then that crazy drunk on the field.

Maybe there were just three innings left. And maybe the sun was getting low. But, boy, he'd wanted a win.

Duke suppressed a bitter laugh. Stupid idea to call the game—but that was Ned. Guy must share a soft spot for the kid. In a way, they all did. Duke could still see the kid's face when his—what was it? Not his father—came crashing onto the field. Screaming at the boy all kinds of curses and threats, telling him the boy's mama was fit to be tied looking for him.

That shame was a feeling he remembered well. More than one time his own old man came to Duke's schoolyard screaming,

"Donny! Donny boy! Git your hide home 'fore I skin it!"

And it wasn't until that moment, hours after as he sat on his balcony, that he realized something else. The man was drunk. Here in Picksville. A dry town.

Somewhere, somehow, someone could get a drink.

He heard the click of a doorknob and turned to look over his shoulder. Through his open bedroom door he saw Ellie Jane, fresh from her bath, standing in the threshold.

"Mr. Dennison?" she said, after giving a soft knock on the doorframe.

"Out here." Though he was sure she could see him.

"Are Dave and Pop home yet?"

"Nope. Guy must have given him some trouble."

"Oh, well…" Her voice trailed off as she fiddled with the ribbon at the throat of her gown. It was the pink and white one. The one she wore late at night. Or early morning. Whenever she had to run past him in the hall. Any second she would bolt out of his doorway and lock herself away until the morning. These were times he might sit up and talk with Floyd. Or sit alone on his balcony and smoke. But tonight, his head still buzzing from the game, he didn't want to be alone.

He stood from the rattan chair and poked his head through the French door leading into the bedroom.

"Come out and sit with me?"

"I shouldn't. It's late, and with tomorrow being Sunday—"

He held his hands up, imploring. "I just want to talk to somebody about the game."

"Well, I don't know if I'd be much good at that," she said, although she did move one shoulder and half of a foot into his room. "I'm afraid I only know as much as you and Ned tell me."

"Come talk to me." So he wouldn't have to go down to the jail. Find the single prisoner in the town's only cell and ask him where a fellow could get a drink to celebrate a near victory. "Just for a while."

"I have to get up early in the morning. The church picnic—" She was backing away.

"I'll go with you. Tomorrow morning."

"To church?" She looked suspicious. And amused.

"Ten minutes. I'll even put out the cigar."

He watched her walk across his room, her robe conforming to her body with each step. Small, narrow frame—nothing like the creation women achieved with their corsets and bustles and all those other contrivances designed to keep a man at bay. Her hair fell in waves and curls, her face floating soft in the middle of it.

It wasn't the first time he thought women had the whole thing backward. All those buttons and hairpins, lace and puffs, thinking they're making themselves beautiful. In competition with each other, maybe. But for a man, what a waste. If Ellie Jane Voyant looked like this sitting on her front porch on a Saturday night, Floyd would be warding off the suitors with his gun.

Duke ushered her through the door with a grand gesture, even offering her his generous rattan chair, pulling out the high-backed wooden one from the bedroom desk for himself. He settled on the edge of its seat, his hands clasped loosely between his knees. Then unclasped. Then clasped again. He shouldn't have offered to give up the cigar.

"You did a lovely job at the scoreboard, Miss Voyant."

"Well, thank you, Mr. Dennison." She was twirling a lock of hair. Maybe he should offer her the cigar.

"We should bring that up to the big games."

"Bring what?"

"A beautiful woman to work the scoreboard."

"Oh, Mr. Dennison, please." She sank deep into the chair. Flattening her body within the pink-striped gown. Disappearing beneath a sheet of curls.

"I mean it." Hints of his old self were coming out from the corners of his brain, smoothing his tongue. Moment by moment, she was becoming just another girl. After the game. In—or near—his bedroom. "That way, even if you're losing, you've got something pretty to look at." He delivered the line with a practiced wink.

She laughed. A soft sound. "I'm afraid your charms are lost on me, Mr. Dennison. You're a little too—"

"Late?"

"I was going to say *rehearsed*. But how refreshing to know you see me as a lost cause." She gripped the arms of the chair and was about to stand when Duke was seized with a certain panic. He didn't want to be alone. Not here on the balcony. Maybe not in his bed. He never slept alone after a game.

"Ellie Jane. Wait." He grabbed her hand as she walked past him, not relinquishing it even as he stood behind her. "That isn't at all what I meant."

"It's late." She wrenched her hand away and moved through the door back into his bedroom, with Duke following close on her heels.

"That's what I meant to say. *Late.* I meant, is it too late? For me. Because you're in love with somebody else."

She stopped walking. Didn't turn around but stopped dead in the center of his room.

Her shoulders slumped. She became smaller. "I'm not."

Duke knew she'd never turn around on her own power, and he didn't trust himself to touch her again. Not yet. So he circled around, coming to a stop in front of her. Then, testing himself, he reached out and took a thin, bundled curl between his thumb and finger, satisfied with that silken touch.

"What about Ned?"

Her nightgown, untied at the throat, revealed a perfect triangle of pale white skin that now flushed pink as every other flannel stripe.

"Don't be silly."

Still, she didn't move. Not nearer to him. Not away. He held on to those few strands, relishing this connection to her, willing her amber eyes to look up into his, and feeling a tiny breath of triumph when they did.

"He's in love with you." Duke took one step closer.

"We've been friends since we were children." She didn't back away.

"But you weren't friends when I got here."

"No—well, yes—"

Her eyes darted about, but he followed them, trying to keep himself ever present in her vision. Not sure whose escape he was preventing.

"Has he ever kissed you?"

"No." A whisper.

"Not a quick one behind the schoolhouse? Under the mistletoe in the cloakroom at Christmastime?"

"No," she said with a giggle, and he moved in closer. Cupped his hand around the back of her neck. Felt the weight of her hair on his arm, trapping him. Warmth seemed to radiate from her very skin, and he smelled her bath soap—a scent now so familiar he imagined he could be anywhere, with anyone, and the slightest waft of Snowberry would bring him back to this woman. This night.

"Have you ever been kissed, Miss Voyant?"

"You know the answer to that, Mr. Dennison."

One week ago, earlier this afternoon, he would have known the answer. But this was a different woman. All the prickles had fallen away. Not a thorn in sight. Anywhere—at least he intended to find out.

Duke brought his other hand up and ran his finger gently across her lips.

"I'd like to kiss you now."

"Why?" Her lips puckered around the word.

"Because you're a beautiful woman." But even as he said it, he knew that wouldn't be enough of a reason. So he took his hands away completely, stuffed them into his pockets, and took a stab at something close to the truth. "Because I haven't kissed a woman since I quit drinking. Because tonight I found out what it's like to play baseball sober. And I—"

"Just want to know what it feels like?"

He gave a slow nod.

"I don't love you, Mr. Dennison."

"I don't blame you."

She stood there, seemingly rooted before him, her face raised, her eyes closed, her lips parted as they'd been when they last said his name. A clear invitation. Which he accepted. He took his hands from his pockets, brought them up to cradle her face, and pulled her near.

If Ellie Jane Voyant was expecting something sweet and chaste, she was due for a great disappointment. The moment Duke's lips touched hers, something shattered. Her hands were up around his neck; he encircled her waist with one arm and buried his hand to the knuckles in her hair. Their kiss deepened as they drew closer together, and he felt himself bathed in sweet Snowberry, bound by soft pink stripes.

And then she was pulling away.

"I have to go." She spoke against his cheek.

In lieu of an answer, Duke brought his lips just beneath her ear, grazing them down her neck. He hooked his thumb around the ribbon of her nightgown, pulling the stripes away from her skin.

"Stop." She brought her hand up to reinforce her command, and he grasped her fingers, bringing them up to his lips. She persisted her protest, saying, "This isn't right."

He abandoned his kisses and drew away just far enough to bring her face into focus. "Because you're thinking about him?"

"We've been friends since we were children."

"You keep saying that."

"Because it's true."

"But you aren't children now, are you?"

"No."

"So what are you waiting for?"

"I don't know."

It was a good enough answer for Duke, and he swooped in again, refusing to believe that her first protest still held. And Ellie Jane herself seemed to have forgotten her objections, because she pressed herself harder against him and allowed his hands to roam the length of her.

There'd been a time, soon after he'd been brought to the sanatorium, when he feared he was making a devastating exchange. Sobriety for manhood. Never again being able to make love to a woman. But tonight, as he held Ellie Jane in his arms, felt her warm and pliant against him, the small of her back, the curve of her waist, his fears became unfounded. Clearheaded, he drank her in. Wanted to swallow great gulps of her. To take sip after sip until she was fully consumed. He took one step back toward his bed, and she followed.

Another, and she followed. One more, and they'd be ripe for falling. Then it would be a simple matter of—

"I'm sorry." Ellie Jane planted her hands firm against his chest and pushed him away.

"You're wonderful." He drew her back to him with no intentions of being thrown out on his third pitch when a power greater than Duke Dennison intervened. The power of an American duplicate Mercedes engine just outside the house.

Ellie Jane heard it too, and she spun out of Duke's embrace, coming full circle to face him, clutching her gown to her throat with one hand, the other brought up to cover her flushed face.

"Oh, Lord, forgive me," she said, her eyes wide.

"Go." Duke stepped out of her way, clearing a path. He heard the click of her door followed quickly by Dave Voyant's booming voice calling upstairs to see if anybody was still up.

"In here," Duke called out too breathless to say more. He hustled himself back out onto the balcony and reached for his abandoned cigar with a shaking hand. His lips, still longing for her soft skin, were wrapped around it when Dave stepped outside to join him.

"Everything all right?" he asked, and Duke wondered if he was imagining the hint of suspicion in Dave's eye.

"Yep." Duke craned his neck to look over his shoulder. "Floyd with you?"

"Pop's going to stay at the jail tonight. I'm going to take him a change of clothes when I leave in the morning."

"Leaving early?"

"First light."

Duke turned back to look out over the yard.

For a while neither man spoke. The second chair remained, and had Dave come home just a few minutes earlier, Duke would have invited him to sit and smoke. Join him in replaying every minute of the game. But he couldn't sit and shoot the breeze with a man whose sister still loomed—soft and warm—between them.

"Ellie Jane already in bed?"

"Yep," Duke said, not turning around.

Without a hint of invitation, Dave settled himself onto the second chair, comfortably propping one foot on top of his knee. Duke stared at that foot. Scuffed leather, perfectly still. Suddenly he was aware of the violent shaking in his own leg, and he clamped his teeth down on his cigar and willed it to stop.

"So, let's talk about that kid."

Duke felt a calm, a comfort spill through him. He leaned back in his chair, mirroring Dave's posture, and looked his friend in the eye. "Didn't I tell you?"

"He's pretty phenomenal."

"Think he can make it?"

"Come on, Duke. He's a kid. How old is he?"

"Twelve."

"Think you had it at twelve?"

"I think he throws better at twelve than any man I've ever hit against."

Dave held up a deflecting hand. "Look. I'm not saying the kid's not good. But none of that's going to change the fact that he's a Negro."

"They've got their teams."

"That's true. And in a few years—"

"But doesn't that seem like a waste?" Duke abandoned his casual pose, lunging forward in his chair. "Not a waste of time. I know he's young. But think what he could do for—".

"For whom, Duke? For the league? There's a lot of talented men out there. And a lot of bigots. Even if the rules changed and he could get on a field, he wouldn't last an inning. Not any time soon."

Duke took a puff of his cigar and watched the smoke dissipate in the starlit air.

"So let me ask you this," Dave continued. "Why do you care?"

One more puff, and he held the cigar out over the balcony and watched the ash fall. "Guess he reminds me of myself when I was a kid."

"Yeah? You were that good?"

Duke chuckled. "Not even close. But I had that hunger, you know? That drive. And I lost it somewhere." His voice faltered on that last word, because he knew exactly where he'd lost it. In the bottom of one bottle after another. But Dave knew that too. Better than anyone. And his companionable silence now allowed Duke to leave it unspoken.

"Tell you the truth," Duke continued, once he regained his composure, "I didn't even realize it was gone 'til I met him."

"Think you've got it back?"

Always the reporter. Asking questions. But the fact that he'd asked set like a rock in his gut. He took another tasteless puff. "You were watching. How'd I look?"

It was a long, long silence. And the answer filled every bit of it.

"Look, it was your first time out since—"

"Give it to me straight, Voyant."

"Well, the good news is," Dave adjusted his round spectacles, "you were easily the best player out there."

"Except for the twelve-year-old."

"You looked a little rough."

"Think I'll be ready to go back?"

"Yeah."

"But not yet."

Now it was Dave's turn to stare at the ground. "Looks like you've got a good thing going here. Just keep playing the game. Relax. It'll come back."

"And Morris?"

Dave sighed. "You worry about your own self."

Duke stared him down, waiting for a more acceptable answer.

"I've got a few contacts," he said eventually. "I'll see what I can do."

After a while, when the conversation dwindled to little more than quiet observations and meaningless sounds, Dave excused himself to retire to his father's room.

"One last thing." He clamped a hand on Duke's shoulder. "I don't suppose I have to tell you to keep your hands off of my sister."

"No." Duke hated lying to a friend, but hated more the idea of tarnishing Ellie Jane in her brother's eyes. "No problem there."

"Good. Because I think something's sparking between her and Ned Clovis."

"That's great." Duke stood, stretched, and dropped the stub of his cigar into a pewter ashtray balanced on the balcony's railing. "Ned's a good guy. He deserves her."

"You're a good guy too." Dave fashioned his hand into a toy gun and pointed it playfully at Duke. "Just not good enough for my sister."

Duke managed to keep the laughter up until Dave left the room and closed the door. Then he undressed, laying his clothes carefully over the back of the chair that had been returned to the little writing desk. He wanted to take a bath, wash the dirt of the day off, and fold himself in any lingering Snowberry steam, but he heard Dave in the bathroom, washing up, and decided he could wait until morning.

Instead, he climbed into bed and pulled the blanket nearly up to his chin. Normally he couldn't stand to have any covers at all, but the night sweats were holding off until nearly dawn. The door to the balcony was open, filling the room with the chill night breeze and moonlight.

Tonight he could not will himself to sleep. He was too busy tasting cigar and Snowberry.

His fingers curled around soft leather and softer cinnamon hair. He saw numbers on a blackboard and pink stripes. Every bit of it was so crystal clear, it was like living the morning and the day and the night all over again.

He lived it and relived it, not closing his eyes until dawn touched his door, and the single crank of Dave's automobile left him here to live another one.

PART 6

RALLY

FIRST CONGREGATIONAL CHURCH OF PICKSVILLE

12 Spring Street
Picksville, Missouri

REVEREND LYNDON G. PORTER, PASTOR

ORDER OF SERVICE

Welcome

Opening Prayer

Congregational Hymn . . . . . "Ye Fearful Saints" #72

Focal Passage . . . . . Philippians 4:5–8

"Let your moderation be known unto all men. The Lord is at hand. Be careful for nothing; but in every thing by prayer and supplication with thanksgiving let your requests be made known unto God. And the peace of God, which passeth all understanding, shall keep your hearts and minds through Christ Jesus. Finally, brethren, whatsoever things are true, whatsoever things are honest, whatsoever things are just, whatsoever things are pure, whatsoever things are lovely, whatsoever things are of good report; if there be any virtue, and if there be any praise, think on these things."

All church members and visitors are encouraged to come to the churchwide picnic being held across the street in Center Park immediately after the service.

It wasn't the first time he wished Marlene would open her diner on Sunday morning. He supposed even a bachelor like himself could manage to fry up a couple of eggs before leaving for church, but it never seemed worth the bother. Instead he reached into the basket that held two dozen rolls he bought from the bakery to bring to today's picnic when, being the second Sunday of the month, the First Congregational Church of Picksville joined together for a common meal.

In the winter they gathered around the long tables in the hall built adjacent to the sanctuary, but on pleasant afternoons like today, those tables were moved across the street to the park where families would fill their plates before returning to quilts spread out on the grass.

He avoided this gathering every month, unsure of exactly how he'd fit in. But today was different. He would bring the basket to the table, mingle with the other church members, and saunter over to the Voyant blanket where he would fall in with Duke and Floyd. And Ellie Jane. Smiling at the thought of it, he pulled out two rolls and ate them, standing in the tiny upstairs kitchen where he'd grown up eating meals not much more complicated than this.

Before leaving for church he took one last look in the shaving mirror above the washstand. The five days' stubble was gone, leaving his face smooth and tan from a week of working outside. Earlier in the morning he'd allowed the blade to hover just above his lip as he contemplated allowing the moustache to grow, but he'd never been one to follow fashion, and there seemed little point in starting now.

Ned straightened his tie, buttoned his vest, and shrugged into his best suit jacket. A series of hooks hung on the wall, from which he took a gray bowler hat and placed it on his head. Looking in the mirror again, he positioned the hat to angle over his left eye, then his right eye, then moved it back, as if knocked there by surprise. In the end, he put it back on the hook. He ran his fingers through his hair to comb it, ignoring the jar of pomade on the shelf. The last time he used it, the results were disastrous. Declaring himself handsome enough, he picked up his Bible and walked downstairs.

He'd come back for the rolls after church.

The streets surrounding the town's Center Park were empty this early on a Sunday morning. There was still an hour before any of Picksville's three churches would open their doors, but Ned always liked to arrive early. In the winter he would start the furnace, shovel the snow off the walkway, and salt the steps leading to the door. In warmer months he set up circles of chairs outside for the various Sunday schools that met on the lawn. He placed songbooks and bulletins in the pews, moving along quietly as if Reverend Porter were at the pulpit, praying or practicing, and when Mrs. Porter began warming up the organ, Ned relished the vibrations that came from the floor, ricocheting around the empty room, giving him his own private concert.

This morning, try as he might to keep his mind on the tasks at hand, he could think of nothing but yesterday's game. The exhilaration of standing at the plate while two players scrambled for position. The puff of dust when the ball collided with the catcher's mitt.

And always, just over his shoulder, Ellie Jane—watching *him* for a change—every time he turned around.

What would have happened if the game hadn't come to such an abrupt end? Would he have had the courage to walk her home, leaving Duke to chum it up with his admiring teammates and fans? It wasn't exactly a Saturday Promenade, but something close to it, and they'd been talking with each other in one way or another for most of the evening. The insurmountable obstacle of the past silent six years had been conquered, and Ned was a new man, standing at the top of a new inning, ready to bring his dreams home.

And he was going to start this morning.

While the First Congregational Church of Picksville didn't have officially assigned seats, its members were not known to stray from their pew of choice. Visitors were rare, and there seemed to be direct, divine intervention to make room for new members only after old ones left vacancies due to death or disfavor.

Ned's own Bible was waiting for him at the far end of the fifth pew—right on the aisle—where he'd been sitting ever since he was a little boy squeezed between his parents. The space was waiting for him when he came back from school, and it seemed enormous the first Sunday he sat there alone. Since then, he'd learned to share his space with a family from Ohio who seemed intent on edging him out by having one child after another. But he didn't intend to budge. From here he could see Ellie Jane Voyant, just across the aisle and two pews up, sitting primly alongside her father.

But after yesterday, two pews and an aisle seemed so far away.

Mrs. Porter stepped away from her organ, joining Reverend Porter on the front steps to greet the congregants trickling in. There wasn't much time. He scooped up his Bible and eyed the pew across the aisle, then the one in front of it—just behind the Voyants'. That's where Mr. Poplin and his wife usually sat, but Ned was sure they would understand his ousting from the Ohio pew.

He felt a touch on his shoulder and turned to see Floyd Voyant standing with his hand outstretched in greeting. *Morning, Ned.*

Ned shook Floyd's hand, giving it a purposeful grip. He wanted to start up a conversation, maybe ask about that man from last night. Maybe he could keep Floyd talking until the two men just naturally migrated to the Voyant pew and sat down together. But something caught his eye over Floyd's shoulder. Ellie Jane, her cinnamon hair tucked beneath a broad-rimmed hat with a long pale blue feather spilling from its brim. Her lemon-yellow dress, trimmed with blue lace, was one he'd never seen before.

Whatever words he planned to say to Floyd were lost as he watched her walk up the aisle. The minute their eyes met, her cheeks flushed—more than just the touch of yesterday's sun. It intensified the closer she came, and she pulled her eyes away. Whatever hopes he'd allowed himself to build clotted when he saw the man just half-a-step behind her.

Duke.

He was wearing an impeccable pale blue linen suit with a crisp blue-and-white striped shirt. He carried a brand-new boater in one hand and smoothed his hair into place with the other. His sharp brown eyes scanned the room until they landed on Ned, at which point they narrowed briefly before taking on a friendly glint. His free hand lingered at Ellie Jane's elbow, as if on the verge of giving her a proprietary steer, but she flinched away at his touch and the flush on her cheeks turned to fire.

What had Duke done?

Ned somehow summoned a smile and said, "Good morning," offering a nod to Ellie Jane. Although he couldn't hear her voice when she returned the greeting, it was clear the distance and discomfort that had hovered for so many years had returned. There'd been an intrusion between the easy camaraderie of yesterday and the awkwardness of this morning. Despite his misgivings, the gurgling mass of distrust deep in his gut, Ned held his hand out to Duke, whose crushing grip did nothing to disguise the sweatiness of his palm.

Hello, Ned.

Years of being locked away from voices made Ned adept at reading faces, and Duke's face said plenty. Tension marked everything about this moment as a lie. Duke didn't want to talk to Ned, and he didn't want to be at church. This was a man who wanted an escape, but Ned gripped his hand harder, offering none.

As more and more congregants entered the sanctuary, Ned moved out of the aisle and backed into his accustomed seat, clearing the way for the Voyant family to take theirs. And the three of them seemed like a family indeed as Duke slid in first, then Ellie Jane, and Floyd on the end. Meanwhile, the Ohio family filed in from the opposite end of the pew, and Ned found himself wedged in a hand's width away from the youngest boy.

Reverend Porter positioned himself behind the pulpit and raised his hands in greeting the congregation. Ned mouthed a response, not wanting to give little Ohio a reason to nudge his brother in the ribs and giggle like he did every other time Ned spoke out loud. He followed the church leader's words as closely as he could—this was the time for church announcements—and Ned surmised much of this was about today's picnic lunch. He thought about the two dozen, minus two, rolls sitting in his kitchen and wondered how many one bachelor could eat before growing sick of them because suddenly it seemed the Voyants' blanket would be mighty crowded.

His eyes bored into the back of Duke Dennison's neck. He'd seen a magician once—one of the many diversions an adventurous boy in a big city could find—who had made his beautiful, scantily clad assistant disappear in a puff of smoke. If Ned's eyes held half the power of that magician's wand, Duke would be nothing more than a pinkie ring left spinning on a pew.

Suddenly there was a shift all around him, and *everybody's* eyes were focused on Duke. Those in the front were turned in their seats, and from the back there was a rippling effect as worshipers craned their necks to get a better look as Duke stood, hat in hand, putting on what he must have thought was a humble expression. Ned looked hard, focusing on Duke's face, knowing the words coming out of it were as smooth as the man's shave.

He was talking about the baseball field, and the crowd followed his hand as he generously gestured toward Ned. Then about yesterday's game…and today's. Apparently inviting everybody to come after the picnic. To play, to watch. A few men in the congregation had been there—some watching, some playing—and they nodded enthusiastically in one collective promise for an afternoon game. Any thoughts of spending an afternoon sulking in the apartment above the feed store disappeared. He would go to the picnic, sit with Ellie Jane, and see to it that, barring an indisputable home run, Duke Dennison never made it across the plate.

With that thought, Ned, smiling his biggest grin, stood to make a grand summoning gesture and—without a single thought to the Ohio brothers' teasing—said, "We'll choose teams at three."

With the announcements over, Reverend Porter called the congregation to prayer, and Ned dutifully bowed his head. He kept his eyes open ever since the one Sunday when, caught up in an earnest conversation with God, he was nudged back to church by the Ohio boy's pointy elbow in his lower ribs. Now, staring at the floor between his shoes, he entered into his prayer acknowledging his agreement with whatever Reverend Porter was entreating from the pulpit.

After that he unleashed his own heart.

Six years, Lord. Six years in silence. And then yesterday…

He ventured a look up and saw Ellie Jane's head dutifully bowed, as was her father's. But Duke sat straight up, staring forward.

Something tugged his sleeve and he looked over to see the Ohio boy wagging a chastising finger. Ned wrinkled his nose, stuck out his tongue and, once the boy had his own freckled nose pressed against his clasped hands, returned to his shoes.

…and then yesterday it all seemed possible. I don't know what happened. He angled his head, peered over again, and saw Ellie Jane's lips moving in silent agreement with Reverend Porter's petitions. *I don't want to lose any of it, Lord. Not her and not*—him? The game? Rubbing elbows with a hero?

I'm a man, Lord. And I haven't felt—

He hunched forward in his seat and planted his elbows on his knees, his hands dangling in front of him. Then he closed his eyes and allowed his hands to speak for him in loose, abbreviated signs.

I haven't felt like a man in such a long time. Not since I came home. Don't let Ellie Jane—his finger made a spiral at her name—*fall in love with him. I know I can't dictate Your will, Lord. But let me try again.*

There was a commotion all around him and he opened his eyes to see the whole congregation on their feet, songbooks open. Ned grabbed a book and, after a quick glance down the pew to Mrs. Ohio, turned to the correct page. He smiled as he scanned the lyrics.

Ye fearful saints, fresh courage take,
The clouds ye so much dread
Are big with mercy and shall break
In blessings on your head.

He remembered the tune from childhood—somber and pon-
derous. Floyd Voyant was going to his toes on the higher notes; he'd
always had a strong, clear tenor. From the approving looks Ellie Jane
gave him, Duke Dennison had a pleasing voice too, though Ned
couldn't imagine the man was familiar with the song.

Blind unbelief is sure to err
And scan His work in vain;
God is His own Interpreter,
And He will make it plain.

Surrounded by a silent "Amen," Ned sat down and took his
Bible in his hands. He'd never been able to follow all of Reverend
Porter's sermons, but he picked up what he could and waited until
the congregation was brought to the key passage. At that time, Reverend Porter made it a point to catch Ned's eye, articulate, and wait
for confirmation before going on. Today it was the fourth chapter of
Philippians. One of the church elders was asked to stand and read
the chapter aloud, and Ned followed along. His heart lingered,
though, on the eighth verse:

…whatsoever things are true, whatsoever things are honest,
whatsoever things are just, whatsoever things are pure, whatsoever things are lovely, whatsoever things are of good report;

if there be any virtue, and if there be any praise, think on
these things.

Not knowing what Reverend Porter had in mind for this passage, Ned sat back and decided to simply obey. To think on those
noble things. For the rest of the hour, he thought about the beauty
of a perfect pitch, the excitement of a play at home, and Ellie Jane at
sunset.

MORRIS

Sunday, May 21

I know the good Lord says if you hate a man you've committed murder in your heart and if that's true I killed that fool Darnell at least a dozen times. But not last night. For a while my heart was so far and above anything he could do to me but he wasn't worth my hate. Or my pity. Or even another thought.

Until he come stumblin onto that field stinkin of Cousin Eddie's home brew. It was like lookin at somethin in that history book Mr. Ned gave me. George Washington or someone like that. Like I know who he is but he don't have nothin to do with me.

Then it just all turned to shame. Because everybody there knows he's mine. All them guys that struck out swingin, all them who lost their chance to show this is a white man's game—all of them know. Once I walk off that mound I ain't nothin but that boy Morris hustlin for their nickels and dimes. And given time I'll be just like him. Shiftless. Drunk. I can throw strikes enough to sit them down but I'll never throw good enough to make me white.

I'll always lose the big game.

But I wasn't thinkin about none of this before he showed up. There's no room for any such bitterness when your mind can only range twenty paces straight ahead. And that's all I saw down the line. Mr. Duke's glove. Seems the whole world came down to my eyes, my arm, and that mitt. Standin up on that hill with that ball in my hand—that's the biggest taste of power I ever felt. Like the whole world's sittin on my shoulders but pullin me up. Standin me straighter. So it took me a while to hate that Darnell for takin it all away.

Lookin back now I should have taken him out. Whole time he's screamin at me about how my mama's worried sick, that he's gonna rip my hide when he gets me home. Like he has a right. Tellin me I ought to be ashamed duckin out'a church like that. Whole congregation turnin the church out lookin for me. Man ain't been inside a church since I known him. Outside, yeah. Waitin at the door to beg a dollar off my mama. Cashin in on that Holy Spirit love.

I could of shut him up. Fastball right between the eyes. I can see that face all round and brown just like what I been hittin all night. A few more seconds and I probably would have. Then Sheriff Voyant took him off. The thought of that fool in jail just set me free.

Until I got home. And had to face Mama.

Now Mr. Duke tells me I got to get some ice, put it on a pillow, and prop up my arm when I get home. He tells me that in the middle of all that noise and I say, Sure. In my head I'm thinkin I got as much a chance of findin a chunk of ice in Satan's kitchen as in my house. And if I got any pain in my arm I don't know it. I'm just thinkin about what I got to say. Tryin to remember everythin I told Mama about school and wonderin what all Darnell told her about the game. Makes me see why God don't want us to tell lies—it's like crossin a stream on slippery rocks.

It's a long walk home and it's full dark when I finally reach my door. My head's swimmin with so many words, such stories that might fill a book. But when I walk inside I see my mama on her knees. Her head bent low over our sofa where I'll lay my own at night. Now I've seen Mama prayin before. Leadin it at church—out of her seat, in the aisle, hands raised up and eyes fixed on that bit of heaven she thinks she sees. And I heard things comin out of her mouth that I just don't know what they mean. But I ain't never seen her prayin like this. Her face and body all tucked in together. I haven't made a sound openin the door so she don't know I'm here. The only sound in the house is her whisperin, Sweet Jesus bring my baby home.

Every lie I had in my head gets swept away. Here I am God's answer and I'm not about to tarnish that with anything that ain't the whole truth. I'd tell her everything. About the money I made and how I made it. About Mr. Duke and the baseball field. How I can throw and what that can mean for me. And her. For a minute I think I don't want to go to California alone. I'll take my mama with me and we'll start off new together, someplace where it won't matter so much what color we are. Someplace where the world is still a little new and needin just about anybody it can get.

So I whisper real quiet, Mama?

And she stops prayin. She turns her head just the littlest bit and looks at me then lifts her face clean up and says, Thank You Jesus. Praise You Lord!

She gets up off her knees and I can tell it's not an easy thing for her to do so I walk on over and offer her my arm. The same one I been pitchin the ball with all night. By now I know why Mr. Duke wants me to put ice on it because it's throbbin. But I don't show none of that when Mama takes a hold and I pull her up to her feet. She's got tears streamin down her face and her eyes look up—just a little—at mine.

Mama says, Morris baby, I was so worried about you.

I tell her I know and I'm sorry and I got so much to tell her but I don't know where to start.

I look down where her hand's clutchin at my shirt. I can feel her rough skin snaggin the new cotton. I'm so busy lookin at that hand I don't see the other one raised up—don't even know it's been raised up until I feel it on my face slappin me so hard it sends me reelin back. But not too far because she never lets go of my arm. She hauls me back to her and hits me again, this time right up the side of my head, her palm landin right against my eye.

She says, Do you know what it does to a mother not knowin where her son is?

I just shake my head but not too hard.

She tells me she bout lost her mind when she turned around, lookin for me when church was done and wasn't nobody who knew where I was.

When I tell her I'm sorry she lifts her hand to me again but I bring my hands up protectin my face and beg her, Please, don't.

Then she asks me real quiet, Where'd you go?

I say, I just slipped out. When you all were singin and praisin wasn't nobody lookin at me. Didn't call no attention to myself. I just walked out the door.

She says, That don't answer my question Morris Bennett. Where did you go you got to slither out of the Lord's house to get there?

I don't know if Darnell didn't tell her where he was goin or if she just wants to hear it from me. So I tell her everything. From the first time I met Mr. Duke until Sheriff Voyant was draggin Darnell off the field. Mama's eyes are gettin bigger and bigger the whole time I'm talkin, like I'm the one who just slapped her. And by the time I'm done talkin she got her eyes rolled up high and she's sayin, Lord, Lord, why You give me this fool for a child?

Now it's my turn to get angry and I tell her I ain't no fool. Mr. Duke says I could make it a job playin baseball just like him.

Mama laughs right out loud at that. She says, How many Negroes you figure they have playin that game?

Her laugh makes me smile because I know the answer to that. And this wasn't ever even a thought in my head until Mr. Duke put it there and it won't last long after he goes. I tell Mama she don't have to worry. That I ain't plannin on goin anywhere soon.

She says, What about that money I got stashed away?

I tell her right now I don't have enough to take me nowhere.

But that ain't true. I could buy me a ticket tonight and be in California by the end of the week. Nearly every day I tell myself I ought to go. And if I ever asked myself why I don't I got the answer right here with this woman who's openin her arms to me and callin me Baby.

Holdin me close and tellin me she'll kill me dead if I scare her like that again.

I tell her we're playin baseball again tomorrow afternoon. That she can come watch if she wants. She says she might but I know she won't. And I tell her that I'll go to a church on Sunday mornin—won't be ours but it'll be somethin. But I know I won't do that neither.

Instead I wake up this mornin and she's still sleepin. She does that her mornins off and I usually do too. But today I have a restless spirit. I don't want to wake her but I have to go. So I walk up to her real quiet and sit on the edge of her bed. When she sleeps like this, seems like all the hardness goes away. Her face is almost beautiful—like what I know her heart is deep down. Like if she could spend her whole days sleepin my daddy might not have gone away.

I lean in close and whisper, Mama?

She stirs a bit and when she opens her eyes her whole face turns into this smile. And for a minute I'm a child again and she's about to tell me that I bring the sun into her sky.

I tell her, I'm goin to try to make up what I did to God and go to the Second Baptist Church just down the road from our own.

She says, That's fine—just keep your heart open and your ears closed because them Baptists don't have it all just right. Then she rolls over and goes back to sleep.

But I don't go to the Second Baptist Church. Don't know why exactly. Maybe I'm just tired. Wantin a little peace. Instead I'm sittin here in the park—never seen it so empty before. Guess everybody in town is in their church or in their bed. Nothin much to be doin outside of those. I can hear them singin from the churches all around me. Seems they sing so slow like their spirits are all tied up in some fancy wrap. Can't imagine their women cryin or their men on the floor eyes up to Jesus. Maybe in their church they like to sit real still so the Holy Spirit will know how to find them. Kind of settle in the gaps and fill up the room. Not like our church where we keep Him hoppin.

But then even this quiet settles down into a quiet I don't know I've ever heard. Round my house even dead of night you hear people talkin. Hear them fightin when the man comes home late or hear them lovin each other in the dark. This is white quiet. I don't know if we could ever sound like this on my side of the railroad tracks.

Must be the preacher's time. All that talk about Jesus and His life and His love—can't be too different from church to church. I ain't never had a Bible of my own but I heard enough of it to know what it says and the same Lord that loves me loves them just the same.

It's like what Mr. Duke taught me about pitchin baseball. Every man—short, fat, tall, or slim—has the same strike zone. That same invisible box between his knees and his heart. Some churches just swing a little higher than others.

I wonder what kind of noise they'd make if I took it upon myself to just wander right in. How loud would those heads be turnin around? If that would rattle them out of what they know to do. If it would throw them off their worship game.

But I don't because right now I'm in the sweet spot. Like I'm square in the middle of a perfect throw. God's lookin down and seein me—one black boy in the middle of a green, green park surrounded by lily-white noise.

This mornin this is my church.

ELLIE JANE

She kept her eyes fixed on Reverend Porter. Ash-colored hair rose in thin, independent tufts from his spot-mottled scalp. His liquid blue eyes were magnified threefold behind his thick glasses. Today he wore the green suit, one of four he kept in predictable rotation. If a month had a fifth Sunday, Reverend Porter came to church in church sleeves and pin-striped pants, handing his church over to a traveling evangelist.

His soft, high-pitched voice seemed incapable of convincing even the darkest heart that there was a smudge of sin in it. Since he first took the pulpit nearly ten years ago, Ellie Janc had sat under sermon after sermon, nodding her head sagely as it went from pigtails to plumes, sanctimoniously agreeing with each biblical truth.

Well, that was certainly not the case this morning.

"Fourth chapter of Philippians," Reverend Porter directed. "Brother Merrick, will you read for us?"

Deacon Stanley Merrick sat three rows directly behind the Voyant pew. Any other Sunday, she would have turned in her seat to give him an encouraging nod, but this morning that was impossible. If she turned to her left, she risked looking at Duke Dennison; if she turned to her right, she risked moving her body and touching him. As it was, he now sat a respectable four inches away from her as she pressed herself up against the length of her father's strong arm, and if she ever did give in to the temptation to send Duke a sideways glance, she would see only the brim of her hat and a cascade of feathers.

Not that she was tempted. Not in the least.

Deacon Merrick's deep, rich voice intoned behind her.

" 'Be careful for nothing; but in every thing by prayer and supplication with thanksgiving let your requests be made known unto
God.' "

And hadn't she always?

" 'And the peace of God, which passeth all understanding, shall
keep your hearts and minds through Christ Jesus.' "

Unfortunately, today her heart and mind couldn't be further
away. This morning she'd given no thought to the idea of entering
the house of the Lord. She wore extra padding beneath her bustle to
hide her figure and a high-collared dress, even though the blue lace
trim irritated the bottom of her chin. She chose a hat to cover her
head, not because she was entering into His holy presence, but
because between its brim and the feather both her eyes and the world
around her were well hidden. In fact, the last time her heart and
mind were fully kept on Jesus Christ, well, there were only two people living in her house.

" 'Finally, bretheren, whatsoever things are true—' "

Like the fact that she'd stood, in a near state of undress, crushed
in the arms of a would-be ardent lover?

" '—whatsoever things are honest—' "

She'd told him, flat out, that she didn't love him. She just wanted
to know—needed to know how it felt…

" '—whatsoever things are just—' "

But to allow herself to be taken so freely? To give over her body
to one man when her head swam with the images of another?

" '—whatsoever things are pure—' "

Hardly.

"'—whatsoever things are lovely—'"

Undeniably, Duke's arms were strong. His lips soft. His fingers, warm on her skin. Lost in her hair. Stroking the base of her throat. He told her she was beautiful. He thought she was wonderful. Was he sitting beside her now, thinking those same things?

"'—whatsoever things are of good report—'"

And if he was, what must he think of her? What a lot of good it would do after last night, trying to point him toward any kind of moral existence when all it took to topple her off her prim tower was a simple—albeit deep—kiss on a balcony. Not even a balcony but a bedroom. *His* bedroom. Steps away from his *bed*.

"'—if there be any virtue—'"

If there be, indeed. Two Sundays ago there was virtue. Last Sunday there was virtue, even if the situation was primed for corruption. But this Sunday, oh, how it festered in question.

"'—and if there be any praise—'"

To see Ned this morning, having left him with what seemed to be unspoken promises. What must he think? Not only had she betrayed their budding trust, but to have done so in such a sordid fashion. To have transferred such improper, lust-driven satisfaction to his faithful, sweet self...

"'—think on these things.'"

As if she could think of anything else.

By the time Deacon Merrick sat down after reading the passage, the scriptures weighed upon her like one hot brick after another dropped on the base of her neck. She concentrated on Reverend Porter knowing that, any moment, he would fly down from behind the pulpit, haul her to her feet, and drag her to the front of the congregation. *Here is a woman about whom there is nothing honest or pure or lovely. She has no virtue. She deserves no praise.*

Not that Reverend Porter had ever flown out from behind his pulpit. In fact, he never even stepped out from behind it until the congregation was nearly all filed out after the service. No, he simply droned on and on in his soft, high voice about how wonderful it is to think only of wonderful things while Ellie Jane sat motionless under his mild-mannered attack.

Next to her, Duke sat perfectly still too. And what thoughts were swimming through his head? Her lips, soft and yielding? Her body sliding up against his, bringing herself closer? Her hands locked behind his neck…?

She shook her head, as one suddenly roused from a dream. The motion brought the long blue plume on her hat to brush against her nose, tickling. The strength and volume of the ensuing sneeze brought Reverend Porter to a shuddering halt, as he clutched the side of his podium with one hand and brought the other up to readjust the glasses on the end of his roundish nose.

Ellie Jane sent up an apologetic smile and gingerly moved the feather out of her face.

The reverend cleared his throat and returned to his sermon, repeating the previous thought.

Seconds later, she felt his breath on her cheek.

"God bless you."

"Thank you." She refused to turn toward him.

He lingered for two, three more heartbeats before returning to his place while Ellie Jane tried to keep her mind on whatsoever things that were not Duke Dennison.

Why couldn't this be a sermon on the evils of drink? Mayor Birdiff's reelection was due; certainly it was time to promote his temperance platform from the pulpit. How much more pleasant this would be if Duke were the one sitting here with the great glow of

illumination on his sin? If he'd been here for last week's sermon—
well, she couldn't exactly recall last week's sermon—but certainly
something would have wormed its way through his hardened heart.
When she first invited him to go to church, she envisioned some
deep truth to penetrate clear to his soul, sending him staggering up
the aisle to fall at the altar, claiming Jesus as his Savior. Renouncing
his drink. Renouncing his women. Renouncing even the cigars that
lent a pungent sweetness to his mouth…

Ellie Jane shook her head again. The plume dislodged again.
Not willing to risk another sneeze, she took in a sharp breath and
held it, exhaling only after the impulse passed, with a hard and
pointed puff that blew it back off her face.

It was going to be a long morning.

ᔕ

When the congregation finally stood for the benediction, Ellie Jane
allowed herself to breathe. As the sanctuary filled with the sound of
shuffling feet and conversation, she stood in her pew, tapping her little foot, wondering if everybody had always taken so much time and
care in exiting a building. She soon discovered the reason for the
delay, as member after member—men, women, and children
alike—were making their way *up* the aisle, their eyes fixed on Duke
Dennison, their hands already extended for an introduction and
embrace.

At the head of the pack was Mrs. Lewiston, wearing the same
Sunday bonnet she'd worn since Ellie Jane could remember. Her
small, shaking hand was encased in a white lace glove, and she left
more than one little boy reeling in the wake of her plump passage
through the pews.

"Now, Ellie Jane," she said in her weak, watery voice, "aren't you going to introduce us all to your young man here?"

"He's hardly *my* young man, Mrs. Lewiston." She forced a smile. "As you can see, I think the entire town plans to lay claim to him."

"But what an honor that anybody would consider me so." Duke reached out and took Mrs. Lewiston's gloved hand and—right there in the middle of church—brought it to his lips. Still bent low, he looked up at the older woman and lifted one eyebrow. "That is, of course, unless you have an opening for yourself."

"Oh, you scoundrel," she said before sending Ellie Jane a wink. "You'd better keep your eye on this one."

She was still giggling when Mr. Lewiston, standing at the open church door, summoned her with a none-too-gentle bark of her name. Left with the stunned faces of the small crowd gathered around them, Ellie Jane turned to Duke and spoke low and close. "You would do well to remember where you are. This is the house of the Lord."

Then she wedged her way behind her father who was engaged in an animated conversation with the mayor's secretary and excused herself time and again as she clambered over skirts and shoes and children to make her desperate way out.

She burst through to the newly noon daylight and grasped the railing along the steps leading up to the door. People trickled past as she took large, gulping breaths. A few paused to look over their shoulders and offer a smile or "Good morning," and she managed to get herself together enough to return their greetings in kind. She even managed to make some polite conversation about the excitement of the game last night and her predictions for this afternoon. It wasn't until she heard a distinctive voice behind her calling her name that she wished she'd just kept running.

"Ellie Jane?"

How, in just two days, had the voice of Ned Clovis become so familiar? And how could the mere fact that he was calling to her bring about the same unsettling combination of thrill and fear as those few moments in Duke's arms? Her breath caught at the thought of it; she couldn't bring herself to turn around. She sensed him moving behind her, around her, and coming face-to-face with her as he stood on the other side of the railing.

"Are you all right?"

She nodded.

"You seem upset."

She shook her head.

"Let's walk." Ned offered his arm and she took it, allowing him to lead her down the remaining stairs. Once she stepped onto the ground, neither seemed to know just what to do until Ellie Jane noticed a sidelong glance from Mrs. Lewiston. She released her grip and held her Bible in a double-fisted clutch.

"What are you bringing to the picnic?" Ned accentuated his words with hands.

She stared off to the side at the crowd behind him, feeling the words crowd against her lips but terrified to open her mouth. If she did, she didn't know if she would blurt out "pickles and cheese" or a full confession of her amorous activities with Duke Dennison. So she kept her mouth closed tight and willed Ned to go away.

Instead, he came into her field of vision, grasping her shoulders and stooping until he was looking up at her, close enough that the feather in her bonnet grazed his face.

"Ellie Jane? What's wrong?"

When she didn't answer, he dropped his grip and, with silent agreement, they walked out of the churchyard and turned left, not speaking, not touching. Ellie Jane had never walked home from church with a man—had never walked *anywhere* unchaperoned with anyone. Part of her hoped everybody would take notice and finally release their grudge; the rest of her wanted to run into the nearest hole, away from prying eyes.

After they had taken just a few steps together, Ned touched her shoulder and said, "Wait here," before he walked across the street and into the park toward a bench where young Morris Bennett was sitting, one lanky leg crossed over the other, staring up into the trees.

Feeling uncomfortably alone, Ellie Jane followed.

The poor boy looked awful. The left side of his face was swollen and bruised, and the shadows beneath his eyes gave him an air of fatigue far beyond his years.

"What happened?" Ned pointed to his own eye.

Morris answered with one word. "Mama."

Ellie Jane felt a tugging in her heart. She'd never been one to have a strong maternal drive. In fact, her experience with children was limited to the few who habitually annoyed her during church services. Then again, she'd never thought of Morris as a child; in fact, until recently, she'd never thought anything much about him at all. But she did recognize that look of shame—the embarrassment of having been rejected by those who should embrace you—and she found herself reaching out to touch the boy's face.

"Does it hurt?"

He didn't flinch. "Not anymore."

"Well, you should put a piece of meat on it. If you'd done so last night it wouldn't be as swollen as it is."

Morris smiled. "Don't got meat at our house."

Ellie Jane took her hand away. "Oh, I'm sorry. Maybe I could—"

Ned caught her hand in midair. "I think it looks fine." Then, to Morris, "Would you like to join us for lunch?"

"Oh, I don' know 'bout that…" Morris's eyes trailed off to the groups of Picksville Congregational parishioners setting bowls and baskets of food on long wooden tables.

"Go to my house." Ned gestured in the general direction of the feed store. "I have a basket of bread in the upstairs kitchen. Bring it here and wait for me."

Ellie Jane hoped she was keeping the shock from showing on her face. He was a nice boy to be sure, but—

"I ain't a part of your church, Mr. Ned."

"It's God's church." Ned's arms spread so wide and high, Ellie Jane got a picture of a picnic big enough to seat the whole world. "Go get the bread."

Morris looked to Ellie Jane who, finding herself swept up in Ned's open arms, offered the boy a welcoming smile. "Of course we'd love you to join us." And to her own great surprise, she meant it.

Ned clapped his hands and gave Morris a pointed directive.

"Yes, sir." He smiled despite the swelling of his face. "Anything else?"

Ned thought for a second. "Yeah. Look around the storeroom and bring a blanket."

Morris tipped his cap to Ellie Jane and took off across the park. She watched for a moment before resuming her way home. Ned fell right into step beside her.

Join *us* for lunch. *Us?* Did he mean the congregation as a whole? Or had Ned Clovis just invited himself to sit with Ellie Jane and her father? And Duke, of course. Not that there was anything wrong with either scenario. It just seemed to be a matter of poor taste to make such assumptions. After all, there might be—

"Stop." He stepped in front of her, causing a near head-to-chest collision on the corner of her street. Ned hooked one finger under her chin and forced her head up. "I told you. If we are going to talk, I need to see you." His fingers beckoned the space between them.

"I wasn't talking." Her spine prickled in defense.

Ned laughed and molded his fingers as if forming the mouth of a pursed-lipped puppet, opening and closing them in rapid succession.

"Oh, my goodness!" Ellie Jane laughed. "I didn't realize. I'm not accustomed to—" She stopped herself, not wanting to delve into years of walking alone, talking to no one, but talking—or singing— anyway. Apparently, she'd come to tune out her own voice.

"I'll try to remember." She spoke with the kind of whisper most people used when talking to themselves. But it was enough for him to understand.

"Good." He gave her a slight tap on the end of her nose.

She kept quiet the rest of the way.

༄

When they arrived at her home, Ned held the little iron gate open, allowing Ellie Jane to pass through and lead the way up to her front door. He followed her across the threshold, catching the screen door and ushering it silently into place.

She had a flash of a thought—how quiet life with this man would be. Years spent living with her father had worn both of them down to creatures of comfortable, companionable silence. Still, there was the odd occasion when one would holler to the other from room to room, not to mention the fact that Pop tromped around the house with such a heavy step, sometimes her china figurines rattled on their shelves.

And Duke Dennison was a veritable fountain of noise. He talked and talked and talked. When he wasn't making plans for the town field, he was telling the exploits of his own career. Then there was the singing. And the humming. And the swishing, gargling, crunching, chomping. He snapped his suspenders, snapped his fingers, always jangling and rattling something.

But Ned seemed content in his cloud of silence. Even when he spoke, it seemed his voice was fighting through layers of cotton batting. He stood now, his arms heavy at his side, moving only his head as he took in the details of the room, a warm nostalgic grin on his face.

His reaction intrigued her. Nobody ever smiled upon entering this room; so few ever did.

"I remember this room," he said, as if answering her question.

Ellie Jane, in the process of unpinning her hat, said nothing.

"I was here for your brother's birthday party, back when I was…" He looked at the gas light fixture in the ceiling, calculating, before flashing a series of fingers. *Twelve.*

She remembered that party and all the begging she and Dave did before Pop would allow such an afternoon. Little as she was, Ellie Jane had made the cake herself; it was messy and lopsided and delicious. They'd found an old punchbowl and filled it with weak lemonade, and there were stacks of little sandwiches and apple slices.

The boys played horseshoes in the backyard while the girls—the few that had been invited—sat in this very parlor, some with their feet dangling loosely from the sofa. At the time she saw it as a glimpse into her future, being the very busy lady of the house. But two weeks after the party, Ned put a caterpillar in her hair, and the parlor had never again been so full.

She hadn't thought about that afternoon until this very moment, and she realized she'd just indulged herself in the same fallacy, entertaining the idea of a quiet life lived with Ned Clovis, contrasting it with that of Duke Dennison, when the more likely scenario—especially given last night's indulgence—showed her living out her days here alone.

She was still struggling with her hat, now a mass of pins and plumes, when Ned stepped in, taking full advantage of his height, and worked deftly to extricate the complication from the top of her head.

"There," he said. "Where should I put it?"

Ellie Jane pointed to one of the wing-backed chairs and, with no hesitation or invitation, headed for the kitchen.

During the dark morning hours following a sleepless night, she'd packed her contribution to the church luncheon: jars of pickled cucumbers, carrots, and cauliflower. She'd sliced half a round of cheese and laid it out on a plate, wrapped tight with a dishcloth. Then there was an English pea salad with fresh herbs and a mayonnaise dressing, left overnight in the icebox but now nestled among the other delicacies. At the time the furthest thought from her mind was actually picking up the basket, and now, when she grasped its thick handle and attempted to do so, her arms and back and shoulders refused to comply.

She knew Pop was planning to check in on last night's prisoner, and Duke was probably still holding court in church. So, frustrated, she followed her first instinct and called to the next room for help.

She was in the middle of yelling, "Mr. Cloo-ooo-vis?" when the folly of it registered and, still clutching the basket handle, she doubled over, self-consciously giggling at her gaffe.

Then, much to her surprise, the kitchen door swung open, and there he was, looking puzzled at finding her in a state of such mirth.

"I thought you might need help."

Not trusting herself to speak clearly, Ellie Jane simply strained to lift the basket one more time, then looked helplessly at Ned and shrugged.

He smiled, walked across the room, and grasped the handle—almost close enough to touch her fingers—and in one smooth motion, lifted it off the table.

Ellie Jane felt herself on the verge of inner collapse, shot through with every bit the same thrill she'd felt last night, and Ned hadn't touched her.

She couldn't imagine what would happen if he ever did.

N ot counting the occasions he was dragged to a wedding or funeral, Duke had been to church exactly three times in his life. The first was when he was a kid in the city. The minister who rounded him up for the train out west took all the kids, lined them up, and made them Christians.

"Good people don't adopt heathens," he'd said.

Duke would never forget the feeling of that holy water dribbling down his collar. The thought of it was enough to stand him up straighter at every stop, hoping one of those "good people" would take him home.

Later, he'd think about it every time Stan Dennison threatened to send him to hell. He'd think, "I ain't going to hell. I'm a Christian." He'd taste the wafer and the wine those times when his old man's hand brought forth the taste of blood.

Then once when he was growing up, his mother heard about a traveling evangelist setting up his tent in Laramie, and she somehow convinced his father to take the family there. At the end of the service, when everyone was weeping and wailing and falling to their knees, his mother dragged young Donny up the aisle and asked the preacher to cast the demon out of him.

"My husband ain't never had a drink, nor never thrown a fist until this devil child came into our home."

Duke knew that wasn't true: The man could barely stand the day he signed the adoption papers, and the woman had faded bruises the first time he saw her. Still, the evangelist stooped to Duke's level, took the boy's scrawny shoulders in his ring-encrusted hands, and stared into his eyes.

"I can see 'em," he'd said.

"See what?" the mother asked.

"Demons! I see their faces and I know their names."

"Oh, sweet Jesus!" It was the first time Duke ever heard the woman say that name in anything close to a prayer. "Can you do anything about them?"

The evangelist looked up. "Have you given your offering to our Lord?"

She nodded.

"Have you given all you have?"

She bit her lip, then reached into her little drawstring handbag and took out a few more coins she dropped in the bucket conveniently passing by.

"Then I say, Demons! Depart!"

The next thing Duke knew, the man had smacked him in the head with the meat of his palm. Then again just as he recovered from the first blow. There were five smacks in all, and by the end of it, Duke could barely stand, and the throbbing between his eyes was as bad as any thrashing he'd ever had from his old man.

"Woman," the evangelist said, "I send you home with a new child. As he is healed, so will your husband be."

Duke remembered relying on his mother's guiding hand to lead him out of the tent. The pain was receding behind a crust of numbness, and his vision was doubled, but if it meant his old man would put down the bottle and stop knocking him around, it was worth the sacrifice.

Later, when they got home and Stan Dennison learned what his wife had done with the last of their money, he turned his fury on the demon-freed Donny. The boy lost consciousness for two days, and when he woke up, his mother had packed a lunch, his clean clothes, and his baseball glove.

He was fourteen years old.

The third time was about a year ago, just before he signed with the Cubs, after a long night's drinking caused him to wake up in the Giants' dugout. In between cups of coffee and cold slaps to his face, Christy Mathewson, the guy everybody called the Christian gentleman, told him he should go to church.

"Not again," Duke had said, but he watched Christy close that day. Not only the power of his game, but the way he moved. The way he talked to people and how people talked to him. A gentleman. A true one, and Duke wanted that. If he had to find it in a church, so be it.

He fought off drinking the rest of the day. And the next. Until Sunday morning came and he made his way to the first church he could find. He sat in the back, unable to control the shaking in his hands. His body. The preacher hollered with the voice of that long-ago evangelist. Saying that each and every sin was like a stone thrown into the face of God.

He noticed the people around him. Staring. Not the kind of stares he got when he was out on the town after a game. Not like kids lining up to touch his hand. Or girls waiting outside his hotel lobby. But staring with the eyes of people ready to cast out a demon.

So he left.

Now, this morning, he listened to Reverend Porter up there with that soft voice saying that today's sermon would be about the importance of filling their lives with things that were true, honest, lovely. Saying this to a man who hadn't done a true, honest, or lovely thing in his life.

Yesterday was no exception.

There had been moments during the game when he felt he deserved a pat on the back—seeing this town come alive, shaking off a little more of its stuffiness with every new inning. The feeling he had seeing Morris on the mound was what he always imagined a father's pride would be. Like he was showing the kid off. If the game ended differently, he might have put the boy on his shoulders and paraded him around.

There were even a few moments during the afternoon when he fancied himself a kind of Cupid. Watching the sparks between Ned and Ellie Jane gave him a warm feeling—like doing something good for two good people.

But he'd sure dropped that one in the dirt.

True. Honest. Lovely. Everything he wasn't; everything Ned Clovis was. And Ellie Jane, for that matter. Until he took her in his arms and knocked her down.

He was every bit the monster Stan Dennison was. Worse, maybe. Because when his old man knocked you down, you could see it coming. It started in his eyes, then traveled to his fist. As a kid, Duke may not have been able to escape his father's blows, but he was never surprised by them either.

Not like Ellie Jane. Poor girl—he hated what he did to her. The look on her face when she left his room. The undercurrent of it all as he talked with her brother. Worse, what he did today. All the smooth talk, sly jokes, rehearsed charm. Like a dog trying to cover up his mess. It was a lot easier when he was drinking. Then he didn't have to think about anything. Bourbon covered everything, buried it in the dark corners of his mind. But when it was just a crisp, clear morning, he had to work that much harder. Smile brighter, flash more teeth, lean in close to tease.

Then came the moment when Reverend Porter asked him to stand.

"Ladies and gentlemen—and all you boys out there—we have a very special guest with us this morning. Mr. Donald Dennison."

If the good people of this church had any sense, they'd use this time to tie him to a rail and run him out of town before he could do any more harm. Instead, he turned to see a tiny pool of smiling faces. Ladies in hats and men in starched collars.

Duke called upon his charm. "Good morning." That would have been it, had Porter not urged him to tell the congregation about the field. About yesterday's match.

"None of this would have been possible," he concluded, "if it weren't for my pal Ned Clovis."

It killed him to say it. There weren't many men on this earth he could call "pal," and the minute he said it he could taste Ellie Jane's Snowberry skin on his lips. He'd seen the way Ned looked at him when he walked in. The man was smiling now, standing up and inviting everybody to choose teams at three o'clock, but he'd sensed something earlier. Duke knew it. And it made him sick. Made him feel dirty.

Made him want to come clean.

That's what made sitting in church so unbearable. Sure he'd been sober for months, cleaned up his life, lost himself in something the reverend up there would deem true and just. Maybe even lovely. But he couldn't think of any of that now. All he could see was the shame in a kid's face and horror in a woman's. Because of him. Because of what he wanted. Because that's what he could have instead of a drink.

Duke studied Reverend Porter. He was a small man with a high, quiet voice. Reminded Duke of a piglet in robes. Harmless and sweet. He thought about the first time he'd been in church and wished this reverend could do what that long-ago minister had done. Just yank him up off the pew, throw some water on him, and wash away the past. Or maybe something like that tent revival man. Haul him to the front, smack him around, and drive the devil out of him. He couldn't remember the preacher at the Chicago church. Only the eyes of the people, looking at him. Knowing what he was.

Not like the crowd at the Picksville Congregational Church. Once they stood for the final prayer, he was pressed on all sides by people. Reaching out to him. Wanting to shake his hand. One sweet old lady who saw him as a harmless flirt.

But Ellie Jane knew better. She couldn't get away from him fast enough, the way she ran out of that church. When Duke saw Ned staring at him, it was clear he knew better too.

Duke was grasping the small, soft hand of Reverend Porter when he saw Ned, slicing through the crowd to get to him. Suddenly Duke's shoulder was trapped in a vise, and he was being dragged away. One backward glance showed Ned's smiling face as he waved with his free hand, but soon Duke found himself being tugged through a side door into a narrow hallway, his back thrust against a wall.

Ned loomed above him, their difference in height more prominent than ever. His finger inches away from Duke's face.

"What did you do to her?"

It wasn't the first time he'd been asked that kind of question. But this morning, the old instinct—to smile and slick it over—was gone. He looked into the eyes of the man he called "pal" and broke down. The back of his throat burned; tears threatened to crowd out of the corner of his eyes.

"I'm sorry."

Duke had only known Ned as the grinning, good-natured Picksville son, and he didn't recognize the man he became at that moment. Ned's face, usually so fluid in its expression, hardened like wax, and the hands—ever ready to speak for him—were balled into fists.

"Tell me."

"I kissed her." Duke spoke as clearly as he could, in a half whisper just in case some nosy resident came into the hall. For a brief moment, he thought about giving Ned a sign, like bringing his own hand to his lips, but such a demonstration seemed vulgar at best. So he took a deep breath, tilted his head up so Ned could fully see his face, and repeated his confession. "I kissed her."

"You *kissed* her?" Ned's expression was a mixture of rage and relief. He brought his hand up in a gesture of finality. "That's it?"

Duke put up his own hands in surrender. "I swear."

"When?"

"Last night. After the game."

A deep breath, and then a question spoken so quietly Duke might have imagined it.

"Why?"

Duke was at a loss. He stood empty before his friend and gave the truest answer he could think of. "I just...wanted to."

Ned seemed to take this answer and turn it around in his head for a moment. Slowly, he seemed to warm to the idea, and the hardness in his face softened, and Duke knew what he was thinking. Ned understood, because Ned wanted the same thing.

"Tell me," Ned spoke without the hint of threat, "are you going to do it again?"

There was a space for hope between the question and the answer, and Duke grabbed it.

"No," he said. "Not again."

Ned balled his hand into a fist again, but instead of holding it restrained at his side, he brought it up, suspended between the two men. With his other hand, he touched one finger to his closed lips, then placed it, open-palmed, over the fist.

"Promise?"

Duke repeated the gesture. "Promise."

The tortuous weight of the morning lifted, pumped out of his body as Ned shook his hand before bolting out the door that led to the side yard of the church, leaving Duke alone. He felt lighter. Lifted. And clean enough to face Ellie Jane.

⌒

He would get that opportunity soon enough, though not before the endless ordeal of going to the Picksville Congregational Church would be over. Still reeling from his pardon, he made the mistake of walking back into the sanctuary, only to find it nearly empty. A few souls gathered at the back near the open door. But empty enough that Duke's footsteps echoed on the polished wood floor.

Alone in church. He hated being alone. Anywhere. But this seemed like more than solitude. He felt insulated. Packed away. Wrapped in batting.

He reached down and touched the back of the pew. The wood was worn down to silk, rounded on the edge from the weight of so many shoulders. He sat down; it creaked beneath his weight. And he waited to feel something. Whatever it was that brought people back here time after time. What that minister wanted him to be when he was a kid in New York. Whatever might have appeased his father. Or healed himself.

But there was nothing. Nothing but muted conversations in the cloakroom. And then a scattering of sound. Footsteps. Small ones.

Duke turned around and saw the boy. Little kid—the one sitting next to Ned during the church service. He ran in from the back of the church but came to a skittering halt the minute he saw Duke looking at him.

"Sorry." The kid's eyes were as round as quarters.

"What for?"

"Not supposed to run in church."

"Why not?"

The boy scratched his head. Pondering the question of the ages. "God says."

"Well then," Duke said. "You'd better listen."

Nodding sagely, the boy took careful steps until he reached the pew he'd been sitting in earlier that morning. He dropped to his knees and crawled underneath, clattering around for a few seconds before emerging with his prize.

"What've you got there?"

"A horse." He held up the toy.

"Are you supposed to play with toys in church?"

The boy considered the question, scratching his head again. This time with the horse. "Sometimes." He drew the word out, convincing himself.

"Good to know." Maybe Duke would come back.

He stood to leave, and the boy—already forgetting rule number one—ran out ahead of him. Duke walked up the aisle, touching each pew as he passed. By the time he got to the back, even the cloakroom was empty, and as he walked out onto the front steps, he saw the congregation scattered across the short green grass in the park across the road from the church. Several long tables were set up in a row with platters and bowls and baskets of food set upon them.

He stood on the steps, frozen. Feeling as alone as he'd felt inside. Then, finally, a familiar face made its way up the street.

"Mr. Duke?"

He walked down the stairs at a quick clip, meeting Morris at the edge of the grass. Under one arm he had a folded blanket. Slung over the other was an enormous basket covered in a blue-striped kitchen towel. One glimpse beneath showed a pile of gold-crusted rolls piled to the rim.

"These is Mr. Ned's." Morris leaned in close, as if sharing a secret. "He invited me to join you all in your lunch, if that's all right with you."

"Us all?"

"You, Mr. Ned, Miss Ellie Jane, and the sheriff—once he checks on…" The boy's voice trailed off, but Duke knew.

"I think that's a fine idea." Just then Mrs. Lewiston appeared at his elbow and, after another bout of inane giggles, took Morris's basket to one of the tables. "It'll give us time to talk before the game."

"I don't know if I can get away again."

That's when Duke noticed the boy's face. Swollen, bruised. He wanted to ask who hit him, but he knew. Talking about it wouldn't make it heal. And nothing could ever really make it go away. Instead, he put a companionable arm around Morris's shoulder and walked him toward what he considered an ideal spot—half shade, half sunshine. He and the boy worked together spreading out the blanket, but neither sat down. They just stood there, holding court at the blanket's corners as those who'd been given the bum's rush from the sanctuary now came by to meet the man. The legend. Though Duke was quick to point out to all of them that the true star of last night's game was Morris.

"He's got an arm, this one," Duke said more than once to the crowd assembled around them. "Come watch this afternoon. Or, better yet, come see if you can get a hit off him."

With each word of praise, Morris seemed to stand taller. Duke couldn't crawl inside his skin, but he had a feeling the bruise on his face hurt a little less with each passing moment. He knew Morris would come back to play again. There was nothing like the game to heal the wounds of home.

Just then, the same old man who'd stood up to read out of the Bible started hollering for everybody to quiet down for the blessing. A quiet rippled through the people, and all the men gathered at Duke's blanket—Morris included—took off their hats and bowed their heads. Duke did too, and while he never was one to close his eyes when Ellie Jane was saying grace at the Voyant house, this time he did. After all, Morris might be looking. Or that little kid with the horse.

When he opened his eyes, he saw Ellie Jane and Ned just walking up. He wasn't the only one who noticed either. That same ripple that got everybody quiet to pray worked backward, and soon all the women were whispering and pointing. Subtle as a frog in soup as his ma used to say.

But Duke saw what they saw, and he knew.

Mrs. Lewiston mowed down all the gossips making way to relieve Ellie Jane of Ned long enough for the man to carry the basket to the appointed table. Leaving Ellie Jane alone.

If Duke didn't say it now, he never would. And if he never did, he'd never be fully rid of the rock sitting square in the middle of his chest every time he looked at her. So, after instructing Morris to hold down the blanket until he returned, Duke made his way through the crowd.

When he was a kid, one of his jobs was to go out and check the traps his father had set in the woods around them. He always hated it when there would be a rabbit—very much alive—watching him with twitchy, panicked eyes, looking for some mode of escape. Forgetting it had nowhere to go.

That's what Ellie Jane looked like now. She clutched at the throat of her dress just as she had her robe the night before.

"Whatsoever things are pure."

She'd traded the silly hat with the enormous feather for a simple straw boater that nestled at the top of her head, cushioned by the mass of curls pinned beneath it.

"Whatsoever things are lovely."

Two more steps and he was close enough to touch her. But he didn't. Instead, he stood before her, his hands clasped behind him, and, with an apology and a promise, set them both free.

PART 7

HOME TEAM

ARREST RECORD

20 May 05
Arrest: One Darnell Buddy, Negro
Age: 35
Height: 5 ft 6 in
Weight: 134
Charge: Public Intoxication, Disorderly Conduct, Assault
Sentence: 3 Days…20 May—23 May 1905
Fine: $5.00
paid 5-23-05

Tuesday, May 23

Before it was just Mama and me I had a daddy livin in the house and his mama besides and there was always music. Daddy blew a mouth harp and my grandma would sing songs she remembered learnin as a child. Mama was never one to join in but I'd see her workin round the edges of the room, maybe hummin a little bit or keepin time with her sweepin.

Grandma stayed with us no matter if my daddy was around or not. One time after we knew Daddy was gone for good Grandma took me in her lap like she always did of an evenin and started to sing me a song. Mama heard it from clear outside and came runnin in sayin, Don't you bring your slave songs into my house old woman. This ain't no cotton field.

I remember gettin real still on Grandma's lap and kind of shrinkin down. Not hidin just tryin to get small.

After that my grandma had to sneak me songs. She'd call me over and whisper them in my ear. My favorite was the one about Joshua. I'd be folded up in her lap or gathered up against her heart and she'd pat the rhythm out on me.

Joshua fit the battle of Jericho, Jericho, Jericho. Joshua fit the battle of Jericho and the walls came a tumblin down.

When she came to the part about blowin the ram horns I'd

*fill my cheeks with air and hold it until she sang, For the battle
is in my hand. Then I'd let it out makin the sound of crashin
walls.*

*Then she'd tell me the story, fillin my head with pictures of
the city. Walls higher than the trees made out of stones bigger
than our house. Imagine that, she'd say. Thousands and thousands of those big ol rocks. And the Lord just turned them to
dust.*

*I'd tell her I felt sad for all them people in the city but she'd
hush me and say we weren't to question the Lord's decisions.
She'd say sometimes He had to clear the clutter to do His work.*

*Now Grandma would probably rise up out of her grave and
pull me down in it if she ever heard me say the name of Duke
Dennison and God's Joshua in the same breath. But I can see
them both the same. Ever since he worked to build that field it's
like more and more of a wall fallin in town. I always thought all
white people knew each other walkin around their town like one
big body with a thousand legs. Everybody actin out the ideas
from the same mind. But maybe not. Because now people are
comin out of the dust to play the game.*

*And they're playin every day. Since that first Saturday base-
ball has become as regular for them people like eatin supper.
Every evenin after five o'clock they just show up. Make up teams
from whoever's there. Mr. Duke doesn't even head up a team
every time. One Sunday he even made the calls so Mr. Ned could
play. Every time I think to myself this will be the last time I'll get
to play they choose me again the next—sometimes first thing.*

*Course that don't mean Mr. Duke knocked down the biggest
wall of all. The one runnin down the railroad tracks separatin
my side of town from the rest of Picksville. Sometimes I feel like*

*the lone trumpet call flyin back and forth between the two with
people on both sides and wonderin just who I am and what I'm
doin. I know my mama don't approve though she never gave me
another beatin after that first day. But she never come to watch
me neither.*

*Some evenings I see her durin a game walkin right past the
field on her way home from work. And she ain't the only one—
there's lots of us who make their way cross the tracks every day.
But did one of them even stop and look? Here's one of their own
standin on high ground, forcin grown white men to swing a stick
at air and they don't even bother to turn their heads.*

*Except that fool Darnell. When the sheriff let him out of jail
on Tuesday he came to the field and sat down right on the track
to watch. Made me nervous at first and the other team got three
hits in a row. But those were the last hits they got and for the rest
of the game all I threw was smoke and fire.*

*Still when it's over there's guys slappin my back and sayin,
Good game son. And not just the ones on my team but the others
too. Them that got a hit are braggin to their buddies and them
that didn't kind of shake their fists and smile and say, They'll get
me next time. All in all I'm bounced around until Mr. Duke sees
Darnell waitin for me and asks if I'll be alright.*

I say, Yeah he ain't nothin when he's straight.

*So Mr. Duke tells me to go on home and rest up. He'll see me
tomorrow. But he walks with me clear over to where Darnell is
waitin, introduces himself like Darnell is any other gentleman in
town, and hands me off.*

*Me and Darnell start walkin, quiet at first. He looks smaller
to me today like he's had some of his spirit sucked right out of*

him. And he smells bad. Worse than usual. We're walkin slow
and I think both of us would have been just fine if the other
never spoke a word but a fool like that can't never keep his
mouth shut for too long. And before we hit the top of the first
street leadin into our part of town he says, Don't let them fool
you.

I tell him, Ain't nobody foolin me.

And he just laughs not botherin to bring his hand up to
cover his old yellow teeth the way he does whenever my mama's
around.

He says, Oh you they fool alright. Up there throwin that little ball just how they want.

I say, I'm throwin a ball they can't hit! How does that make
me a fool? More than that Mr. Duke is still payin me ten cents a
strike. Even in the games. He says I throw that good. That if I
was playin in the big leagues they'd be givin me a thousand times
more than that.

Darnell just makes a hummin sound. Then he starts tellin
me about a time when he was up in the city. How he saw this
man that used to go around in the streets playin this little organ.
He had a monkey that went around with him. Every time the
man finished a song that monkey would go around in the crowd
holdin out his little hat.

He says, That man couldn't play organ for nothin and he
wouldn't have made a dime if he didn't have that monkey beggin
for it. People was givin their good money to a cute little monkey
with a hat. And you Morris my boy, he says, ain't nothin more
than their beggin monkey.

I tell him, Don't nobody give me money except Mr. Duke.

He says, They're givin you a lot more than money. They givin you respect and ain't no price on that.

Which makes me feel like I'm winnin this argument and when I say so Darnell stops walkin and looks me straight in the eye and says, It's because you ain't nothin but a boy. A child. He tells me to just wait. Wait until their little monkey is old enough to do more than throw a ball. Wait until he's old enough to take their jobs and love their women. Wait until he's a man fully grown makin them look silly with their sticks.

He leans in closer, close enough that I can see the wet pink skin holdin back his eyes, and says, Why do you think there ain't no Negroes playin with the big white boys?

I want him to go away and stop speakin all this darkness to me but he has one more question. I can feel his breath on my face when he says, Tell me Morris. Do you ever get a hit?

And I don't say nothin because we both know the answer to that. No. Been up to bat a dozen times, and ain't never touched it to the ball.

I say, None of them can pitch to me. I always get a walk.

Darnell makes that hummin sound again and asks, Ever get hit with the ball when you're at the plate?

I feel a burnin behind my eyes and say, Once.

He asks, Did you ever score a run?

And I think of all the times I walked in from third. Or second. Never once runnin across that plate.

He says, Mark me boy. They done decided what your place is. They gonna keep you there.

We part ways after that. Darnell heads up the path to Cousin Eddie's where he'll get a bottle of hooch and disappear until he needs money for the next one. I'm standin at the corner with more than two dollars of monkey money burnin in my pocket.

So I run. Not home to Mama but back across the tracks past the field where Mr. Shiner's rakin the dirt through the park where I was invited to stay at a white church picnic—all the way to Miss Ellie Jane's street where she's walkin with Mr. Ned on one side and Mr. Duke on the other.

Usually when I'm on a street like this—with nice houses and fences and all—I keep myself real quiet tryin to blend in with the street. But this time I run right up behind them and shout, Hey!

Mr. Duke and Miss Ellie Jane stop and turn around. Then Mr. Ned does too and the four of us stand there starin at each other until Mr. Duke in that deep smooth voice of his says, Yes Morris?

I got hurt burnin up inside of me like I haven't felt since I don't know when. I don't want to hate this man and not just because I don't want that fool Darnell to be right. But because white and rich as he is he needs me. Ain't nobody ever needed me before.

But I don't want to need him not the way Darnell says so I reach in my pocket and pull all the money I have out of it and throw it down at his feet and say, I'm not goin to be your monkey boy no more Mr. Duke.

I'm scared to death that he's goin to laugh at me because I see a tiny snip of funny in his eyes but he don't. Instead he squats down in the street and picks up what I dropped, scoopin the dollar and dimes and nickels into his hand. Then he turns to

Miss Ellie Jane and Mr. Ned and tells them he needs to speak
with me alone if they wouldn't mind. I see the look on Mr. Ned's
face and I know he wouldn't mind walkin his girl the rest of the
way home alone.

So they leave and Mr. Duke waits until they're a piece away
before he says, Son what the h*** are you talkin about?

I tell him everythin Darnell told me about that monkey and
the music and the hat. And I got more pride in myself than to be
anybody's toy. That I know what it means to work an honest job
for honest pay. That I been doin that all my life before he got
here and I'd be doin it long after he was gone. That I had a plan
to go to California and I had the money to take me there without his stinkin strike dimes. And I knew exactly how much he
gave me. And I was givin it all back. And I was never gonna
play his stupid game again.

Mr. Duke stands there his hand full of our money, shakin the
coins a little like he's goin to throw them down tryin to roll a
double. He says, Morris do you like playin ball?

I tell him, Yessir.

He asks do I know how much they want to pay him to play?

I say, No sir.

He tells me, Ten thousand dollars. Before he even walks on a
field or hits a single ball.

When I say that makes him one big ol monkey he laughs and
says he guesses so. But that's what they think he's worth so he takes
it. It's his job, all he knows how to do.

I say, Well nobody's payin you to play here with us are they?
Of course not. And ain't nobody else earnin nothin on that field
either. So I tell him, All I want is to be the same as everybody
else. Same as you.

Fair enough, he says. He puts the money back in his pocket then holds his hand out to shake mine. Just like he did that first day I met him. Course that time he was payin me to tote his bags but I'm seein a whole different world between bein paid to work and bein paid to play. He tells me to keep the rest he's paid me and I don't want to but he says I could always use it to buy somethin nice for my mama so I agree.

Then we both say everythin we have to say. Except for the questions. He asks me if I am still gonna play ball here and I say I'll be here and play as long as people will pick me. I ask him how much longer he's gonna be here in town and he says just long enough.

Neither of us want to ask the next question. The one about what's gonna happen then. Now's not the time because it seems like we're two brand new people just meetin each other. So I say good-bye and he does too but not before askin me to come by a little earlier in the afternoon tomorrow to get me some battin practice. Because he promises that one day I'll get a hit.

ELLIE JANE

When she and Ned reached her front door, Ellie Jane turned and asked the same question she'd asked the evening before. "Ned, would you like to stay for supper?"

"Is your father home?"

"No, he's at the station."

"Then I'd love to." He smiled what she had come to identify as the "prince" smile. Charming and controlled, warm and reassuring, it gave the inflection to his words that his voice could not.

That's what she'd noticed during these days as the two circled round and round each other like two birds in a yard. Rather than impressive displays of color and plumage, Ned called to her with his face and his hands. He beckoned her with wide-eyed appreciation whenever she came into view. When she spoke, he leaned in, closing whatever space lingered between them, never wavering in his concentrated study of her mouth, her eyes. His hands—ever fluid—moved in constant accompaniment to the lyrics of his speech, making each conversation a kind of dance. Little by little, she learned a few steps until, in times like this simple front-porch invitation, there seemed little distinction between the voice and the hand. In fact, once they'd crossed the threshold into her parlor, she couldn't remember if she'd heard his answer or seen it. She might as well have been as deaf as he was for all it mattered. She simply *knew*.

It was late, nearly seven o'clock, and the dusk falling on the street outside seeped into the dark Voyant parlor. Ellie Jane moved expertly through the semidarkness, moving to light the lamp on the end table near the window. The heavy drapes were still open, the view slightly obscured by the sheer curtains behind them. She drew the curtain aside, just enough to peer through the clear glass and see Duke and Morris engaged in what seemed to be a very serious conversation.

It wasn't long before she felt Ned beside her, reaching his own hand higher than hers, leaning close to look out the same window. "Quite a pair, aren't they?"

Because they could not stand face-to-face, she didn't answer, but then the question didn't beg a response. It was just a statement, a little truth spoken to tie them all together—the two in the parlor, the two in the street.

"Do you think he loves you?"

She shook her head, slowly, clearly.

"Do you love him?"

She twisted her body to face him. He was gazing above her head, out the window, so she lifted her hand and touched his face, feeling the tension in his jaw. He seemed to be fighting for control, so she waited until he looked down before she shook her head again and whispered, "No."

He closed his eyes and captured her hand, turning his face to bury his lips in her palm.

The current from his touch raced up her sleeve, threatening to bust the line of tiny buttons that stretched nearly to her elbow.

"Duke told me—" He gripped her hand tightly to him.

"I'm so sorry," she said, pleading.

"—he kissed you."

He couldn't see her, so she shook her fist, just a little, trapped as it was, and when he opened his eyes she waited until he was fully focused on her face.

"It didn't mean anything," she said, resisting the urge to shout.

"Of course it does." He released his grip and she felt like she'd been dropped to the floor.

"No!" And this time not only did she shout, she grabbed his arms to hold him in place. "It doesn't matter!"

But it did, to him, she could tell. Any hope she had that she'd be able to put such wanton behavior behind her disappeared in the pain in Ned's face.

"Oh, my." She covered her mouth with her hand. "What you must think of me." In the resurgence of her shame, she brought both hands to cover her face and wailed. "It was a moment of weakness. I was thinking of you, but he was just so—"

Somewhere behind her jumble of words she heard his voice. How long he'd been talking, she didn't know, but when she peeked above her fingers, he was smiling down at her.

"It matters because I love you, Ellie Jane."

"You do?" She pulled her hand away and tried her best to look irresistible.

Apparently, she succeeded.

His kiss was soft and warm, gentle and chaste against her lips. She felt a certain heat spreading through her body—not the rolling explosion that rocked her the night she kissed Duke, or even the electric current from a few minutes ago, but a slow, steadily growing fire, melting her from within. Every bone turned to wax, dripping down inside, hardening into a relentless ball at her core, then starting all over again.

It ended too soon, in the middle of a melting moment. When Ned drew his lips away, she kept her eyes closed and tried to follow, opening them only to find that he stood tall above her, looking down with eyes that, even in the growing shadows, held flickers of all that had nearly consumed her.

"I've waited six years to do that," he said.

"Why?"

"Because I couldn't even get you to look at me."

"No," Ellie Jane said, harnessing all those lonely years behind her question. "Why did you wait?"

He bent low and placed one more quick kiss on her lips. "I didn't have a choice."

She was moving toward him again when she heard the latch on the door. Instead of falling into Ned's arms, she ducked beneath them, sending him into a full spin. By the time Duke walked into the parlor, Ned and Ellie Jane were standing respectably side by side, betrayed only by the fluttering curtains and her sharp, shallow breath.

Duke stopped short at the edge of the carpet. "Am I interrupting something?"

"Of course not." Ellie Jane smoothed her skirt. "I was just about to start supper."

"In the parlor?"

No good could come of pursuing this conversation, so Ellie Jane simply said, "Excuse me" and headed for the kitchen. There was a pot of spring vegetable soup—left over from last night—on the stove. She touched the side of the pot and found it was still warm. Pop must have stopped by for supper before going to the office. It wouldn't take long to get it boiling again.

Ellie Jane took a long match, lit the burner, and gave the soup a stir. A taste brought to her lips told her it was good, but not special, and she wanted something delightful for this night's dinner.

She took a dish of hard-boiled eggs out of the icebox, peeled them and extracted the yolks, mashed them, and mixed them with the yolk of a fresh egg and a little flour. By the time she'd rolled this mixture into several little balls, the soup was boiling, and she plopped each one in, careful of the splatter. Then she washed her hands and set about tearing chunks from the round loaf of Irish soda bread she'd brought home from the bakery yesterday and placing them in the towel-lined basket in the middle of the table.

She pulled three bowls down from the cupboard and set the table, adding a pitcher of water and a cut glass dish of olives. Then butter. Then salt and pepper. In between each addition, she made a detour to the door, laying her ear against it. No conversation seeped through, which was odd because she couldn't imagine Duke Dennison sitting quietly with anybody for any length of time. Not even Ned. So right after the salt and pepper, before the fetching of spoons, she opened the swinging door just a crack—enough to see into the parlor.

"Mr. Dennison?" Silly question, really, given that he wasn't there. But Ned was. He'd littered the coffee table with little slips of paper and was carefully peeling another off a bundle held in his hand.

Ellie Jane hadn't yet caught his eye, so she had this moment to look at him, soft in the lamplight. She'd never tried to picture anybody sharing her life here with her father, but Ned Clovis was as much a fixture as anything, and in this new light, he fit.

"Did you call?" Duke bounded down the final steps and into the peaceful scene.

Ned looked up, glanced at Duke, then brought his eyes on Ellie Jane.

"I, um, just wanted you to know that supper will be on in a few minutes."

"All right." Duke sat next to Ned on the sofa, and Ellie Jane noticed for the first time the sheaf of papers clutched in his hand.

"What are you two up to?"

"Stats." Duke held up one of the slips. "Ned's been keeping track of it all. Who's played what, if they hit, how they hit—"

"Fascinating," Ellie Jane said, barely able to recall the outcome of the game that ended less than an hour ago. "And what do you intend to do with all this information?"

Duke held up the papers. "Compile it, here. Get it all in one place."

"I see." Suddenly, the two men in the parlor seemed more like overgrown boys. "And why are you doing this?"

Duke and Ned turned to each other, then back to Ellie Jane. Ned shrugged, and Duke said, "It's what we do."

She had no argument for that, and frankly she didn't care, but returning to the kitchen seemed like a lonely option.

"Tell you what," she said, "put that away for now, come eat supper, and afterward you can work at the table. The light's better in here, anyway."

Ned picked up his papers, putting them in meticulous order before handing them over to Duke. The two of them walked past as Ellie Jane held open the door. She somehow resisted the urge to touch Ned as he walked by, but she could not ignore the wide, satisfied grin he gave her as he did so.

"And no baseball talk at the table," she admonished for no good reason except to see if they would obey.

And they did.

The meal was companionably silent at first, just the clink of spoons against the bowls. She thought she noticed a slight hesitation when Ned encountered his first egg ball, but it passed with what she

swore was a wink as he took a chunk of the bread and dipped it into
the broth.

"You are a very good cook."

Duke, sitting opposite Ellie Jane, kindly said nothing.

"Thank you." She sent a pointed glance at Duke, just in case. "I
try to avoid meat whenever possible."

"Oh." Ned lifted his bread. "This is good too."

"I bought that at the bakery."

Ned pointed at the dish of peach preserves and raised an eyebrow.

"Mrs. Finneworth gave those to me."

As if on cue, both men reached for the dish, Duke a little more
eager.

The olives?

Ellie Jane would never have believed it possible to point sarcas-
tically, but Ned did, so her answer matched his tone. "God. Then
the cannery. Then the grocer."

There was a small ripple of laughter around the table, then back
to the quiet. When the last crust of bread was slathered with the last
of the preserves, Ellie Jane cleared the table. She made a pot of tea and
poured the rest of the hot water from the kettle into the sink before
sprinkling in soap flakes and adding cold water from the tap. She
washed and rinsed each dish, setting them to dry on the drainboard.

The men talked quietly behind her, filling in the tiny boxes
drawn on the paper with all sorts of letters and numbers.

"Struck out twice, swinging."

"Walked in the first inning."

"Bats right. Throws right."

"Hit a double, got thrown out at third."

At one point Ellie Jane turned around, her soapy hand on her
hip. "How in the world do you know all of this?"

Ned pursed his lips and tapped his forehead. "I remember everything."

She was drying and putting away the last of the bowls when the parlor clock struck nine. Usually she was upstairs in her room by this time, her hair taken down, brushed and braided, her Bible open to the day's reading. She and her father rarely had guests, and certainly none that stayed until this late hour, which left her at a loss as to what good hostess etiquette required. Ned showed no sign of leaving, Duke no signs of asking him to, and by this time it was unclear as to which guest belonged to whom.

"My goodness," Ellie Jane said, relying on the ancient feminine art of dropping a hint, "it certainly has gotten late, hasn't it?"

Neither man replied.

"Well, then. I suppose I'll just go into the parlor and do a little reading." At least that part of her evening routine could get done.

Wary of the idea of even walking to her bedroom with two bachelors in the kitchen, Ellie Jane went to the bookshelf beside the desk and found her mother's Bible. She opened the front cover and saw the dates listed.

November 10, 1877—Married: Floyd David Voyant and Claire Eloise Mitchell

September 9, 1878—Born: David Jonathan Voyant

October 15, 1881—Born: Elijah Jane Voyant

October 25, 1881—Died: Claire Eloise Voyant

None of this was new of course. When she was a very little girl, Ellie Jane would often take her mother's Bible and simply hold it close to her, loving not only the stories within it, but also the stories of this very book. Her father told her that Claire would take this book to bed with her every night and read—sometimes for hours— with Floyd sleeping beside her. When she was bearing her children, she'd held it to her breast until the midwife wrenched it away, and she'd gone to her final sleep with it resting by her side.

Tonight, though, this front leaf held a melancholy twist Ellie Jane never considered. Her parents had less than four years together before Claire Voyant died.

"Four years," she said out loud, and her heart heard an echo from just a few hours ago.

Six years.

Six years, Ned had loved her. Well, he hadn't actually *said* that he loved her all that time, but like so many other unspoken words between them, she simply *knew.* Six years—two years longer than her father had loved her mother. And, after all this time, her father had never loved again. Written as it was in the front page of this Bible, it seemed like such a little bit of time when indeed, it was so much more. It was an entire life, entire lives, really, changed and created and left as legacy.

She took the Bible over to the wing-backed chair next to the lamp and turned up the light a wee bit. She'd been reading in the book of John, but tonight something new tugged at her, and she put her finger in the page marked by her mother's tasseled bookmark and opened to the fourth chapter of Ecclesiastes:

> Two are better than one; because they have a good reward for
> their labour. For if they fall, the one will lift up his fellow:
> but woe to him that is alone when he falleth; for he hath not
> another to help him up. Again, if two lie together, then they
> have heat: but how can one be warm alone? And if one pre-
> vail against him, two shall withstand him; and a threefold
> cord is not quickly broken.

She read the verses over and over, marveling at her reflection within the words, how very alone she'd been just weeks ago. Tonight she couldn't get the men out of her house fast enough. This, admittedly, made her blush at the heat generated at the thought of "when two lie together," but that was chased away by the image of the threefold cord. She and Duke and Ned in the kitchen this evening. She and Duke and her father on others. Duke and Ned and Morris playing a makeshift game long before the town joined in.

She cocked an ear and heard a third voice coming from the kitchen. Low and deep, the voice she pulled from her earliest memory. Her father must have come in through the back door as he often did when he came home late. Soon his voice broke away and he was beside her in the lamplight.

"You're up late, Ellie." He bent to kiss her offered cheek.

"We have company."

"I see that. What are they doing in there?"

"Stats."

"And why, exactly?"

Ellie Jane shrugged. "It's what they do."

"Well, at this hour, they need to do it another time. It's getting late."

"You tell them, Pop. I don't have the heart."

He winked at his daughter, stood upright, and walked into the kitchen.

Knowing the situation was well in hand, Ellie Jane stood too, leaving her mother's Bible on the table. She had just turned down the lamp when the door to the kitchen opened, outlining Ned in the light coming from the kitchen.

"I've been asked to leave."

"Oh," she said, startled. "I figured Pop would have you leave by the back door."

But of course he hadn't heard her, and he would not have understood her in these shadows. Any moment he might turn back and leave through the kitchen rather than risk making his way through in the unfamiliar room. Thinking, *woe to him that is alone when he falleth,* Ellie Jane reached through the darkness and grabbed his hand.

Fingers intertwined, they moved together, until they were at the place where this evening began. The front door. The front porch. And a kiss in the moonlight full of promise.

25 May 1905
8:16 a.m.

TO: Mr. Donald Dennison
Picksville, Missouri

FROM: Dave Voyant
Chicago Times-Herald Offices

Duke—
The owners request your return. Selee and
Chance want you on the field 29 May to
practice. On the roster 2 June. Guess you
are ready after all. HA! HA!
Hope all is well. Have NBL contact with
Union Giants.
Kiss my sister for me. HA! HA!
Dave

NED

In many ways his life went on as it had since he'd come back to Picksville. He still woke every morning, uneasy with the profound silence that came with the new day. Minutes before, in his dreams, he might have been hearing his mother calling him home for supper or the taunts of his childhood friends—sometimes coming through utter darkness. How odd it seemed to open his eyes to a soundless half-light with the echoes of music and voice lurking in the last strains of sleep.

Breakfast was still the corner stool at Marlene's counter, hotcakes and eggs and lately two cups of coffee, but there had been a decidedly different air to the restaurant these past few days. No longer huddled over newspapers and conspiracies, men sat in open conversation from table to table. Their expressions jovial; their bodies animated.

But there had been big changes too, like the fact that he kissed Ellie Jane Voyant once in the twilight, once in the moonlight, and had every intention of doing so again. He stared at his stack of hotcakes and planned just how and when and where he would do so. The satisfaction he felt must have registered on his face, because suddenly Marlene's fingers snapped within his line of vision. He looked up to see her questioning face, framed by the blond braids wound about her head.

What are you smiling about?

"Delicious." He used his fork to point at the untouched stack. Then, to prove his point, he cut away a generous bite and stuffed it in his mouth, determined to chew until she went away.

Minutes later, Duke and Floyd walked in. The baseball star

hadn't been given the hero's reception—that mixture of reverence and suspicion—in weeks. He was just another citizen. Marlene would have his coffee on the counter before he sat down.

For Ned, the arrival of these two meant only one thing. He swiveled in his seat just in time to see Ellie Jane, obscured from the nose down by the lettering on Marlene's window. The hotcakes turned sweeter in his mouth, and he swallowed hard, fighting the urge to wipe away the lingering syrup on his lips. He'd watched that little front-facing profile march past this window for years, but this morning she stopped, right before disappearing behind the capital "D," and looked inside.

It would have been imperceptible to anybody but him. In fact, he would have missed it too, if not for the years spent waiting for such a sign. With no invitation and no social obligation, she lifted her hand—just to her shoulder—and waved. This time it was Ned who responded not with the slightest nod of his head, but a broad, sticky smile. When he returned to his breakfast, he swooped past the knowing eyes of Duke Dennison and the sheriff, who adopted a stern expression and tapped the silver star on his vest—*Be careful*—punctuated with a fatherly wink.

Having devoted a week to building the field at the railroad station left things a complete mess at the feed store. Earlier, at breakfast, when Duke tried to convince Ned to meet him at the field and help get in a little batting practice for Morris, Ned had to hold up his hand and adamantly refuse.

"Some of us work," Ned told him, and his friend quietly dropped the subject.

Now, as he stood among a dozen unpacked crates after telling half-a-dozen people to come back later when he had things organized, the thought of standing on the mound and throwing a few balls across the plate seemed much more appealing. Especially knowing that just beyond the chicken wire backstop, in the middle of the platform, was a little octagonal room where, if he were brave enough, he could sneak inside for just a minute and—

Stop.

Ned wedged a crowbar underneath the sealed lid of a wooden crate and pried it loose.

Ellie Jane is not the kind of girl to let a man take such liberties in the middle of the day.

He sifted through the packing straw and lifted out a jar of green pellets.

But I can walk her home tonight.

On he worked through the afternoon, arranging his inventory, sweeping the stockroom floor. He even gave some attention to the front room, wiping down the counter with a sweet-smelling linseed oil and knocking the corner cobwebs down with a broom. All the while he allowed his mind to wander with much purer plans, like handing chores like these off to Ellie Jane.

Ned pictured her standing behind the counter, a pencil lodged in her hair. She would take it out to write orders on the little pad kept on the top shelf. And every day, when he left to meet the two-o'clock train, she'd take off her apron, take the pencil out of her hair, and go with him to the station. As they waited on the platform, he'd tell her how this was always the highlight of his day, how he always hoped she would look at him. How he knew, if he could get her to look at him just one time, she'd never be able to look away.

Then, to his relief, it was two o'clock. Time to see her again.

He went out to the barn behind the store and hitched his horse to the wagon. This foray out to the railroad station was just about the only driving he ever did. Fran, the gentle bay, knew the route by heart. The reins were slack in Ned's hands, and he kept his eyes on Fran's black tail swishing rhythmically with each step.

All of a sudden he saw a new tension ripple through Fran's body. He barely had time to get a new grip on the lines when the horse reared up and back, throwing her head and twisting it almost full around to where Ned could see the whites of her eyes. Once her hooves were planted on the ground again, she took off, careening a crazed course through the street, nearly running the Picksville pedestrians off the sidewalk in front of the post office.

Ned pulled tight and tried to make soothing sounds. He saw the angry faces of the people and noticed they were pointing accusingly all around him. Too afraid to turn his attention away from settling his horse, he simply continued to fight for control only to find the situation becoming more and more dire with each second.

Then he saw it. Just out of the corner of his eye, coming up along the right side of his wagon, an automobile. It was a red, two-passenger runabout. One young man drove, another twisted in the passenger seat, mouthing something with a cocky tilt to his head. A minute later the car turned left at the intersection of Spring Street and Center Avenue and disappeared.

Ned caught his breath, Fran found her footing, and townspeople went about their business. Still, the automobile left one question in its wake.

Who was that?

Not that automobiles were unheard of in Picksville. Mayor Birdiff had one, of course, as did Mr. Coleman and a number of other businessmen. There was, however, that unwritten rule about driving in the town square, and with the exception of driving a certain baseball player home from the train, Ned couldn't remember a time when anybody had ever broken it.

Ned tried to place the men in the car but recalled more of an impression than actual features. One thing was sure, he didn't recognize them. They were young, unshaven, and apparently idiots.

He hopped down from the wagon seat and ran a reassuring hand over Fran's neck. When he looked up, he saw Morris trotting down from the corner to meet him.

Did you see those guys? Morris pointed in the direction of the vanished auto.

Ned grudgingly acknowledged the existence of such fools.

Goin' to the train?

Ned nodded and gestured to invite Morris to come and help him out.

Morris shook his head and held up a telegram. *For Mr. Duke.*

Ned smiled and made a dismissive gesture then reached into his pocket and pulled out a quarter. Morris took it and put it in his own pocket, along with the telegram.

Five minutes later Ned pulled up next to the station. The train was already there, so he wasted no time finding the conductor and signing for his delivery. Twenty bags of feed corn, a case of bird seed, two cases of Milk Oil mange cure and flea treatment, and an assortment of cardboard boxes. Morris would earn his two bits today.

He backed the wagon up to the platform and picked up his first bag, loading it onto the tailgate while Morris dragged it to the front of the bed. He glanced over his shoulder with each trip and smiled at Ellie Jane behind her ticket window glass.

Once the first ten bags were in, he left the rest of the loading to Morris and made his way across the platform to the booth. He walked right up, planted his elbows on the little ledge, and leaned forward, almost touching his face to the glass.

"Good afternoon, Miss Voyant."

Hello, Mr. Clovis. She even offered a small curtsy.

He beckoned her outside. She shook her head. He made a pleading gesture. She shook her head more vigorously. He was about to fall to one knee when he felt a tap on his shoulder. Morris.

"Finished already?"

The solemn, worried look on Morris's face caught his attention, and he followed the boy's gaze behind him to the empty baseball field. Empty, that is, except for the two men who were unloading a canvas bag from the automobile brought to a stop right next to the bleachers.

He turned back to Ellie Jane, who was hunched down, trying to see past him.

Who are they?

Ned shrugged and was starting to walk away when her hand reached through the arch cut in the glass at the bottom of the window and grabbed his.

"Don't worry," he said. "I'm not leaving."

He clapped the kid on the shoulder and the two walked down to the platform. When the last cardboard box of hoof treatment was loaded, he told Morris to hop up in the wagon and handed him the reins. He gave him another quarter too.

"Can you unload for me?"

Morris nodded. *Anything else?*

"Yeah. Tell Duke to come down here."

DUKE

Five more days, according to the telegram. Two weeks ago this would have been the best news he could hope for. Proof that he could escape from the crawling underneath his skin. But today it looked like the end of something. Still, there was good news, maybe. For the boy. He fished in his pocket for a dime.

"No thank you, Mr. Duke." Morris held up his hand. "I said I'm not gonna take no more of your money."

"This is different. This is work." He took Morris's hand and placed the coin inside.

"Well, then, I thank you, sir."

They were standing on the front porch—Duke having stepped out after Morris refused to step in.

"Anything else?"

"Yes, sir. They's two men down at the field."

"Well, they won't get much of a game at this hour."

Morris wouldn't be amused. "I don't know who they are. They ain't from here. Mr. Ned don't know them neither." And he went on with his story. Something about a car and Ned's wagon nearly colliding in the street. "And they was hollerin', 'Sorry!' and all that, but they just seemed mean. I think Mr. Ned's worried about leavin' Miss Ellie Jane down there alone."

Duke didn't hesitate. "Let's go." He went inside briefly to drop the telegram on the end table and ran upstairs to grab a cap and the canvas bag with the gloves and Ned's bat. He and Morris walked at a pace too quick for conversation.

He noticed the car first. He knew plenty of guys who owned them, but other than the fact that they ran on gasoline and had wheels for steering, Duke knew nothing. Didn't want to. They were noisy and dangerous and seemed impractical on Chicago's crowded streets. But this was a decent one. Not new, but not like other rattletraps he'd seen. He didn't care about the car, anyway. He just wanted to know who was driving it.

Ned was sitting on one of the benches on the platform, and he stood as soon as Duke came into view.

"What are they doing?" Duke asked, forgoing any sort of greeting.

"Just playing. Hitting out to each other."

"Well, let's go have a meeting."

Duke couldn't shake the knot he felt in his stomach—it had been there since he saw the look on Morris's face. He almost told the kid to stay on the platform. Safe. Let him and Ned handle this. But he didn't. Maybe because he knew the boy thought of himself as a man. Maybe because the knot didn't get unbearable until they'd nearly reached the little set of bleachers. It was one thing to tell him to stay. Another to tell him to go back. He wouldn't do that to any man.

Duke planted his feet, folded his arms, and watched. They were young, probably not twenty years old. One stood at home plate, tossing a baseball high in the air and calling his hit—"two!"—before knocking the ball straight toward second base as it dropped. The other guy would scramble back, stepping on the base to make the play, then throw the ball back in. A few more hits and it would be time to switch.

That's when they saw Duke. At least, that's when they acknowledged him. The two men met between the mound and home plate then, converged their course, and headed straight for where Ned, Duke, and Morris stood at the bleachers.

The two strangers were equal in stature. Medium height. Medium build. The one walking in from the plate had a face that looked like unbaked biscuit dough. Flat, round, white, with a little pointed nose stuck right in the middle of it and shallow, wide-set eyes. He balanced the bat on his shoulder as he walked but dropped it in the grass behind him when he stopped. The other was darker but handsome, Duke supposed. Given a haircut and shave. Neither smiled. Or offered a hand in greeting. Or looked at anybody but Duke.

"Good afternoon." Duke appointed himself the obvious spokesman. "Don't believe we know you fellows."

"This here's Raymond." The accent was thick and Southern. "And they call me Peach."

Duke gave a sidelong glance at the automobile. "You two up from Georgia?"

"Not necessar'ly," the one called Peach said. His voice was high and thin. Like it was coming through a tin can string.

Duke clenched his jaw and offered his hand. "I'm Don. This is Ned. And Morris."

The two shook Duke's hand and reached for Ned's. When it came to Morris, though, there was only the briefest nod on Morris's part. No acknowledgment at all on theirs.

"Got you a nice field here." Peach twisted at the waist, surveying it. "Don't remember this place havin' somethin' as nice as that."

"You've been here before?"

"Once or twice. We kind of go all over."

The one called Raymond turned a baseball over and over in his glove, studying the laces.

Every hair on the back of Duke's neck stood on end. He knew guys like this. Coming up from their dirt farms. Classless. Ignorant.

"Well, Peach. I see you've got some equipment. You fellows play on a team somewhere?"

"Not yet. But Ray here, he's been to a couple of club tryouts. And I'm fixin' to do the same next year. How 'bout you?"

Without warning, Raymond tossed the ball to Duke, who brought his hand up to catch it without blinking an eye. He inclined his head toward Ned. "We run kind of a pickup league. Guys just show up and play."

Ray held up his glove, but Duke had no inclination to throw the ball back.

"Really?" Peach said. "When do you play again?"

"No telling." Duke spoke quickly. Ned was standing right beside him, able to follow Peach's questions but probably not Duke's answers. "So you might want to move on. You might make it to Springfield by nightfall."

"What makes you think we're headin' for Springfield?"

"Just a friendly suggestion."

"Yeah? Or maybe we could give you a ride back to Chicago, *Don.*"

Something spread cold inside him. This time, when Raymond held up his glove, Duke tossed the ball over.

He turned his back on the two men and crooked his finger, bringing Ned's face down closer to his. Without speaking out loud, he mouthed the words: *You and Morris. Go.*

Ned's eyes darted over to the ticket booth.

Take her too.

When Ned began walking away, Duke told Morris to follow.

"Yer friend sure don't talk much," Peach said before the two were even ten steps away.

"My friend's deaf." Duke pointed to Ray. "What's his problem?"

Peach smiled, revealing small gray teeth. "Aw, he's just shy. Heckuva ballplayer, though."

"I'm sure he is." The coldness had congealed now, settling across the top of his shoulders. "And how about you?"

"Oh, I do awright, I guess," Peach said. "But I ain't nothin' next to you, Mr. Dennison. Or can I call you Duke?"

Shy Ray let out a chuckle, like this was the joke he'd been waiting for all day. But Peach had lost any hint of humor.

Now the cold was a single, icy spot right at the base of his skull. "How'd you find me?"

"Y'er playin' baseball at a train station." Peach's voice had the pace of someone talking to a fool. "People travel. People talk."

Duke looked over to see Ellie Jane sitting in Ned's wagon seat, and Morris climbing up beside her. Ned handed Morris the reins, gestured some instructions, and gave the bay a friendly slap on the rump.

Then, to Duke's relief, he began making his way back. After all, if Duke learned nothing else at church, he'd discovered that Ned Clovis could more than hold his own in a fight.

He took a deep breath and aimed for that perfect note of authoritative charm. "So. Have we met before? Or are you just a fan?"

"Neither one." He cocked his thumb back toward Ned. "You sure you want your friend to hear this?"

"I told you," Duke's voice was smooth. "He can't hear anything."

"You 'member a place called Nellie's? In St. Louis?"

"I've been in a lot of places." He kept his words even, but his mind was already racing, trying to place just where and when he'd met this guy. And what he'd done.

"Well, it don't surprise me you don't recall. You was pretty well lit up."

"Done a lot of that too."

"Well, that ain't no secret, is it?"

Duke flinched at the remark, recovered, and formed a mask of steel.

"So this was about two years ago. 'Round about September?" Peach turned to Ray for confirmation.

"Yep." It was the first sound Ray made.

"Yep," Peach confirmed. "So we's at this place called Nellie's. Nice place. Cold beer. And a bunch of us was drinkin'. Me and Ray here, a few others you never got a chance to meet."

He went on to tell a story typical of just about every night of Duke's life since leaving home when he was fourteen. A dark bar. A crowd of guys. A lot of booze. Maybe a woman or two. And Duke, sitting alone at the bar. Quietly downing one drink after another. Wanting to be left alone.

"We was just wantin' to get you into the cel'bration."

"I don't celebrate much." But the picture was trying to come clear from the darkness around it. Like looking through a stereoscope. This flat-faced kid punching Duke in the shoulder. Light, good-natured. Then Duke punching back. Not so light. In fact, maybe hard enough to cause that bend in Peach's sharp little nose.

Ned wasn't taking his eyes off Peach, who strode about like an actor on a stage.

"We was just tryin' to get you into the party! Next thing I know, I'm on the ground and I got this crazy guy beatin' me."

"Look, man." Duke held out a hand, trying to smooth things over. "I was drinking a lot in those days. Did some stupid things. I'm sorry. What do you want from me now?"

"Do you know what we was celebratin'?"

"No." Of course not.

"Just made the cut. The first one, anyways. On my way to the Cardinals."

Duke narrowed his eyes, trying to refine his vision. Picturing this guy at the plate.

"Don't bother tryin' to place me now. I didn't make it." Peach stood perfectly still now. "See, I got into this fight the night before the second round. Got my face busted up, a couple of cracked ribs."

"I've known plenty of men who played with cracked ribs." Including himself.

"Yeah? You know a lot of fellows who play with broken arms?"

"I didn't break your arm." He was pretty certain, anyway.

"Naw. Not you. But them goons that pulled me off of you sure could. Same ones that hauled me in for drunk and disord'ly."

Now Duke remembered. The meeting the next day with the manager. Hearing how they covered for him. Again.

He shook the shame off. "Looks to me like you've healed up. You can try out again."

"I did." He let out a rueful laugh. "Didn't make it."

"I'm sorry." He'd been saying that a lot lately. "Maybe I can help you out. Put in a good word for you."

"Maybe your word don't mean as much as you think it does."

"So what do you want?"

"Well," Peach scratched his chin, "I didn't really know 'til I got here. But now I think I do. I want a game."

"A game?"

"Sure. Just a chance to see how I would'a done playin' in the big league."

Duke felt an overwhelming sense of protection for the men who'd faithfully gathered here over the past weeks. He didn't want this guy anywhere near them.

"This is hardly the big league."

"Nope. But you're a big league player."

"Fair enough." He looked over at Ned, and he knew his friend was already stacking the team. "You want to play with me? Or against me?"

Peach and Ray looked at each other and shared a grin.

"Buddy," Peach said, "I wanna beat ya."

"Well, then." Duke offered his hand. "Be here at four o'clock."

PART 8

TAKE A KNEE

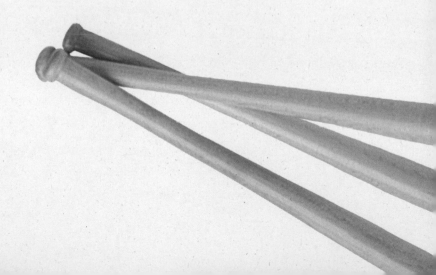

MORRIS

Thursday, May 25

So today I got a taste of what it means to be a man. Mr. Ned
hands his rig over to me like it's nothin and tells me to take his
girl home. I don't know how many people know she's his girl yet
but the way they was talkin to each other ain't no other way to
put it. He just tells her to get in the wagon and go home and she's
not a bit happy about that sayin she's got a job to do and people
gonna need their tickets and she never left in the middle of the
day. But Mr. Ned? He just gets this look on his face and the
whole time he's talkin his hands is flyin, makin tiny little snaps
and I'm thinkin, Boy-o. This is a man in charge of his woman.

Course she's complainin the whole drive home. I tell her that
Mr. Ned's just lookin out for her. That we all had a bad feelin
about those guys and wanted to be sure she's safe and all. That
turns her tale and then she can't stop talkin about what a good
guy Ned is. She calls him a sweet man and I don't want to tell
her that callin a man sweet on my side of the tracks don't mean
anythin she'd wanna know. But as it is I can't say nothin because
I don't never get the chance. Seein her locked up in that little
booth all the time I never knew that woman could talk so much.
I never knew any woman could talk so much. And I guess that's

just more showin the wisdom of God pairin up a woman with that mouth and a man with them ears.

I take Miss Ellie Jane right up to her front gate just like Mr. Ned told me though it took some doin to get that horse not to go straight home. She invites me in for some iced tea and somethin to eat but I tell her I got to go unload this stuff for Mr. Ned. Then she tells me to come on over after I'm done. A boy who works that hard needs to eat.

And I ain't got nothin to argue with that.

I'm a little worried about backin the wagon up to the storeroom but luckily Miss Fran knows all about that too. I'm worried more about what's goin to happen when somebody comes by and sees this Negro boy out with the keys to a white man's store. Sure enough I get just one box carried in and when I come out for the next one there's old Mr. Shiner.

I'm haulin off a bag of seed corn and old Mr. Shiner says, Boy! What do you think you're doin?

Well he might be an old man but that don't mean nothin so I start talkin real fast tellin him how Mr. Ned sent me to unload all this for him. Then he starts laughin a little and tells me not to be scared, that he's worried about my arm is all. Then what do you know? He starts helpin me. Just like that he grabs a sack and I tell him where to put everythin because I've done this a dozen times with Mr. Ned and he's got the whole place straightened up I don't wanna be the one to leave a mess.

When we're done old Mr. Shiner asks do I know how to unhitch a team. Which I don't because I never have and he takes old Fran and the wagon into Mr. Ned's barn and does it for me.

And now I don't know what to do. Mr. Ned done give me another two bits to finish this up for him but I ain't never seen a

Negro tippin no white man a quarter. But it don't seem right for old Mr. Shiner to do all this work for free. So I tell him Mr. Ned paid me fifty cents to take care of this load and I'd be glad to give him half.

Old Mr. Shiner considers that for a long time then he says, Young Morris that seems fair to me. And he holds out his hand.

Nothin ever felt that good.

Bein a man of my word I go back to Miss Ellie Jane's even though I feel a little guilty cause I hadn't done all that work myself. But she's expectin me after all and a fellow just doesn't turn down iced tea when he can get it. I think about stoppin by the post office and the mayor's to see if there's any runnin for me to do to make up the quarter I just gave to old Mr. Shiner but then I figure if Miss Ellie Jane is gettin an afternoon off I deserve one too.

I go straight through the front gate and I'm makin my way round to the back when Miss Ellie Jane opens the front door and says, Morris dear come on in.

Now Mr. Duke's asked me in plenty of times and I always tell him no. But who knows when I'll ever get the chance to be asked in to a nice white lady's parlor? So I take off my hat and dust off my shoes real good and feel grateful that I'm wearin my other new shirt that's mostly clean.

When I walk in it's like nothin I've ever seen. Not even in books. I never thought of a room bein so soft before. Velvet drapes with golden tassels and a thick rug with flowers and vines. There's wallpaper with what looks like puffy scrolls all over it. The lamps on the tables have rounded globes and there's a sofa with big buried buttons on the back that looks like it'd just swallow you up the minute you sat down. One whole wall ain't *nothin but books. Hundreds of them looks like. More here than in the mayor's office. And a desk. A real desk with a rollin top— not a kitchen table with one short leg. I think if I could sit at a desk like that I could write forever.*

Then there's the stairs with a blood-red carpet runnin up the middle and a banister so scrolled and polished it looks like silk spillin down the rail. It's the most beautiful thing I can imagine and I think one of these days I'm gonna climb a staircase just like that and wind up in heaven.

Course I don't say any of this. I ain't no sniveler. I just say, You have a lovely home Miss Voyant.

And she says, Why thank you Mr. Bennett.

Then she asks me to join her in the kitchen for lunch.

I've heard Mr. Duke talk about Miss Ellie Jane's cookin so I don't know what to expect. And I've been tryin to be a better boy for my mama so I'm hopin it won't be nothin she wouldn't approve. When I walk in I see a plate all laid out with a fork and napkin. I sit down and Miss Ellie Jane says, I hope you like macaroni.

I say, I sure do.

Then she fills my plate with cooked macaroni that's got butter melted with it and some kind of flavor that I don't know but it's real good. I try not to eat too fast but there's a whole pot of it and Miss Ellie Jane says she already ate lunch so I can have as much as I want. I'm shovelin it in and she tells me it's good to see someone appreciatin her cookin for a change.

When I've eaten so much I'm not sure if I can move she asks if I have any room left for dessert and I feel a little spot open up for just that purpose.

She says to be patient because she's not much for sweets herself. Then she takes a biscuit out of a wooden box on the counter, cuts it open, and lays it out on this little plate that has all kinds of birds and flowers and vines swirlin around it. It's almost like a flat bowl because next she spoons some canned peaches over the biscuit and then pours Borden milk all over the top of that. If that ain't enough she gets out this tiny jar and a tiny spoon and sprinkles somethin all over the top.

My mouth's waterin so just watchin her put it together and by the time I take my first bite you'd think I was hungry all over again. I ask her what it is she put on the top and she tells me it's cinnamon.

I say, You know Miss Ellie Jane that cinnamon looks just like the color of your hair.

And she looks so pleased. She kind of touches her hair and says, Why thank you Morris. She says if she can't have a peaches and cream complexion she'll just have to settle for cinnamon hair.

Now I have no idea what any of this means but it don't matter. In short order I've eaten everythin on this little dish and there's still some peach juice and cream in the dish. When Miss Ellie Jane gets up to run some water in the sink I lift that dish up to my mouth and drink it all down. Then I swig down my tea. Then I can't move.

She was right there when Mr. Ned made me promise to stick with her until either he or Mr. Duke or her father came home but I know I can't just sit here in her kitchen all afternoon. Just as I'm wipin my face with the napkin—like I think I'm supposed to—she says, Well Morris since you've been appointed my guard how would you like to spend your time?

And how do I answer that? So I say, Well do you have any-thin here that needs doin?

She gets this smile and tells me that as a matter of fact her father just strung a hammock between the two trees in the back-yard but nobody's had a chance to know if he did it right. So would I like to test it out?

She must think I'm four years old. But again a chance to stretch out between two shade trees on a spring afternoon? When's the last time in my life I ever had such a chance?

I tell her I don't think I'll be much of a guard if I'm swingin in a hammock. And she tells me not to worry. She'll be workin in her garden.

So off we go to the Voyant backyard where I first learned to throw a ball. She settles down on her knees in the patch where I'd throw to Mr. Duke. I settle myself down in the ropy mesh between the trees that used to keep my pitches straight. Right away she starts hummin. I close my eyes and feel the sun on my face, and the last thing I hear before Mr. Duke wakes me up is Miss Ellie Jane singin about glimmerin worms.

At first I think it's goin to be like any other game until we get to the field and I see them two from the car. I ask Mr. Duke what they're doin here and he says it's a long story that he'll tell me later.

The other thing I notice is that him and me aren't goin to be part of the team pickin. That's headed up by young Mr. Shiner and that red-headed high school boy. They'll each pick six. Duke and me'll round out one team and them two strangers will finish out the other.

Then it's time to play ball.

There's a tension to this game that ain't like any other I've known. Maybe it's because I know Mr. Duke so well that I can see he don't have none of the joy on his face like he normally does. When our team's up to bat he's pacin between players. And when I'm on the mound he's behind the plate just about beggin me to strike this or that fellow out.

Guess I only ever knew the man that wanted to play and today I met the man who wanted to win.

But all that tension works some kind of magic because we ain't never played a game like we did today. I shut them out for three innings straight and they leave us with men stranded on base. Miss Ellie Jane just keeps the 0's on the scoreboard. Then they get a couple lucky hits off me and Mr. Duke and them Vick brothers hammer three in a row and the next thing I know we're all tied up with numbers.

And then it's about to be over. Last inning. All tied up. When we flip the coin right at the start our team gets last bats. Somethin that gives Mr. Duke the only smile I'd seen on him all day.

First up, one of them Vick brothers gets thrown out at first. Then the other one goes down swingin.

Then it's my turn.

After all these games and all this time I still hate gettin up to bat. Cause I still ain't never got a hit.

That red-headed high school boy is pitchin and any other time I know he'd step out and walk me. But before he throws his first pitch that pasty-faced stranger comes in from first base and trades him out. His buddy's the one been catchin and I step out so they can take a few practice throws.

That's when Mr. Duke calls me back over to the bench.

Now listen, he says, crouchin down real low to look me straight in the face. You hear that bat hit that ball you just drop that stick and run.

I ask him, How do I know if I hit it far enough?

And he just laughs and says, You'll know.

So I get up to the plate and that flat-faced pitcher throws one real high and I'm up on my toes tryin to chop at it. Behind me I hear Mr. Ned say, Streeiike One! the way he does in that goosey voice of his and I wish I could beat myself over the head with this bat for takin such a stupid swing.

The next one though is just perfect and I know why I hear these fellows talkin about hittin the Sweet Spot because when the ball hits that stick just right there's nothin better. It goes flyin up, up—what the Duke would call a real moonshot—high and deep. The sky's lookin a little purple because evenin is about to fall and the sight of that pearl flyin against it is just about the prettiest thing I've ever seen. So I just stand there lookin until Duke tells me, Run! You blamed fool! Go!

And just like that I'm off like a shot truckin down to first base listenin to all them town people screamin my name, every one of them yellin, Go two! And I don't even think about slowin down at first base cause that man is just standin on his bag, glove out and ready. But out of the corner of my eye I can see the outfield scramblin around so I just touch first and head down the line. The second baseman is starin me down thinkin he

*might crowd me out but I ain't never been one to scare off so
easy.*

*But as soon as I get past second there's a change. All them
players on the field are talkin now. The ball's up in play and
they're gunnin for me. I slow down in the baseline thinkin I
might just go back and shore up at second. Everybody's yellin my
name half of them tellin me to run! The rest tellin me to go back!
The other players are screamin too, callin out plays and shoutin,
Fire it in!*

*Somehow through all that noise and mess I hear Duke's
voice. I guess it comes across so clear because he's not really
shoutin at all. Not loud and frantic anyway. He's standin just
in front of our bench and kind of wavin his hand tellin me,
Come on son. Just go for home.*

*I figure he must see somethin goin on behind me but I can't
waste any more time lookin so I pick up my speed, gettin ready to
take that final turn. Then just as I'm roundin third I hear the
sound of the ball landin in somebody's glove and all the heat and
hurt's behind me. If I turn back I'll be out for sure so the only
choice is to keep on runnin.*

*The catcher's up and a pile of dust is spreadin so high I can't
be sure where I am but I figure if I just keep on goin forward,
runnin straight, I'll make it home.*

*Duke's voice is right in my ear tellin me, Keep goin! I think
I hear the ball flyin past my head as the third baseman throws it
to the catcher. Duke is tellin me, Slide! and it never occurs to me
not to obey. I drop right then, no more control over my body
than if somebody'd tied a rope to my boots and yanked me those
last few feet. There's a blur as I speed past that catcher and he*

must have had that ball gripped pretty tight in his glove but I never felt a single stitch of it.

The dust clears a bit and I open my eyes, starin straight up at Mr. Ned whose arms are open wide like some kind of welcomin angel.

Safe! he says, and Duke picks me up on his shoulders paradin me all over the park like I was the newest soul in heaven.

Later that night Duke, Ned, and me sit drinkin Coca-Cola in the moonlight and I'm thinkin that I ain't never had a day more perfect than this. And Duke tells me, Morris this could be your whole life.

And I say, I can't believe that.

He says, Maybe not right now. That I might have to work for it a bit. Maybe sweepin up or cuttin grass. But he thinks I can do it. He thinks it'll happen. And all I have to do is want it.

I stop and think. Do I? And I don't know. What I want most of all is for the dream to find me and it never will if I don't let myself be where it'll land.

So I say, Yes Mr. Duke. I want it.

And he slaps me on the back like I'm a man as big as him and tells me we're leavin in the mornin.

ELLIE JANE

Ellie Jane was stirring the oatmeal when she heard the knock on the door. Well, *knock* might not be the best word for the sound emanating from the parlor.

Pop sat at the table, reading his paper. "Who in the world?" He slammed it on the table as he stood.

Whoever was on the front porch seemed determined to pound on wood and glass equally until someone from the Voyant house— or anyone from the Voyant neighborhood—saw fit to let him in.

Ellie Jane dropped the spoon into the pot, turned the flame down under the burner, and ran out of the kitchen, close on her father's heels. The two of them collided with Duke at the foot of the stairs. He was already fully dressed—unusual for this time of the morning.

When they reached the door, Duke and Ellie Jane stepped back and allowed her father to do the honors. He'd barely turned the knob when the door burst open, and a familiar person spilled inside.

It was that man Darnell, the one who had made such a scene at the town's first game, every bit as wild-eyed as he'd been that evening.

"Where's the boy?" He tried to push past Pop, but the older man held his ground and kept Darnell at bay with little more than an outstretched hand.

"Now you just hold on there a minute."

"You!"

Ignoring, or oblivious to, her father's stature, Darnell lunged for Duke, grabbing his shirt front and hauling him close to his dark, worn face.

Pop wedged himself between the two while Ellie Jane stood back, unable to be angry with this intrusion.

"Darnell," her father spoke with authority, "you need to calm yourself down and tell us what this is all about, or you're going to find yourself in trouble again."

"Ask him." He practically spat in Duke's direction.

All eyes turned to Duke, and Ellie Jane watched his face change from surprise, to realization, to something that looked like fear.

"He's not here," Duke said. "Yet."

"You a liar!"

Ellie Jane moved to close the front door, lest Darnell's shouts wake whoever might still be sleeping in the neighborhood. Pop continued to stand between the two men, like a schoolmaster holding two scrapping boys at bay. "Now, Duke? What do you mean *yet*?"

"This fool say he's goin' ta take Morris away."

"Take him away?" Ellie Jane spoke up, feeling compelled to speak on Morris's behalf. "What is he talking about?"

"Back to Chicago," Duke said simply. "With me. Today."

She wasn't sure what part of Duke's statement was most shocking. "Today?"

Even her father seemed surprised, and that didn't happen often.

Duke avoided their eyes, busying himself straightening his cufflinks and sleeves. "I checked with Coleman at the station. There's an eight-o'clock train."

"And you thinkin' he's yo' boy now, ain't you?"

"I never thought—"

"Well, he done tol' his mama last night he wasn't goin' to go wit' you. She cried and cried and he swore he wouldn't never leave. So, sorry, Mr. Duke man. Looks like you lost your own personal nig—"

"Stop it!" Ellie Jane could have slapped him. "Don't you say such things about that child. Or about him." She came along Duke's side. "Now, Mr. Dennison, this man is simply worried about Morris. Where do you think he might be?"

"Maybe at the station?" Pop's deep voice offered a soothing touch of calm.

"I asked him to come by here first," Duke said. "But maybe—"

"Nope," Darnell said, keeping his eyes narrowed on Duke. "Just came by there. Besides, he ain't goin' away, so he got no need to go to the station."

Her father reached for his hat on the rack by the door. "Still, Darnell, let's you and I go look for him." He turned to Ellie Jane. "You two stay here in case he shows up."

As he was being hustled out the door, Darnell turned and pointed a long, dark finger at Duke. "If anythin' happens to that boy, so help me I'll—"

"I'm sure he's fine," Pop said. "Now let's go find him."

After the door closed behind them, the room seemed doubly silent. Ellie Jane and Duke stood deep within it for a few minutes before Ellie Jane said, "Come on. Let's wait in the kitchen."

"Might as well. Doesn't look like I'm going to make that train."

The oatmeal had turned into something not even she could justify, so she simply poured them each a cup of coffee—real coffee, no less—and sat down, prepared to listen.

First, without a word, he handed her the telegram.

"When did you get this?"

"Yesterday."

"This says you've got a few more days."

"Yeah. Well, things can change pretty quickly."

"Is it something to do with those two men?"

He wrapped both hands around his cup. "They were here looking for me."

"Oh, my goodness. Duke, are you in trouble with the law?"

"Nothing quite so simple."

"Then what is it?"

"What it is, is a long story."

Ellie Jane rested her elbow on the table, her hand on her chin. "So tell me. I love a good story. Dave always tells the best, and since he's not here, it's up to you to play big brother and keep me entertained."

When Duke looked up at her, something in his face turned him into a man she hadn't seen before. His eyes, always deep brown, were flat and dead—nearly black. And they seemed to be weighted down, pulled to the table or the coffee or his hands in front of him. Never to her. He didn't look at her once as he launched into his story.

She wasn't prepared for the outpouring to follow. Just as the man across the table from her now seemed a stranger, the tale he told revealed a man she didn't recognize. A dark, disturbed, violent man—someone so foreign to the charming, debonair stranger she'd brought into her home, he seemed almost mythical.

"That wasn't you, Duke." She reached across the table and placed her hand on his, trying to still the shaking that reappeared after such a long absence. "That was the drink."

"It was me, all right." His eyes were dark. "I've been rotten all my life. The drink just set it loose."

"You can't believe that."

"No reason to believe anything else, Ellie." He used her familiar name, the name her father and brother called her. "Never heard anything else."

"Well, I'm telling you something else. You're a good man."

He looked at their grasped hands. "How can you say that? After…what I did to you."

"It's forgiven." She gave his fingers one last squeeze before letting go. "And forgotten."

Duke raised one devilish eyebrow. "Forgotten?"

"Almost completely." She let a little bit of the devil come through her own voice, knowing the temptation was conquered and gone. Those moments locked away in a warm memory, though she knew he didn't see it in the same rosy glow. "Is that part of why you want to leave? To get away from…" She didn't want to dangle the budding love between her and Ned in front of him, especially if Duke was still burning with desire for her.

"No," he said with a chuckle that knocked her down to a more respectable peg. "It was them two. I just had a feeling they meant trouble. And if they followed me here, they'd follow me away."

"That's very noble of you, Mr. Dennison."

He grinned sheepishly. "Either that or I'm a dang coward. Not wanting to face them alone."

"Oh, you're hardly alone. I think it's safe to say you've won the affection of the entire town."

"And you?"

"Me?"

"Are you going to miss me?" There was no hint of flirtation in his question, none of his usual guile or conceit.

"We both will."

"You and Ned?"

She felt herself blush. "I meant me and Pop. You've become quite a part of the family. But I think, yes, he'll miss you too."

The parlor clock chimed the quarter hour. They sat in that certain silence that comes with waiting.

"So," Ellie Jane ventured softly, "are you going to tell me about Morris?"

"What do you mean?"

"He's a child, Duke. He has a home and a mother."

"And Darnell. Don't forget Darnell."

"The point is, you can't just *take* him like some kind of…souvenir."

"Is that what you think? Look, I wasn't much older than him when I left home. Alone. I just thought he's a kid with a lot of talent who could use some help."

"Help?"

"Maybe get him a job with our club for now. Until he's older. Then maybe help get him on a team. Dave says he has some connections. I just figured if somebody could see…"

He seemed so full of pain at this moment and something near loathing. For what, she wasn't sure, until he spoke again.

"I already screwed things up for at least one guy. And who knows? I might have screwed it all up for myself."

"What do you mean?" She held up the telegram. "They're waiting for you to get back."

He stared into his coffee. "I'm scared, Ellie."

"Of what?"

"I've never played without drinking. Never stepped onto a field completely sober."

"You have here."

"It's not the same."

"Why? Because we're just a bunch of small-town nobodies?"

"Partly." He deflected the halfhearted slap she gave to his shoulder. "But because here it didn't matter. Here it's all fun. People enjoy the game."

"And they don't in the big leagues?"

"I didn't. Not always. I guess I just want to take all of this back with me."

"So, you're taking Morris."

He sighed. "I don't want to be alone." He took a quiet sip of coffee, grimaced, and set the cup down. "But I guess you know all about that."

It took a moment for Duke's remark to settle in, and when it did it sprouted thorns. One that pricked at the scabbed-over pain from years of loneliness. Another that pricked at his exposing it again. And somewhere, deep down, a small one at having to acknowledge the role this man at the table had in bringing it to an end.

"You know," she said, mirroring with her own sip, "I was never entirely alone. I had Pop."

"Yeah."

"And I had God."

Up went that eyebrow of his.

"Just remember," she reached out to him again, "if you're ever feeling alone, you can always talk to Him. I spent a lot of nights—"

"Saturday nights?"

"Some, but others too. The point is, I hope you found a little bit of Him here, that you'll take Him with you when you go."

"I went to church one time, Ellie. That doesn't mean I've found God." Duke made a shallow, dark sound, something like a laugh. "Think He knows where Morris is?"

She smiled. "You should go. He loves you, Duke—"

"That's ridiculous."

"No, it's not. We all need somebody. And judging from that Darnell's behavior, Morris will need you there when they find him."

NED

Ned held to the truth that all business proprietors fell into two categories: those who swept their front walk before opening, and those who swept after closing. The exception was Mr. Poplin, who could be found broom in hand throughout the day, but then his patrons were mostly ladies who appreciated the extra step taken to keep dust off of their skirts.

Ned was a morning sweeper, for the sheer reason that his father had been a morning sweeper, and probably his father before him.

And so it was that he was out in front of the feed store, lost in thought in the early morning when he saw an unlikely sight—Floyd Voyant and that man Darnell striding up his street. Darnell walked freely beside the sheriff, so it didn't seem like an official jaunt, but the two had such serious, set faces it wasn't a pleasure stroll either.

"Hey!" Ned leaned the broom against the wall, trotted over to meet the two men, and, with his face and body, asked what the two were doing at this early hour.

Looking for Morris. Floyd's face looked grim.

"He's not at your house?"

You knew?

Ned gave a curt nod and wondered if they'd lain awake most of the night thinking about it too.

He looked straight at Darnell. "Did he come home after the game?"

'Course he came home after the game. The man's face was sneering, as if insulted by the question. *Why you think he wouldn't come home?*

Floyd said something to calm the other man down and communicated the rest. Apparently, Morris wasn't in his bed when his mother woke up in the morning.

Ned checked his watch. "Go to the station. He'll be there."

He ain't leavin'. Darnell was obviously exaggerating his words, either because he knew Ned was deaf, or because he thought Ned was stupid. *His mama said, "No."*

"Then he'll be here to say so." Morris was a good kid. He wouldn't leave Duke waiting and wondering. "Let's go."

He'd somehow assumed the role of leader as the three men made the familiar trek from the feed store to the railroad station. He didn't know if Floyd and Darnell were speaking to each other or not, but he had one constant conversation going on in his head.

Please, Lord. Let him be safe.

And the Lord replied in a voice as clear as any other Ned ever heard.

He is.

When they got to the station, they gathered on the platform, the better to survey the surrounding area. Then, off in the distance, a figure came over the horizon. Small and dark, every bit the size and color of the boy, but not the boy. The figure was still a good way off when Ned could make out the anguished face and the worn dress. The woman wasn't walking; she was marching, pumping her arms and legs like a woman headed for war.

Darnell hopped off the platform and met the woman as she crossed the tracks. The two engaged in an animated conversation. Hands flying, aggressive postures, faces enraged. He remembered Morris's bruised face that Sunday morning after the first game, and his heart sank thinking what fate might be in store for the boy when these two got ahold of him.

Please, Lord. Let me find him.

The pair headed toward the station. For the first time Ned noticed the paper clutched in the woman's hand. As soon as she was close enough, she thrust it out at Floyd.

What does it say?

Floyd unfolded the paper and held it out at arm's length, allowing Ned easy access to read along with him. It was a page torn from a ledger book, the same kind he'd given Morris months before. The handwriting was small and surprisingly elegant.

Dear Mama—

I know I said last night I wasn't goin to go away with Mr. Duke to Chicago. And honest I didn't want to lie. There just wasn't a way to say the truth and make you happy at the same time and I didn't want to have to remember you bein mad at me.

So I'm goin. Not just because of baseball and not because of Mr. Duke. I know no man can make a life for another. It's up to me and the Lord. I've seen what the Lord can do for me here and it ain't enough anymore.

I left you some money in the kitchen jar and I have enough to keep me from bein beholden to anyone. I love you Mama. And I'll make you proud. I'm about to do something grander than I've ever dreamed.

Your son,
Morris

Ned looked at the mother's face while Floyd read the last words of the letter. The battle mask she'd worn earlier cracked and fell away, replaced by animated anger. She snagged the letter out of Floyd's hand.

If I get my hands on that fool, I swear I'll—

Ned stepped down from the platform and bowed his head to pray again, determined more than ever to be the one to find the boy and stand between him and his irate mother. He repeated it over and over, looking up and down the tracks and across the baseball field, which looked a little less like a diamond this morning. It still had all the shape, but without the game, without the people, it seemed to lose its luster.

Its sparkle.

Or did it?

A tiny flash of light caught his attention from the overgrown grass at the edge of the outfield. It marked the official homerun territory or, as Ned liked to call it, Dukeland, because he was the only one in town who had ever hit a ball anywhere near it.

Ned abandoned the gathering at the station and made his way toward the field. The light wasn't any kind of a constant beacon, but an intermittent beckoning glint. As each step drew him nearer, he knew he was coming closer to an answer to his prayer.

And he'd do anything to turn back.

The first thing he saw was the source of the light. A piece of broken glass. Then another, and another—obviously part of what was once a jar, now shattered, with a few coins scattered in the dirt around the shards. Next to it was a battered black journal, pages open to the sun. Ned recognized the old ledger book he'd given away so many months ago. Numbers graced the top of the page showing what was labeled as a day's earnings. The rest of the page was filled with the same graceful script. A dark hand lay open across the words. One folded page had escaped and flapped listlessly.

And worst of all, a clean shirt—white with blue stripes—stained dark with blood.

Ned felt his own blood drain. Every drop of it starting from the top of his head, rushing past his ears, carrying with it any ability to make sense of the scene in front of him.

Dear God in heaven.

He closed his eyes, blocking out the scene, plunging himself into total nothing. He felt numb, cold. He put his hand to his chest and felt it rise and fall with each breath. Beneath his shirt, behind his skin, his heart pounded so strong he could almost feel it.

Then he opened his eyes and walked closer to the boy in the grass. Knelt down beside him and looked for the same signs of life. Begging God to show him a breath. Preparing his touch to feel a heartbeat.

Nothing. The boy was cold and still, his large brown eyes staring straight up into the sky. Ned reached out and touched his fingers to the lids. When he closed them, Morris looked more like a child than Ned ever remembered.

Bring him home, Lord.

He looked over his shoulder and saw that his absence had attracted the attention of the rest of the party. He stood, not so much as to face them, but to delay the inevitable. To put off the moment when the small dark woman in the faded dress would see the image of her son. Because when she did, her face contorted to a shape he'd never seen before. That was the moment Ned knew why God struck him deaf all those years ago.

To spare him from hearing this woman's scream.

She fell straight into Ned's arms, and he went to his knees beneath her slight weight. He'd never felt anything like the ravaging sobs that convulsed through her body. It was like some force was attempting to tear her apart, rip her right out of his arms, and all he could do was hold tighter. Because he knew if he relinquished even a bit, if he moved his fingers just a hair away from where they formed little furrows in her dark skin, she'd be gone. Shredded right in front of him. And who knew? Maybe that's what she'd want, to be dealt the same cruel blow as the child beside her. To open her eyes again and see him, whole, waiting.

But Ned wasn't going to let her go. So he held her. Rocked her the way he imagined she'd rocked Morris a thousand nights before. In his head he spoke softly, whispering promises until she was taking deep, restorative breaths, and her body barely quivered.

But the real hurt—the thing that killed just a little bit of his own soul—was standing just behind the chicken wire backstop. Ned looked over the top of the weeping woman's head and saw Duke, frozen and small.

Oh, Lord. Not yet.

He needed more time. Time to cover the body, or even reposition the boy to something other than the lifeless sprawl left in the weeds. Instead, he watched, helpless, as his friend stepped onto the field, home plate, straight across the mound, over second, slicing through center field, getting smaller with each step. Floyd followed right behind, eyes downcast, hat in hand, preparing himself for something he'd probably seen far too many times.

As soon as they were close enough, Ned uncradled the grieving woman and passed her gently to Floyd, who offered his strong body to her weak one and guided her away from this nightmare.

Then Ned stood between Duke and the boy, hoping to block the worst of the scene, but he couldn't stand there forever. He locked eyes with his friend before taking one sidestep to the left, revealing the worst.

That's when the battles began.

He saw the man struggle to maintain his steel-jawed composure—

a fight he would lose as his body gave over to a series of shudders. Ned fought his own war, one between the desire to reach out to his friend and masculine reserve. That, too, would meet defeat as compassion won over.

The mother of this child had crumpled into Ned's embrace, but Duke would put up a fight, standing rigid when Ned first clamped a hand on his shoulder before collapsing, breath by ragged breath.

After a while, when he sensed Duke's strength returning, Ned released him. The two men stepped away from each other, keeping their eyes trained to neutral ground. When they met again, each told the other the same silent story about the aftermath of a close-scoring baseball game, and the celebration of a town when the form below them had been lifted high.

They saw the round, flat face of a dead-eyed stranger promising them that the game wasn't over even as the Duke Dennison, baseball royalty, told them to get out of town. His town. Their town, where they'd stood, shoulder to shoulder, watching them drive away in the dusk.

They must have had a change of heart.

A third figure joined them and, setting all past skirmishes aside, Ned and Duke shuffled their positions to welcome Darnell into their little fold. It was one of the few times Ned didn't regret not having clear speech. There was nothing to say.

Duke and Darnell, however, seemed to find another way to communicate. His face now eerily stoic, Darnell reached inside the pocket of his oversized pants and produced a small metal flask, which he touched to his lips. He closed his eyes and tilted his head back, taking long, thirsty gulps.

Ned watched Duke become a man possessed of a new hunger. Darnell must have seen it too, because when he was finished with his drink, he solemnly handed the flask over to Duke, who took it and held it before offering it up as a toast and taking his own generous swallow. When he was finished, he stood absolutely still, his eyes tightly closed until Darnell pried Duke's fingers off the flask and offered it to Ned.

Never having been prone to drink, Ned's first instinct was to wave it away, but this was one of those moments when instinct just didn't ring true. He took the flask, repeated the offering, and touched the warm metal opening to his lips. The drink was bitter and awful; he fought to close his throat around a single sip.

When he finished, Ned wiped off the mouth of the flask with his sleeve and handed it back to Darnell, who swirled it a bit, as if gauging just how much was left. Duke pulled out his ever-present money. He opened the clip, pulled off two bills, and handed them over to Darnell.

This should cover it.

Darnell nodded, pocketed the money, and made his way back across the tracks. After a moment's hesitation, and one long last look at the boy, Duke followed.

Ned sank to his knees and closed his eyes, shutting out every bit of this world, and wept. Until he felt a softness at his side, and small arms wrapped around him. He felt his head drawn to a soft cotton breast, and lips warm against his hair.

The only reason he ever wanted to open his eyes again was to see her face.

DUKE

Just one drink. That's what Dr. Keeley had told him. One drink, and he'd be back where he was.

Well, he was there. Not drunk, but wanting to be.

There'd been a moment when he hoped the booze would do its magic. That he'd take a drink and pull a curtain down on everything around him. That he'd forget about the boy who pitched like fire, and he wouldn't care about the boy on the ground.

A lot to ask from one drink.

So he followed Darnell to the source. The same man who was ready to kill him an hour ago. Some people might say that death has a way of bringing people together. Settling differences. But Duke knew better. If there's anyone a drunk loves, it's another drunk. He and Darnell had a bond stronger than any dead kid.

Most of it was a blur. Something about a guy named Eddie who hated white men more than most. So when they got to the house— if such a pile of wood and tin could be called a house—Duke waited outside. Hands in his pockets. Wondering why that boy's mother would want him to stay here.

When Darnell came back outside, he handed Duke a plain glass bottle full of amber liquid. A fine layer of dirt on the glass. A tiny divot in the cork.

"Now you take that and go on back to yo' people."

"I don't have any people."

"Then you just go on wherever you wanna go."

Just as Duke started to walk away, Darnell called him back.

"You keep that bottle hid. Can't have it in town and don't want no trouble comin' back to Eddie. Or me. You done enough here."

Duke dropped the bottle inside the inner pocket of his jacket. Just the weight of it made him feel better.

He walked back to town, thinking that this was the path the boy took every day. One shack after another. Unorganized, puddled roads. Filth and waste, all of it washed gray, even in this morning light. Had Duke ever walked the kid home—even once—and seen all this, he'd never let him come back.

The path he'd taken in brought him right back to the tracks. But he couldn't cross them just yet because a long train was just pulling out. Picking up steam. That was the eight o'clock. He was supposed to be on it. Him and the kid. Looked like they were both left behind.

He crossed over once the train was gone. A small crowd had gathered at the field—people from town. Most of them standing around helpless. The boy's ma sat on the sideline bench, a few women fawning over her. Out in the field, the two Vick brothers carried a long, blanket-draped bundle on a stretcher to their wagon behind the bleachers. Mayor Birdiff himself was in the middle of it all, looking like he'd pulled a pair of pants on over his nightshirt. Marlene and Gustav Geist circulated, pouring coffee into tin cups.

One thing to be said about this town. News traveled fast. He tried to picture his place among the townspeople, but they were milling all over the field, giving no regard to the carefully designated baselines and boundaries. There was nothing for him there.

He kept walking.

Voices called out to him, but their words flew by. He had nothing to say and even less to hear. Not from Ellie Jane. Not from Ned. He wanted to be alone.

Floyd Voyant stepped in the middle of his path. Full of questions. Where'd those men come from? Where were they headed? What were their names? Each question more useless than the one before. Still, Duke looked at Floyd and saw him as a man he'd never seen before. Taller, if possible. Star blazing on his jacket. Authority and power and hope. Floyd placed his hands on Duke's shoulders and leaned in close.

"I'm getting some men together. We're going to take care of this."

"It's all my fault." Duke hated the weakness in his voice. The catch and the helpless closing of his throat. "They came here for me."

"Well, they didn't get you, did they? And there's got to be a reason for that."

"What reason?"

"God only knows, son. But He does."

Floyd engulfed him in a hug and walked away, joining old Mr. Shiner and his son. The three bent their heads together, then left, moving with a common purpose.

Duke had a purpose too. In his pocket. Just waiting for him.

But not yet.

He found himself at the corner of Park and Green. Turn left, and he'd be on his way to Ned's place. Straight ahead, home. The Voyants'. He couldn't go there. All that velvet and carpet and that constant ticking clock. Instead, he cut straight from the corner. First to third; second to home. Through the park with constant green grass under his feet. Trees over his head. Until he found the bench. His bench—sitting here just as it had been that day. The day he decided to change the kid's life.

It was empty now, as it had been then, and he sat down, the bottle in his pocket making a reassuring *thud* against the slats. At that time he hadn't noticed the church. Right in front of him. Five little steps leading to two wooden doors. Inside, those words.

True. Honest. Just. Pure.

And he was none of those. No matter what Ellie Jane said. Maybe, for a time, he'd been a good man. But that was because of the boy.

Alone, he was worthless, no matter how much gold flowed through his blood.

PART 9

THAT'S THE
BALL GAME

ELLIE JANE

She touched her ear to the door and knocked.

"Mr. Dennison? Duke? Are you awake?"

It was a scene reminiscent of his first days in their home; nothing but silence coming from the other side.

"Duke!" She knocked louder. "The service starts at ten o'clock." Pause, nothing. "There's coffee made."

She pressed her ear closer and managed to pull away just as she heard the amplified sound of the turning knob. She had to grab the doorframe to keep from falling through.

"I'm not going."

She was grateful to have something to hold on to once he appeared in the doorway. His hair hung lank over the side of his pallid face. His mouth was slack; his eyes, empty. He wore the same clothes he'd worn the day before, and they had the appearance of damp rags that had been left to dry on his sagging frame. Never—not after an afternoon of working to build the field or at the end of an eleven-inning game—had she seen him looking like this. He looked like someone had crumpled him up and dropped him in the room.

"Not like that, you're not," Ellie Jane said, once she absorbed the shock of his appearance. "We still have an hour before we need to leave, so wash up and shave. Do you need anything pressed?"

"Stop that. You can't just get all chipper and chatty with me and send me on my way."

"I just thought—"

"Well, don't—" He balled his hand into a fist and pressed his knuckles right between his eyes. He filled himself with one deep breath, exhaled it, and took his hand away. He raked his fingers through his hair, restoring some semblance of his slick style. He flashed a smile that almost reached his eyes, and even his skin seemed to lose the edge of its pallor.

"I'm sorry," he said, a new calm to his voice. "I didn't sleep well last night."

"None of us did," Ellie Jane said, relieved at his transformation. "But I'm sure if you'll take a bath and have some breakfast, you'll feel much better. I'd be happy to fix something for you."

His vest hung open over his stained, rumpled shirt, and he produced his gold watch from its pocket. He snapped it open with a flourish, making Ellie Jane wonder if he knew what a parody of dapperness he presented.

"Don't bother." He dropped the watch back in the pocket. "I still have time to get something at Marlene's."

That slight movement sent something wafting between the two of them. She couldn't tell if the sourness came from his skin or his clothes or his breath, but she tried not to wrinkle her nose as she leaned forward.

"No, you can't," she said, craning to look behind him. Maybe it was coming from the room itself. "She's closed the diner for the day so she can help with the food at the memorial service."

"Well, that's a shame." He shifted his weight, reaffirming his presence, and began to inch the door closed. "I'll get something later."

"Duke, wait." She wedged her toe against the door. "You've got to go. People will be expecting—"

"I don't make decisions based on what people expect from me."

"Oh, really?" She leaned in close to get a whiff of his breath. It was sour and unpleasant, but as far as she could tell, not suspicious. "People expected you to stop drinking, and you did."

"Yes," he said, looking just past her eyes. "And people are expecting me to be back on the ball field day after tomorrow. So if you don't mind, I have some packing to get done."

There was no toe or foot or body big enough to hold the door open after that. In fact, it closed right over the corner of Ellie Jane's good black silk skirt. She tried to tug it free, and rather than risk tearing it, she pounded on the door again, insisting that he open it long enough to free her. When he did, she made one more plea.

"Duke, please. Even for just an hour. We owe it to the family—"

"Do you honestly think going to a funeral will give back to that family what I took from them?"

"It's not a funeral. It's a—"

"Listen, Ellie. If I thought for a minute it would make a difference. That it would bring him back…"

His voice trailed off, and the two stood in silent, stilted grief. She'd run out of things to say. Instead, Ellie Jane took advantage of Duke's moment of weakness and stepped through the door, into his room, and straight into his body. She wrapped her arms around his waist and laid her head against his chest. It was, at first, like holding a straight-backed chair, but soon enough he softened against her and tightened his own embrace.

It was nothing like the moments she spent in his arms that night a lifetime ago. She felt no temptation to do anything other than hold him, like she would any other wounded soul, and it was clear he harbored none of his previous passion.

Tears welled up in her eyes, and she allowed them to seep unchecked into his shirt and wondered if the raggedness of his

breath meant he was crying too. It occurred to her then that, despite
his bluster, Duke was every bit the little boy that Morris had been,
and she held him even closer.

When the front doorbell rang the first time, neither moved. It
wasn't until the second ring that Ellie Jane said, "That must be Ned,"
before easing away from his embrace. At the third ring, they were
standing an arm's length apart, holding each other's hands. His were
cold and damp, and he seemed desperate not to let her leave.

"I have to—" She stopped, midtug. "Oh, Duke. No."

Amidst the chaos of the room, the open luggage spilling over
with half-folded clothes, a bottle sat on the writing desk, morning
sunlight glinting off the amber liquid.

Duke dropped her hands and put his own in his pockets.

"I haven't touched a drop of it, Ellie."

Her head filled with a million things to say—warnings and reprimands and all kinds of chastisement. In the end, though, all she
could think to say was, "Not in my house, Duke."

The bell rang again. Free, she turned on her heel and ran out of
the room, down the stairs, and straight for the door. She flung it
open to reveal Ned standing—tall and clean.

"Good morning," he said, but his smile didn't last the time it
took Ellie Jane to usher him across the threshold.

She pointed upstairs. "It's Duke."

Ned indicated that he would go talk to him, but as he headed
for the stairs, Ellie Jane heard the water running in the upstairs bathroom. Perhaps Duke had changed his mind.

"Come help me in the kitchen first." She took Ned's hand to
lead him away, pleased with how natural the gesture felt. Happier,
still, with how eager he seemed to follow.

Once through the swinging door, Ellie Jane donned an apron

and nodded toward the chair where she wanted Ned to sit. She placed a wedge of sharp cheddar cheese in front of him along with a bowl and a grating box and instructed him to get to work. Meanwhile, Ellie Jane drained a jar of olives and sat at the table with him, chopping them fine on a small wooden cutting board.

After a few minutes of busy silence, Ned asked if Ellie Jane had heard anything from her father.

She shook her head. "No." Pop had assembled a group of deputized men, including the Vick brothers; they'd been given Mayor Birdiff's personal touring car to track down the suspected murderers Peach and Ray.

"We just want to talk to them." Her father eyed the guns each man had brought to the house.

That was yesterday, just after noon, just as Mr. Poplin was delivering a new, clean shirt to Picksville's undertaker.

She didn't share all of this with Ned who, she was sure, would have loved to have been part of the posse, but instead opted to stay home and be a friend to Duke. Right now, she was glad for that decision. How nice it was not to be alone—not only for this pleasant moment looking at him across the table, but also knowing about the man upstairs, newly reverted to a stranger, and the memory of the bottle sitting in the sunlight.

She wondered how she would tell him, or if she should at all. There was already so much ugliness. She would keep these few minutes, pouring her energy into making her special cheese-and-olive spread sandwiches, keeping her conversation with Ned a series of soft smiles.

They worked in such sweet tandem: she mixed the grated cheese and chopped olives with a bit of mayonnaise dressing; he sliced the bread—perfectly thin—and arranged the assembled sandwiches artfully on the tray. He even took one for himself, nibbling a corner before finishing it off in two great bites, then helping himself to coffee.

Ellie Jane was covering the pile of sandwiches with a sheet of waxed paper and her prettiest tea towel when Duke breezed into the kitchen, bringing with him a fresh scent of shaving soap and skin cream. He'd managed to pull a clean, pressed shirt and dark trousers from his bags.

"Think I'll take you up on that coffee, Miss Voyant." His voice was new and robust. He rubbed his hands together like a man ready to dive into a grand adventure and blew across the floor, heading straight for the cups hanging on hooks on the wall. He tossed a "Morning, Ned" over his shoulder as he poured, impressing Ellie Jane with his newfound control.

"So have you changed your mind, then?" Ellie Jane untied her apron.

"No." He took a sip, made the same face he always made at her coffee, then sipped again before turning on his heel and leaving.

She wasn't about to go after him, not with Ned sitting right there at the table. Instead, she threw her hands up in frustration and tossed her apron onto the back of the chair.

"What was that about?" Ned stood and drew her face up to look at him.

"He won't go to the service."

Ned's eyes softened. "It can be hard for a man to show his grief."

"It isn't hard for you."

He smiled. "Maybe I'm more of a man."

She laughed and went to her toes to plant a soft kiss on his cheek before speaking directly into his ear. "You're more man than I ever imagined."

"Do you think I should talk to him?" Ned asked as she returned to her feet.

"There's one other thing." She busied herself folding and smoothing the tossed apron. "I'm worried that he might be drinking again. There's a bottle upstairs. And he's so upset. And if he would just talk to someone—"

Ned gently tugged at her chin, his eyes searching.

Ellie Jane took a deep breath and, bound by a loyalty she didn't understand, said, "I'm afraid. For him."

NED

He spent more than a few minutes pounding on Duke's door to no avail, and when he spied Ellie Jane on the upstairs landing, he gave up, pronounced that Duke was a man who would have to live with his own decision. That's when Ellie Jane shooed him downstairs, and now he stood in the middle of the parlor, holding a tray of sandwiches, waiting for her to get her hat.

There was a hitch in his spirit as he stood there, a heart-wrenching guilt for feeling contentment in the wake of such tragedy, but he couldn't remember when he'd last felt like he was at home. Not because of the parlor—the upholstered furniture, the bookcases, the drapes—but the idea of belonging. He looked around and wondered if he'd want to live the rest of his life here.

Before he could formulate an answer, a movement at the top of the stairs caught his eye. Funny how he always knew just where to look for her, whether in town, in church, or in her own home. Now there she was, her black lace glove poised on the polished banister as she made her way down. Her hair was topped with a complicated mass of black silk and feathers, with a tiny bit of netting draped over one eye, but with each step, his vision of her changed. He could imagine her black-and-gray striped blouse replaced by ivory silk, her little black purse a spring bouquet.

He knew, then and there, that he would marry her. He waited six years for her to look at him, but he wouldn't wait that long again. Now that he had her, he would wait—until after the funeral, until after Duke was gone, until her father returned to grant his blessing. He'd wait until he had her back, and then he'd never let her go.

She walked right up to him and laid her hand on his arm. *Are you ready?*

"Yes, my love," he said, immeasurably pleased at her smile.

They walked together, Ned conscious of matching his stride to hers. The neighborhood streets were empty at this midmorning hour, and he noticed more than one front-room curtain parting as they walked by.

Ellie Jane tugged on his arm. *It's like our own Promenade.*

"Well, then," he said, not missing a step, "I'll call for you at six."

Not tonight. Her eyes were full of apology. And worry. *I want to stay home and wait for Pop.*

"Then maybe I'll just come and sit with you."

She gave his arm a squeeze, and they continued on. Glancing down he could see that she was talking. And talking. Her lace-covered hands flitted around, and though he couldn't hear her words, he knew what she was talking about, because he was thinking the same thing. That there wouldn't be a game tonight—maybe never again. That those long, easy evenings on the field were a bright flash in the town's life, and with one star fallen and the other shooting himself away, it would be awhile before anyone would wish to meet at the bleachers and choose up teams.

In fact, he was dreading that moment at the intersection of Green and Park when a glance to the left would reveal the corner of the unassuming railway station, the little octagonal booth, and the corner of the chicken wire backstop. He found himself slowing his steps even more, and Ellie Jane slowing with him until, at some point, they were stopped, and he followed the line of her lace-covered finger as it pointed.

There were six of them, boys dressed in patched-up play clothes and caps. One on the mound, one at the plate, two at the corners, and two in the outfield. A wobbly throw, a valiant swing, and a soft bouncing grounder making its way lazily to second. Then a change of positions, a new batter up. He wondered what rules they'd devised for themselves, but it didn't matter. He took a moment to wish they'd been here before, on a sunny day when Morris could have joined in, then offered thanks to God for a vision of life. Of new beginnings.

He shifted the weight of the sandwich tray to one arm, offering the other to Ellie Jane, and on they walked, past the station, past the booth, skirting the field, and over the tracks. Ned was no stranger to this part of town, but he doubted Ellie Jane had much experience maneuvering its narrow dirt paths. Floyd had given him directions to the house Morris shared with his mother, and it was there that the friends and family would gather after the services. He steered them toward it and knew he was at the right house when he saw the tiny, sideways shack overflowing with people.

They were Morris's people, mostly, all dressed in their best clothing. But there were a few townspeople too. Besides Marlene and Gustav, he saw Mr. Poplin and Mr. Samms, Old Mr. Shiner, and some woman he didn't know. She stood out among the others, not merely for the color of her face, but for the amount of paint she'd smeared over it.

A large black woman broke from the crowd and made her way toward them. She took the plate of sandwiches, saying, *Thank you,* without looking either of them in the eye. The mournful mother was nowhere to be seen; neither was the unpleasant Darnell. Ned supposed they were already at the church, and by some command, the crowd began a unified pilgrimage to join them there.

It was just a matter of a block or so, but the slow-moving passage of so many shuffling feet made the journey a long, somber one. Nothing like the veneer of comfort he'd felt walking alone with Ellie Jane. She hadn't let go of his arm since he'd offered it to her, and she clutched it tighter and tighter with each step. She spoke to no one, but kept her eyes fixed straight ahead.

The church was just a slightly larger version of every house they passed on the way to it. Plain, white clapboard with a modest cross mounted at the top. The double doors were wide open. Ned, Ellie Jane, and the people from town held back and let the others file in. He couldn't imagine they'd all fit, but somehow person after person disappeared through the doors, and when it was their time to follow, he and the others filed neatly into the last rows and sat down.

Craning his neck above those seated in front of him, Ned could just make out the narrow white coffin at the front of the room. The open lid revealed the outline of Morris's face, soft brown outlined against white silk. Other people he'd seen in death—his mother, his father—looked so different than they had in life. But not Morris. He'd always been a child of peace, and now he looked simply asleep.

A large, impressive-looking man stood at the front of the church and immediately bowed his head in prayer. Ned did too, closing his eyes and opening his heart in agreement with all these people around him. He didn't open his eyes until he felt Ellie Jane's gentle nudge, and that's when he saw the mother, leaning heavily on the arm of another woman, making her way up the aisle. She went immediately to the coffin, touched her son's face, and allowed herself to be led to a seat in the front row.

Then, something broke loose.

It started with the minister at the front—Bishop Tilley, as was recorded on the attendance board on the front wall. Ned could not follow his words, as he didn't establish his spot on the floor behind a pulpit like Reverend Porter did. Instead, he paced the length of the room, back and forth in front of the casket, up and down the aisles. He held an unopened Bible in one hand, which he pounded and waved intermittently. He spoke to the heavens and he spoke to the people, his mouth a continuous flashing white beacon.

Soon the crowd was a little brown rolling sea. Faces raised, hands lifted up. He saw their mouths moving along with him—not in unison, like a congregation engaged in a hymn, but seemingly random utterances.

He looked to Ellie Jane for some explanation.

Amen, she said. *Praise God. Morris is home.*

And then he realized he was sitting in the midst of praise. He knew, of course, of Morris's faith, but to see it played out in front of him was something to behold. Slowly the vestiges of sadness he'd carried with him since finding that small, broken body in the field transformed to something new, and he felt something akin to joy ready to burst forth.

One glance beside him showed Ellie Jane standing at the edge of the same fervor. Tears streamed down her face, yet she wore a rapturous smile.

He saw the same expression echoed in face after face, and he wondered if these people even knew all about the life they were celebrating. That Morris had been a familiar, trusted soul. That he'd had goals and dreams and skill. That he'd touched the heart of a giant and brought together the lives of two lonely people.

Ned had no idea how long the actual service lasted, but when Bishop Tilley yielded the floor to the crowd and they began to line up to pay their respects at the casket, he tugged at Ellie Jane's arm and, exhausted, they exited out the back of the church.

They were joined by Mr. Poplin and Mr. Samms, who indicated they needed to return to their businesses. Mr. Shiner and the mysterious woman soon followed, looking equally bewildered. When Mr. Shiner offered his arm, she took it eagerly, hungrily, and the two staggered off together down the path, narrowly avoiding a collision with a boy running toward them.

Miss Voyant?

Ned recognized the boy from church—the nondescript middle son of the Ohio family. He ran up now, holding out a familiar-looking envelope.

A telegram.

The boy held his hand open long after Ellie Jane took the envelope. *Ain't you gonna give me a tip?*

Ned dug into his pocket and produced three pennies, which he dropped into the outstretched pink palm. The boy scowled at the coins and stood there, expectantly, before closing them up in his fist and thrusting them into his pocket.

Without anything close to a *Thank you,* the boy turned and shuffled off.

With a shaking hand, Ellie Jane gave the telegram to Ned.

I can't.

He opened the envelope and took out the small yellow paper. It was from Dave Voyant, and it was short.

`Pop called. He got them.`

Ned showed the telegram to Ellie Jane and waited for her to look pleased. Instead, a softness came to her face, and she shook her head slowly.

Those poor, awful men.

Ned tried to drum up some sympathy for the guys who were now at the mercy of Picksville's imposing sheriff, but none came. He took Ellie Jane's arm and led her in a slow, easy stroll. "I wish Duke would have been here."

Ellie Jane stopped in the middle of the dusty street. *I'm worried.*

"It'll take some time—"

No. She formed her hand around an invisible flask and motioned it to her lips.

"He's drunk?"

Not yet… But she looked so helpless, and despite the near pure joy he'd experienced inside the little church, anger sparked deep within his gut.

"Come on."

This time when he took her arm it was meant to hurry her along with his stride as he retraced their steps back to town. The nerve of Duke, bringing that ugliness into Ellie Jane's life—into her home. The man was dangerous enough sober; Ned couldn't imagine what he'd be capable of after taking a few drinks.

But that wasn't exactly true. Of course he could imagine it. In fact, he didn't have to imagine it. He knew.

DUKE

He closed the last latch on the final suitcase and looked around the room. Neat as a pin. Just as he'd found it. Like he'd never been here at all.

Except for the bottle, still untouched but still there.

There wouldn't be a train to get him out of here until Monday, but he couldn't stay in this house. Leave it to Dave Voyant to stick him in the one town without a hotel. Never mind. He'd stay with Ned. Should have gone there a long time ago. Ever since they started building the field together. Or at least since the first game. Then he could have had a little peace and quiet in his life, away from her endless chattering.

He lifted one bag off the bed and tested its weight. Heavy, yes. But not impossible. He lifted the second one and tried to take a step. He might be able to make it across the room, but he'd never make it as far as Ned's.

He'd have to find somebody to send back for them.

But he wouldn't need much for one night at Ned's. He took the smallest of his bags—a soft leather satchel filled with his toiletries—and tossed in a couple of clean shirts. He picked up the satchel, put on his cap, and stared at the bottle. All he'd have to do is walk away. Walk off and leave it sitting right on the table. No need to pour it over the balcony. Just go to Ned's and let her dump it out.

Easy.

But then again he was strong enough to hold on to it this long. He could last one more day. Besides, if he left it here, he'd be tempted to come back.

And he couldn't come back.

So he picked it up, felt the heft of it in his hand, and put it in his pocket.

Now he could go.

Duke walked downstairs, out the front door, and through the little iron gate at the end of the walkway. There were people on the street he'd come to know as neighbors, and they offered weak, sympathetic smiles and halfhearted waves as he passed. Mrs. Finneworth came running off her front porch and actually grabbed his sleeve as he passed, saying she was so, so sorry about that little Negro boy.

He said something back to her. Some sort of mumbled charm. Enough to make her say, "God bless you, Mr. Dennison," before returning to her potted plants.

God bless him indeed.

The town was strangely quiet for a Saturday, and when he got to the corner of Park and Green, he heard a sound as familiar to him as any other. A bat hitting a ball. A boy calling a play.

He should turn right. Head up Park Street to Ned's place, but he had to see. Even though he knew—*knew* it wasn't the kid. His kid. Someone was playing the game. So he took the well-worn path and saw the chicken wire backstop looming through the haze in his head.

They were just kids, hitting a ball around. Scrambling a few plays. No rules, no winner. Nothing but the joy of hitting and throwing. Running and catching.

He wanted to go sit on the bleachers and watch, but already he felt the burning at the back of his throat. One more minute and he'd need to either cry or drink.

He turned right and headed for Ned's.

The door to the store was locked and a sign hung in the window saying Closed: Memorial Service. Duke went around to the back and climbed the stairs to the apartment. He'd never been here before, but he figured this door wouldn't be locked. He was right.

It was a tidy, functional front room. Duke dropped his satchel on the table, pulled out a chair, and sat down. The weight of the bottle pulled on his pocket, so he lifted it out and set it on the table in front of him. Then he pushed it away. An arm's length and a bit more.

He was shrugging off his jacket when he felt it. The sleeplessness of the night before. Everything hurt. His back, his eyes, his head. Somewhere beyond this little kitchen room, there had to be a bed, a couch, something. But his legs suddenly weighed a thousand pounds. He folded his arms on the table and buried his head in his clean, starched sleeves.

He should have gone to the church. There had to be a reason people went there when they felt like this. But this hard wooden chair in this bare room was the closest he was going to get today.

"Listen, God." He spoke straight into the table. Tears gathered in his eyes. They trickled along his face, gathering at the corners of his moustache. He thought about that long-ago day, the minister putting a wafer on his tongue, a swallow of wine, and he hoped that was enough to make him be heard. "Floyd says You have a reason. And I need to know. So You have to tell me. Either that," he reached his hand out, almost enough to touch the bottle, "or I've got to just forget it. The only way I know how. 'Cause I won't be able to stand not knowing."

And he waited. Closed his eyes and brought himself to darkness.

⏎

Pounding. The sound of glass on wood. Vibrating through his skull.

"It's gonna kill you this time, Duke."

That voice. Ned's voice. Like something coming from the bottom of a well. Or the bottom of a bottle.

Duke lifted his head and tried to make sense of where he was. The room was full of afternoon shadows; he must have been asleep for hours. He sat up straight, grimacing at the series of clicks down his neck and back.

"Is that what you want?" Ned pulled out another chair and sat across the table.

"I should be dead already."

"What does that mean?"

But he couldn't explain. How he'd spent so many nights in such oblivion it felt like a miracle itself to see another day. How he had entire days—weeks even—that he couldn't remember. How he'd met a guy intent on revenge, and he let an innocent kid get in his way. So when Ned asked him again, he just looked his friend in the eye and told him to shut up.

"I'm not going to let you kill yourself, Duke." Although Ned made no move to touch the bottle. "You're a good man."

"It should have been me." He stretched his mouth, exaggerating every word.

"No. You're—"

Duke grabbed a handful of Ned's shirt, ready to pull him over the table. "Don't say that again. Morris. *He* would have been a good man. I'm nothing."

Ned remained absolutely placid until Duke released his grip. "Do you know where Morris is?"

"I couldn't go."

"Not his body. But *Morris*." Ned made his sign for Morris's name, his hand curled—three fingers over his thumb—swirled in front of his mouth. This time, though, he moved his hand in bigger circles. Taking in his face, his head, his heart.

"He's just gone," Duke said. "I saw him. Spilled out."

"No, he isn't." Ned lifted his head, looking straight beyond the ceiling. He made his hands into sharp planes and moved them, an invisible stairway, one above another and another. "He's in heaven. And do you know what heaven is?"

Duke opened his mouth to answer, but Ned interrupted.

"Heaven is the big league." He popped his fingers wide on *big*, then narrowed one hand to point one finger. "And you, my friend, are not ready. That's why God took Morris. Gives you another inning."

Not ready. Not ready to die. He'd been ready to die since he was fourteen years old. Before that his ma and pa had been ready to kill him. Before that, out on the streets, nobody much cared which side he was on. Ned thinks the booze will kill him? Only if he was lucky. One long, forgetful black sleep. He'd been ready for that his whole life.

"You don't know *anything* about me."

"Really?" Ned reached across the table and picked up the bottle. Then he stood to walk out of the room, motioning for Duke to follow.

Duke did and found himself in the only room he'd even been in that he'd ever describe as "cozy." It was warm and light. A long bed with a well-worn quilt in one corner, an enormous leather chair in another. The walls were covered with page after page ripped from newspapers and magazines.

Ned walked around the room, his eyes roaming over the clippings. Every now and then he paused to pull one off the wall, then another and another, until he had a handful of papers to bring over to Duke.

"Here." He thrust them into Duke's grip, and he began to read through them. His name. Over and over.

Dennison Hits a Miracle Triple
Cubs Look to Dennison to Turn Season Around
Dennison Pulls Through in a Clinch

And there were others too.

Dennison a No-Show at Training
Dennison Thrown Out After Third Base Brawl

Then Ned, still clutching the bottle, began digging through a box, pulling out card after card. He flung them to the floor, and Duke stared down, seeing his own image looking up at him a dozen times over. Duke in a batter's stance. Duke with his fist in his glove. Duke with a bat balanced over his shoulders. And he knew what was on the back of those cards. Numbers and letters for everything he ever did in a game. The lies he told for his biography. People kept these, carried around these little pieces of him.

Right now, he hated it.

He took the handful of clippings and threw them onto the floor with the cards. "This isn't me."

Undaunted, Ned headed for a pile of books on a little table next to the comfortable-looking chair and grabbed his copy of *Spalding's Official Base Ball Guide.* "You're on page 86."

"None of that is real."

"Yes, it is! It's just as real as me. And Ellie Jane. And Morris. But you're about to trade it all." He brandished the bottle. "For *this.*"

"Give that to me." And just when Duke thought he would have to grab it out of Ned's hands, he found the bottle offered to him. His fingers closed around the glass, and he already hated himself a little because of it. "I will decide what I'll trade."

The two men stood, breathing hard. The room had lost its appeal.

"I've got to get out of here," Duke said.

"Then come on."

Ned stormed past him, walking right over the pile of clippings and cards, kicking them back in his wake. Duke followed through the sparse front room and down the stairs.

It wasn't Duke's first time in the storeroom, but it was the first he'd seen it so well stocked and clean. The high windows along the west wall let in the afternoon sun. Just enough light to keep the room from being totally black.

Ned motioned for Duke to make his way to the back, and when he was there, told him to sit down, straight on the floor, back against the wall. Then he closed the door and sat down too.

"Now you can drink." If it weren't for the insulating bags of grain lining the shelves, his voice might have echoed. "No one will know. It's just us."

Duke didn't move at first. Instead, he sat watching the dust dancing in the squares of sunlight, breathing deep the smells of wood and canvas and grain. His head rested back against the wall and he thought he might sleep—warm and comfortable as he felt—but the bottle was there, warm in his hand. And slowly, as if hiding from the man in plain sight across the room, he eased the cork out of the mouth and was raising it to his lips when a sudden movement caught his attention. A split second later, responding to years of instinct, his hand reached up. And caught the ball.

Ned's face was one big grin. Duke returned it in kind and threw the ball back.

"Go ahead." Ned tossed the ball up and down. "Take a drink."

But this time Duke was steeled for the catch. His hand itched for it, even as he lifted the bottle. He could smell the whiskey inside and was set to taste it when—*whack!* The stitches on the baseball stung his palm.

"Fool me twice," Duke said. This time, he gripped the ball in one hand while raising the bottle with the other, giving him only a split second to choose when he saw the familiar projectile heading for his face.

He opened his fingers. Heard the glass hit the floor.

"Sorry."

Duke fired both back, amused to see Ned scramble to catch them. Then he set the bottle upright. And corked it.

"Got any plans for the rest of today?" Ned tossed the ball.

"Nope." Duke returned the throw.

"Good." Ned held it, trying different pitching grips. "You can tell me who you really are."

Ned threw; Duke returned; Ned threw.

"You won't be able to understand from way over—"

"I won't be able to understand everything." He raised his hand and caught Duke's throw. "But I'm not the one who needs to hear it."

Duke didn't say anything at first. Just threw the ball back and forth. Played catch like he'd done a million times in his life. But in the gathering shadows, he saw those pictures. Those stories. He thought about all he'd done. All he hadn't. And he thought about Morris, that pure spirit. He wondered if he'd ever been that young. If he'd ever had so much hope. If he'd ever have a chance to get back to the boy he'd never been.

So there, in the patchy light, Duke spoke. A lifetime of confession. Releasing a little more pain with every throw. And a little less with every catch.

Ned never said a word. He was just there, a steady counterpart until the moment came when Duke had nothing more to say. No ugly bit of his life left unspoken. He'd come to the place where he met the boy. Built the field. Played the game and loved it.

Where he'd learned what it was to love someone so much, he wanted to give over his life for him.

After a time, the waning light brought darkness to the storeroom.

No more light for catch.

No more words to say.

He leaned his head back against the wall. Ned had all but disappeared in the darkness, and when Duke closed his eyes, he did. This would have been the time for Duke to feel alone. But there was something within him. A new presence. And for the first time in his life, before he fell asleep, Donald Dennison lifted his voice in prayer.

"Thank You, God. For another day."

And he slept. Deeper and better than he ever remembered. Dreamless and calm. Perfect and still until morning came and Ned stood before him, reaching out his hand. Duke took it and allowed his friend to haul him to his feet.

Ned had a sheepish grin. "I was supposed to call on Ellie Jane last night."

"She's going to hate me." Duke dusted the lingering grain from his rumpled slacks.

"I'll think she'll understand. We'll talk about it after church." He unhooked the latch, slid open the door, and walked outside.

Once again, Duke followed.

The sunlight was new and blinding, but Duke couldn't look away. He lifted his face to it. Soaked it in. Somewhere behind the warmth, Morris stood on the mound, all wound up and waiting.

AUTHOR'S NOTE

Stealing Home started with one rather gruesome image. I was reading a lovely book called *Glove Affairs: The Romance, History, and Tradition of the Baseball Glove* by Noah Liberman and Yogi Berra. In it, an old-time player recalled how, before the use of leather gloves, players' hands would be like "sacks of walnuts" because of all the broken bones incurred while playing the game. I was instantly fascinated by the idea of athletes so dedicated they would play through that kind of pain for very little money. Often, only for the meals provided during the season. That was passion. That was love. That was baseball.

Many, many thanks to those who've run these bases with me:

- First—Thank you, Bill, for being my champion!
- Second—Thank you, Julee, for seeing this diamond in the rough.
- Third—Thanks to my Monday night group who went through this with me one inning at a time.
- And, finally, Home—I'm so grateful for the ones I have here, with Mikey and the boys, not to mention the rest of my family who gives me such love and support. Even more, though, I give thanks for the heavenly Home I'll get to share with all of my friends and family and readers who have a relationship with Jesus Christ, our Savior. What a team we make!

OTHER BOOKS BY ALLISON PITTMAN

Nonfiction
Saturdays with Stella

Fiction
CROSSROADS OF GRACE SERIES
Ten Thousand Charms
Speak Through the Wind
With Endless Sight

READERS GUIDE

1. In *Stealing Home,* we see four very different people brought together through God's providence. Has anyone ever come into your life through unexpected circumstances?

2. Ellie Jane spends years wounded by childhood taunts. Why are the words of childhood teasing so painful?

3. Ned has suffered years of unrequited love. Can you remember a time when you longed for someone?

4. Morris is a relatively uneducated young man. Yet, in what ways is he one of the wisest characters in the story?

5. Although this story takes place shortly after the turn of the last century, what hints of modern celebrity do you see in Duke's life?

6. What draws Duke to Morris? To Ellie Jane? To Ned?

7. Picksville is a fictional town full of colorful characters. Who are some of the more memorable people in your hometown?

8. Ecclesiastes 4:12 says, "Though one may be overpowered, two can defend themselves. A cord of three strands is not quickly broken" (NIV). What "cords of three strands" are formed throughout the story?

9. Revisiting Ecclesiastes 4:12, where do you see Jesus Christ playing the third strand? How does He serve this place in your relationships?

10. Ned, Duke, and Ellie Jane are at some point involved in a love triangle. How do they serve as an example of grace as that conflict is resolved?

11. Morris's fate marks a tragic turn in the story; yet, what can it tell us about God's greater good?